I dedicate this book to my students and writing clients.
You inspire me to write more and continue to
amaze me with your dedication to the written word.

Darcy Nybo

Cleansing Water

Cleansing Water

Darcy Nybo

For book signings and wholesale enquiries, please email publisher@artisticwarrior.com.

ISBN # 978-1-987982-76-3 (Paperback)
ISBN # 978-1-987982-77-0 (eBook)

First Edition

Author Photo by Kim Elsasser, kimsphotography.com
Book Design by Artistic Warrior

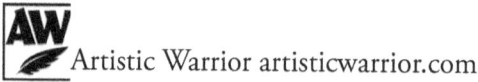

Artistic Warrior artisticwarrior.com

Chapter 1

Ashley raised a blood-stained hand to her forehead and brushed away a strand of hair. She smiled at Dudley, her Siamese cat.

"Marowr."

"I know, I know. I'll wash it off later."

She entered the living room and gathered the glasses, plates, a large knife, and a couple of beer bottles. When she returned to the kitchen, Dudley glared at her, then wound his way through her legs. His staccato cries of "marowr, marowr, marowr" did not go unnoticed. How could they?

"Soon, little one, soon. Be patient." Ashley stepped over to the stove, lifted the lid on her stock pot, and stirred the contents. Dudley stood on his hind legs and leaned his front paws on her calf.

"Marooowrrrrrr!"

"Oh, be patient, just for once." Ashley placed the lid back on the pot and rinsed her hands in the sink. She grabbed a meat patty and a Smokey from the fridge and went out into the yard.

A light April chill hung in the air as she fired up the propane barbecue. It was a great way to hide the smell coming from her newest 55-gallon drum hidden just off the back deck. She grabbed the hacksaw beside the drum, removed the blade from its handle and put in on the lower rack. She hummed as she turned the burner on low and placed the burger and Smokey on the highest level of the grill. Dudley followed her and sniffed at the dried bits of burned fat and meat collected on the ground behind the barbecue. He turned up his nose, strutted back into the house, and plopped himself directly in front of the stove.

Ashley closed the lid on the barbecue and went inside.

"So much to do, such little time," she said surveying the dirty dishes on the counter. She plugged in her Google Home.

"Okay, Google, play Pink, 'You and Your Hand.'" The song started, and Ashley's head bobbed with the music. "You tell 'em, Pink." She pulled open the dishwasher and filled it with the remnants of last night's affair. Dudley sat motionless, staring at the stock pot.

"You know what, Dudley? Someday, I won't have to do this. Then what are we going to give you for treats?" Ashley added a dishwasher pod, closed the door, and turned it on. "Now, to clean myself up."

She bent over, picked Dudley up, and brought him to the bathroom. She learned the hard way that her wily cat would jump onto the stove if he smelled his favorite treat cooking. A $450 vet bill was not easy to forget. Nor was the sight of Dudley walking awkwardly with little booties on his front paws to protect them until they healed.

She closed the bathroom door and put Dudley down. Ashely undressed and tossed her clothes on the floor. Dudley curled up in a ball on her discarded clothing as she stepped into the shower and turned it on. Ashley immediately felt better as the warm water hit her body. Water was magical for Ashley. It absorbed her stress and washed it down the drain. Water, she decided, was the perfect way to wash away everything. Water was cleansing. Water made everything better.

Memories of the previous night rose to the surface. Every drop of water captured her negative thoughts, then slid down the drain. Let the wastewater treatment plant deal with them. They weren't hers anymore.

She thought this one would be different. He wasn't, but she always hoped that someday, and hopefully soon, she would find someone not brainwashed by their upbringing. He was her sixth attempt at finding a suitable mate. Her sixth 55-gallon drum off to the side of the back deck.

At thirty-one, her biological clock hammered at her. She needed to reproduce soon. She hoped her child would be a boy. She would teach him how to treat a woman properly. He needed to learn how to be an equal in a relationship, how to be a decent human.

Ashley opened the shampoo bottle, poured a dollop into her palm, and put the bottle back. As she lathered up her hair, she felt all her destructive thoughts bubbling to the surface, each word, each bad memory, captured in the foaming crown on her head. She sighed, rinsed her hair, and felt immensely better. She turned off the shower, wrapped herself in a towel, and picked Dudley up.

Together, they went into her bedroom. Dudley watched from the floor as she finished drying off and getting dressed. He batted at the corners of the sheets as she stripped the bed.

"It's a pity, Dudley," she said as she gathered the bedding

and left the room. "He was good right up to the moment he wasn't." Dudley followed her into the laundry room.

"He was so close to being perfect, or at least a good one. I had such high hopes." Dudley meowed in agreement. Ashley tossed the bedding into the washing machine, put in detergent, turned it on, and closed the lid.

"Let's see if your treats are ready." Ashley returned to the kitchen and poked at the contents in her stock pot. "Almost done, kitty, almost done."

The dishwasher rang in a sing-song tune, letting her know the dishes were done. She opened it and let the steam waft out. She inhaled deeply.

"All clean," she said to herself and grabbed a dishtowel.

She stopped and unplugged her Google Home. She couldn't take the chance of someone, somewhere, eavesdropping on her conversation with her cat. Ashley believed that was the problem with society today. If you wanted convenience, you had to pay for it by giving up your privacy. Instead, she just unplugged any device that might listen in. It was a necessity, and she was willing to adapt.

Dudley wove his way between her legs as she put each dish, each glass, each cup away. With every clean item, her mood lifted. Ashley picked the large, bloody butcher knife out of the sink, cleaned it and put it away. She felt a huge relief once the last item was put away. She was always amazed at how water erased evidence of the past. It was like it never happened.

She turned off the stove and riffled through the drawer for her large strainer. She placed it across the sink, took the lid off the pot and brought it to the sink. Steam rolled out and dissipated into the air.

"Did you see that, Dudley? Water is magical. Water to steam, steam to air, and poof, it's like water never existed."

Ashley put on her oven mitts, grabbed the pot off the stove, and poured the contents into the strainer. The smell was at once vile and intoxicating. A mixture of beef and pork with a hint of fat. Ashley stopped mid-pour. That smell wasn't coming from the stockpot.

"Damn it." Ashley put the half-empty pot down and rushed out to the barbecue. Her beef patty looked like a hockey puck. She turned off the burner and glanced at the Smokey. It was all shriveled up, its outer casing burst open and burned to a crisp. She turned off the propane and grabbed the tongs. She'd wrap the blade in newspaper and toss it out with the trash for tomorrow's pick up. She'd do the same with the cremated remains of the burger and Smokey. Satisfied that all was in order she looked around for Dudley. He wasn't there.

"Double damn it!" She raced back into the house.

There was Dudley on the counter, trying to reach the contents of the strainer without falling into the sink.

"Shoooo! Get off the counter. You can have it in a minute."

Dudley flicked his tail and jumped down.

"Foolish cat!" She shook her head as she cooled the blade under running water and then wrapped it thoroughly in the local newspaper. She glared at Dudley as she tossed it into the trash.

"You are the most impatient cat I've ever met," she said

and went back to the sink. She poured the rest of the contents into the strainer. She watched as the murky-looking water flowed down the drain, taking the past with it. She turned on the tap again, rinsed out the stockpot, and turned the spray on the strainer. It was hypnotic, watching clean, clear water splash over the contents and remove any remaining fat and goo.

The distinctive sound of a diesel truck pulling into her driveway broke the spell of the water. She turned off the tap and smiled at Dudley.

"Matt's here." She tossed the contents of the strainer back into the now clean stock pot, put the lid on, and placed the entire pot in the fridge. Dudley couldn't get it in there. She ran out the back door and onto the deck.

Matt got out his truck, smiled and waved when he saw Ashley.

"Hey Matt!"

Ashley loved her brother. He was really her foster brother, but a brother, nonetheless. He was great at what he did—helping people bury the past.

"Same spot?" he asked as he took the oversized dolly out of the truck's bed.

"Yep, same spot." Ashley followed him out back and watched him hoist the sealed drum onto the dolly.

She told her neighbors she made a compost tea, like liquid fertilizer, with rainwater and kitchen scraps and sold it to a local farmer. They didn't need to know what was really in there. She ran back inside, grabbed some cash, and returned in time to see the barrel being secured in the truck bed.

"Here you go, Matt." She handed him ten, twenty-dollar bills.

"Same time next month?" he asked.

"I sure hope not." Ashley let out a long sigh. "But come again, just in case. If you aren't busy I could make you dinner next week."

Matt gave his sister a big hug and slowly released her. "Sounds good but let me check my schedule. It's been busy lately. And sis, I think your dreams will come true very soon."

"Thanks, Matt. I sure hope so."

He gave her a quick kiss on the cheek, climbed into his truck, and drove away. Ashley watched as he disappeared down the driveway, then went inside.

A few lingering memories from the previous night bubbled to the surface. He was a one-night stand, but it could have been more if he hadn't been such a jerk. What was it he said? She scrunched up her nose as if the motion would bring the memory closer to the surface. It worked.

"I remember now," she said to the cat. "He said he was in touch with his feminine side. Can you believe that, Dudley? I had such hope until the next sentence tumbled out of his mouth. Something about him not minding washing dishes, doing laundry, and cleaning the house."

She opened a drawer and pulled out a plastic container. "I wonder if he knew why that upset me so." Dudley ignored her—his eyes focused on the fridge door. "I mean seriously, cleaning up after yourself is not women's work. Such a shame. He had great potential."

Dudley tore his eyes from the fridge, rubbed against her leg, and howled.

"MAWAWRRR!"

"Right, I'm on it." Ashley pulled the pot and its contents from the fridge. She grabbed a pair of tongs, picked each item out one by one, and placed it in the container. Eight fingers, two thumbs, and eight toes. She tossed the remaining baby toe and a big toe to Dudley. He pounced on the big one and tossed it in the air a few times before taking it to his bed. He returned for the little toe, hopped back into his bed, and proceeded to strip the flesh off the bones. Ashley smiled as she watched Dudley enjoy his treat. He never ate the bones. She would grind them up later and place them with the others.

She returned the container to the fridge and turned on the kitchen tap. She watched the water as she washed her hands, watched it as it carried all the evidence down the drain.

Chapter 2

Two weeks passed, and Ashley had yet to get her period. Maybe the guy in touch with his feminine side had strong sperm. After ensuring Dudley had all his needs met, she headed out for her shift at the local nursery. Ashley loved working among the plants and imparting her knowledge to customers when asked.

It was also the perfect place to get plastic 55-gallon rain barrels. She was also able to order large quantities of lye under various fake customer names. Now, if only she could get pregnant and right the wrongs of her life through the next generation.

No one understood her, and she accepted that, except for Matt. Matt was the big brother she'd always hoped for, even if he was only a few months older. He understood her. She met him at the tail end of her stints in foster care. They had a lot in common. Both had mothers who deserted them before their fifth birthdays. Both had abusive fathers with a penchant for torture and pedophilia.

Ashley parked her car and stared at clock in her car. She was five minutes early. She closed her eyes and winced as she recalled the sting of a lit cigarette on her bare bottom. Ashley grimaced as she remembered Daddy dearest spending the next five to ten minutes applying and carefully massaging in the ointment. She'd blocked out what followed.

By her thirteenth birthday, she done her research at the local library and learned about alkalines, specifically lye and its corrosive properties. She planned to do it slowly, over time, but she got the measurements wrong and gave her father a glass of iced tea that burned his esophagus and destroyed his stomach. She waited thirty minutes before calling 911. He was dead by the time the paramedics arrived. Ashley lied and said she thought it was sugar and didn't mean to hurt her dear Papa. It wasn't her fault they both came in white bags with blue labels. They were going to learn how to make soap together that morning. It was a horrible mistake. The police believed her. As no relatives stepped forward, they placed Ashley in foster care.

"That's enough of that!" Ashley said as she exited her car. "Time to put on a happy face and tend to the plants."

She entered through the front door and went to the staff room. She donned a bright green apron with flowers and headed out back to water the seedlings. Soon, throngs of avid gardeners would come through the door searching for the perfect plants for their vegetable and flower gardens.

Ashley grabbed the overhead hose and carefully watered the plants. She picked a stray baby weed out of a lettuce six-pack and stuffed it into her apron pocket.

As she watered, she remembered the day she met Matt. She'd just arrived at a new foster home, and she and Matt were put on garden duty. He accidentally pulled several flower seedlings from the flower patch and received a strap across his thighs as punishment. That night, Ashley snuck into Matt's room and put lotion on his welts, being careful not to touch his buttocks. From that day on, they did everything together. They became each other's champions and alibis when things got weird. Kids at school made fun of them, but they had each other, and that was all that mattered.

Now and then, someone sent from the adoption agency would come to visit and take one of them home for a weekend trial to see how they fit in. Ashley and Matt made sure they didn't fit in. If they couldn't be together, they didn't want to be adopted.

"Excuse me, miss." A deep voice startled Ashley out of her reverie. "Can you tell me if you have everbearing strawberries?"

Ashley turned and found herself face to face with a gorgeous set of blue eyes.

"Yes, yes, we do," she said. "Follow me, and I'll take you to the berry section. We have eight types of everbearing strawberries, five types of blueberries, and seven types of raspberries. We even have gooseberries, and blackberries if you're interested."

"Lead the way," the voice with the eyes said.

Ashley nodded and weaved through the tightly placed rows.

"Here you are," she said, sweeping her arm over the strawberry sections. "I recommend the Quinault. They grow best here. However, the Ruby Ann is sweeter."

"Hmmm, how about a starter pack of each? I just moved here and want to start small and see how it feels to have a garden. I moved out of my condo and into a ground-level townhouse with room for a garden. This is all new to me."

As he reached for a six-pack of Quinault, he brushed the

side of Ashley's arm. She felt a slight tingle and stepped back.

"Here, I'll get you the Ruby Ann," she said and handed him the young berry plants.

"Thank you, miss, umm …"

"Ashley. My name is Ashley. And you're welcome." Ashley crab walked around him and headed for more open space. "You can pay for them at the register out front. They'll be happy to help you there."

"Ashley. That's a nice name. It suits you," he said. "I'm Randall or Randy if you prefer."

Ashley nodded and smiled. He was gorgeous but too close to her safe space at work. This one would have to be a catch-and-release.

"Nice to meet you, Randy. Please come back if you have any other questions."

With that, she turned on her heels and headed back to the seedlings.

* * *

The workday passed quickly, as it always did when nurturing the plants. Ashley washed her hands, marveling at how the dirt simply disappeared down the drain. She hung up her apron, dug out the weeds from the pocket, and tossed them in the compost. She grinned when she thought about what tonight's adventures would bring.

It was ladies' night at her neighborhood pub, but Ashley didn't like hunting too close to home. She had ten days or so until she ovulated again, but maybe she could find a few prime specimens before then. She decided to head out of the suburbs and into the city core, where she could fade into the crowd. Hunting was always easy in crowded clubs.

"Goodnight!" she called as she headed to her car. A scattered chorus of goodnights followed her out the door.

Dudley would be waiting for her to give him a snack, and she'd have to change his litter box before she went out. He'd throw a fit and poop on the bathroom mat if she didn't. She maneuvered her car out of the parking stall and headed home. Sure enough, Dudley was waiting at the door, yowling away.

"Hey there," she said, tossing her purse and keys on the side table. "And how was your day?"

The cat purred and snaked its way around her ankles, knowing this was the best way to get a treat. It had been a few days since Ashley ran out of Dudley's favorite treat. He'd have to make do with regular kitty goodies. She went into the kitchen and opened a packet of miniature fish-shaped treats. Dudley sat at her feet like a faithful dog while she picked out five small crunchy bits and threw them into the living area. Dudley was gone in a flash, hunting for the morsels.

Ashley headed into the bathroom and scooped out the daily leavings from the litter box into the toilet. A familiar cramp gripped her midsection.

"Damn it!" she cried out. "Life is not fair!" She opened the drawer beside the sink and pulled out a tampon.

"Fek, fek, and double fek!" She pulled down her pants and panties and sat on the toilet. A tell-tale single drop of fresh blood stained the crotch of her favorite underwear. Another mission failure. She removed her pants and panties, tossing the latter into the sink. She inserted the tampon and sighed. She didn't feel like hunting, but she had eleven to sixteen days to meet a guy she liked, get to know him, and then bring him home. Her one-night stand approach wasn't working.

Discovering their schmuck factor after sex was more trouble than the sex was worth. Besides, disposing of bodies was hard work. She decided she needed to ensure her baby daddy was morally upright, strong of character and body, and not a jerk about women.

The last one was the most important. She wasn't quite sure how the whole nature/nurture debate worked. She only knew her baby daddy had to be a nice guy who didn't treat women like second-class citizens. That meant lots of questions about how they felt about their mom or sisters without coming off as a weirdo.

Ashley composed herself and took a breath. Saturday nights were the best time to hunt, so she had to make herself presentable. She flushed, added water to the sink, and headed to her bedroom to change clothes.

Thirty minutes later, she was refreshed and ready to go. As she headed toward her front door, there was a knock on the back door.

"Who is it?" she called out. No answer.

She opened the door and saw Rocky, her neighbor from across the street.

"Hey Ashley, sorry to bother you, but my wife said you might have some extra lye that she can mix into the garden, and the stores are closed. I want to get it done before the rain tomorrow. Could I borrow a cup?"

"A cup!" Ashley tried not to laugh. "You don't have a big enough garden for a cup of lye, Rocky. You'd kill everything you put it on."

"Oh." Rocky looked down at his shoes. "Well, you see, my wife's been gone for a week, and I promised her I'd fix the pH in the garden, and well, she's due home tomorrow, and I haven't done anything. Can you help a neighbor out?"

Ashley smiled. "You have any ashes left over from your wood stove?"

"Well, yeah, that was the next thing I was going to do, clean it out. It's still chilly at night, so we're using it. Why do you ask?"

"Because wood ashes are safer and easier to use, and you won't accidentally burn the entire garden. Just clean out your woodstove, sprinkle the ashes everywhere, and then water it all down. It's supposed to rain tomorrow anyway, so tonight is perfect. Trust me. It works better than lye or lime. That shit is super caustic."

"Okay, cool," Rocky said, giving her a once-over. "Oh, and another thing, do you think I could get your recipe for that organic liquid fertilizer you make? I bought a big rain barrel and want to mix some up for the garden."

Ashley glanced at the clock. She had an hour to make it downtown, get in line, and get a good spot at the club. She could spare a few minutes.

"Sure, Rocky, it's quite simple. Take three or four cups of

your ashes and drop them in a three-quarter full barrel. Then drop in about four cups of grass clippings and a cup or two of comfrey if you have it. I usually dehydrate my vegetable cuttings, potato skins, tops of carrots, leek tops, etc., and add that a few days later. You don't have to dehydrate them, but they take up less room if you do. Oh, and coffee and tea grounds are good for flowering plants. Stir it daily, and when it stinks, it's ready. But again, be careful, do a test area first. You don't want to kill the seedlings. When in doubt, dilute it with water. Water is the key to an excellent good fertilizer."

Rocky smiled at her. "Wow, thanks so much. I think I can remember that. Beth will be so happy!" Rocky started to leave, then turned back to face her. "Do you think I could buy a barrel of it from you? We can't help but notice that nice young man who comes over once a month and picks up your barrel. You sell them to a local farmer, right?"

"Yes, yes, I do, but I only make enough for him. If you don't mind, Rocky, I must get going."

"Yeah, Yeah. Of course. You look fabulous, by the way. If I weren't married—"

"You are married, Rocky. Good night."

Ashley closed the door and shook her head. She didn't like the way Rocky looked at her. He and his wife, Beth, appeared to be nice enough, but in her opinion, they were a little too privileged. They had two cars, a truck, a boat, an RV, a snowmobile they rarely used, kayaks, and electric bikes with fat tires.

Ashley had a car and a cat. She'd inherited $250,000

when she was twenty-one, money from her asshole father's life insurance. She'd used that to put a large down payment on her little 1,200-square-foot home. It was small, but she loved it. Rocky and Beth had a 3,100-square-foot home that covered most of the corner lot across from her. Fortunately, they had a huge driveway and a triple garage, so all their toys were off the street. They were a few years older than her and childless which made her a little suspicious but never jealous. She'd get what was coming to her in good time. She believed in fate, and her fate was to have a child, a son, so that she could raise him right.

Dudley found all his treats and cleaned his face as he lay on his favorite chair.

"You are one spoiled cat," she said, then left through the front door. It was time to get to the club and find herself a mate.

Chapter 3

Ashley sat in a back corner, near a group of giggling twenty-somethings who were constantly fixing each other's hair and going to the bathroom in pairs. Ashley hated that. But that's what you had to contend with when looking to pick up someone or be picked up. Ashley preferred the former to the latter, but she let the men think they made the conquest.

The band was a tribute band, playing covers from some much-loved eighties hair band. Ashley didn't care what the music was. As long as it had a beat, and she could dance to it. That was pretty much what all species did to attract a mate. Shake your booty, bounce your bits, and hope for the best.

The band finished their last song of the set, and the DJ put on some EDM. The hairband crowd headed for their tables while the younger ones pushed onto the dance floor. Ashley made her way up to the bar and ordered a club soda with a splash of orange. It made it look like she was drinking. She needed her head on straight and her focus laser sharp.

To her left was a long-haired, middle-aged man wearing a "We Are the World" T-shirt that had seen better days. He'd be a pass. Farther down the bar was a thirty-year-old man with a respectable haircut, a nice shirt, and tight jeans. He might be worth another look. She headed toward him when she noticed him place something in the palm of another man's hand.

"Well, damn it," she said under her breath. She didn't want to hook up with a man without morals. He was either a drug dealer or a user. She wasn't sure who was who, but she did know a handoff when she saw it.

"I'm sorry. Was I in your way?" A pair of blue eyes looked down into hers.

"Oh, no, sorry. I was talking to myself." Ashley tried to make her way around the man, but he put his hand gently on her arm.

"Wait, I know you. Ashley, right?"

Ashley felt a glimmer of recognition but couldn't place the man.

"Do I know you?" she asked.

"What?" he said.

Ashley took a deep breath and leaned in closer to be heard above the music's driving beat. "Do I know you?" This time it was a slight holler.

Blue eyes nodded and leaned closer. "I'm the Ruby Ann guy."

Ashley looked at him with a blank stare. Who was this guy, and why did he have a woman's name? "You're Ruby Ann?"

"No!" The man laughed. Ashley liked the way the corners around his eyes crinkled. She liked genuine laughs. Her eyes opened wide as she recognized him.

"Oh my goodness, you're the strawberry guy. Ruby Ann and Quinault!"

He smiled and nodded. "Well, you can call me Randy."

Ashley smiled. She wasn't at work, and as long as she was at the club, he might be a good candidate. She already knew he liked growing things.

"Oh, right! What a coincidence running into you here." She glanced downward, hoping to look coy.

"Hey, this EDM isn't doing it for me. Would you like to go get a snack or something?" He gave her a hopeful grin.

"Well, that depends," she said. "What'd you give that guy you were just talking to?"

"Oh, that!" he said. "Guess that looked a bit sketchy. I was giving him my phone number. I met him a few weeks ago, and he wanted me to do some work for him, but he lost my contact info. I gave him a piece of paper with my number on it. He'll probably lose it again."

Ashley smiled. "Sounds plausible," she said. "Let me get my coat." Ashley put her drink on the bar and headed for the coat check. The noise level was tolerable near the front door, and she breathed a sigh of relief. Clubs were great for picking up men, but the noise level made her anxious. She retrieved her coat, and when she turned around, he was right behind her.

"Shall we?" he said as he opened the door to the club.

They walked in silence down the street to a tapas restaurant. She smiled when he held the door open for her again. At least he had manners.

"Table for two?" the hostess asked.

"Yes, please. The quietest one you've got," Randy said.

Randy took Ashley's coat and placed it on the back of her chair, then pulled her chair out.

"After you," he said.

This guy was either really lame or really nice. Ashley couldn't decide which.

"Thank you." She gave a small nod.

They looked at the menus, decided what to share, and each ordered a non-alcoholic drink.

"So, Randy." Ashley decided to be straightforward and get the facts out in the open right away. "Do you always pick up girls in nightclubs?"

Randy smiled, but it didn't reach his eyes. "I was just going to ask you something similar. Do you always leave clubs with strangers?"

"Touché." Ashley smiled. He was nice and witty, too.

"Truth is, I liked you when I met you at the nursery. I didn't think it would be wise to ask you out then because, well, if you had said no, it would have been awkward for me to go back. And I do need more plants."

"Well, here's hoping we get along then." Ashley smiled as the waiter dropped off their drinks. She lifted hers in a toast. "To friendship and whatever that becomes."

Randy lifted his glass and clinked it with hers. "This dating over thirty is a bit awkward, at least for me. So, how about we get the basics out of the way and then see if we want the night to continue? I'll go first."

"Okay," Ashley said as the waiter brought them their dishes. "I'll start eating first." She lifted a fish taco and took a dainty bite. "Yummy!" she said. "Okay, go. Don't worry. I'll save you some."

"Well, my last name is Hicks. Please don't laugh. I'm not a hick, honest. I'm thirty-two, divorced, and have no kids. We just didn't plan on having kids right away. But then she decided she never wanted them, and I did, so we got divorced. We still chat now and then, but for the most part, it was amicable." He reached over, took a fish taco and bit in. "Wow, this is good. Now you."

Ashley swallowed what was in her mouth and put the remains of the taco down.

"Okay, I'm single, never married, and I do want children. No crazy ex hiding anywhere. Most of the men I date simply disappear after we end it." She popped the rest of the fish taco in her mouth and gave a little moan. "Oh, that is so good!"

Randy tossed a stuffed mushroom cap into his mouth and bit down. "Oh shit! That's hot!" he said, opening his mouth to suck in cool air. "Oh gawd, that must look gross. I'm so sorry." He mumbled through his half-open mouth. He placed his napkin in front of his mouth and sucked air onto his burning tongue. A few seconds later, he bit down, chewed, and swallowed.

"Ummm, okay then, where were we? And by the way, those are hot."

Ashley laughed. "I'll wait then. And it was your turn to tell me something about you. We've already covered babies. How about we dive into sex, politics, religion, and our family and just get it over with."

Randy gave a small laugh. "Deal. Okay, well, I like sex. I'm hetero, not bi or gay or anything else, kind of boring, really. I like to cuddle before and after sex, and I take direction very well."

Ashley held a stuffed mushroom on the end of a fork and blew on it. "Well, that was a bit more than I needed to know, but I'm pretty much the same. Next." She took a bite of the stuffed mushroom and smiled. "Oh yeah, this is yummy too."

Randy took a sip of his drink. "Politics is next. Well, I always thought I was a far left leaning guy, but I took a quiz online, and it turns out I'm just slightly left of dead center."

"No way!" Ashley said as she swallowed the last of the mushroom cap. "I did a test, too, the last election, and I thought I was a big ole right-leaning machine. Turned out I was slightly left of center. How weird is that."

The waiter brought two more plates: bacon-wrapped figs stuffed with goat cheese and some crab cakes.

"Oh, my gawd. This snack is turning into a meal!" Ashley exclaimed as she reached for a fig. "I forgot we ordered so much. Okay, how about religion?"

"That's a tough one for me." Randy placed a fig and a crab cake on his plate. "I started with family and stuff as a regular Christian. Then once I got older, I started checking out other religions and realized they were all pretty much the same. My folks weren't strict about the church, so they didn't mind that I strayed from it. I found I had a lot more I could relate to in Buddhism, except for the not eating meat part or drinking. I like a good glass of wine now and then. Oh, and then I looked into Taoism, which is very similar to Buddhism. It felt more comfortable, but again, no meat. So, I guess you'd say I'm a seventy percent Taoist."

Ashley chewed her fig thoughtfully. "That's quite the

spiritual journey," she said. "I'm glad you found something you can relate to. But technically speaking, Buddhism and Taoism, and a few other isms are philosophies, not religions."

She watched Randy as he cut his crab cake in half and ate it. She smiled as his eyes closed, and he gave a little moan.

"Oh gawd, the food here is fabulous. We have to come back again!" he said.

"Are you asking me on a second date before we've finished our first?" she asked.

"Ummm, yes, I believe I am. But it's your turn now. Religion. Go."

"Okay then. Well, I was raised Catholic. My mom left when I was almost five, and my dad didn't care for church much, but he kept going because he liked getting his sins negated via confession. He died when I was twelve. I lived in a bunch of foster homes where I met my foster brother, Matt. We're still in each other's lives. He's a devout atheist. I looked into lots of religions, including Baha'i, which sounded good at first. Unity of all people regardless of race, gender, etc., but once I got to know more about it, it didn't fit my lifestyle. Some of their laws were great, helping get the planet toward world peace and all. But the others didn't appeal."

"Oh, how come?" Randy asked.

"Well, as you've seen, I don't drink, well, not often anyway. But when I was told it was forbidden for me to drink, that just pissed me off. Then I was told sex was off the table. No sex until marriage, and no gay sex. And that pissed me off because I have gay friends, well, acquaintances, but still. So I left. I looked into a few other religions but finally settled on being a pantheist. They believe God is everything and everything is God, and all religions hold truth."

"That's convenient," Randy said. "I don't mean that in a bad way. I just mean that, well, it's great that it considers a little of everything. Is it organized? Is there a church or space you all meet in?" He looked at the last mushroom and then at Ashley.

"Go ahead, take it. I'll take the extra crab cake." She smiled as she popped the entire crabcake into her mouth. "Dis is shooo good." She mumbled around the food in her mouth.

Ashley took her time savoring the last of the crab cake, then looked Randy in the eyes. "And no, I don't go to a group or a church. I simply believe we were all stardust and will return to be stardust, and in between, our consciousness just kind of hangs out and experiences stuff."

"Interesting." Randy wiped his mouth with his napkin. "I'll have to look into that."

"It's pretty cool," Ashley said, "and a lot of famous people were pantheists. Einstein, Beethoven and the Carls: Jung and Sagan. Even writers like Ralph Waldo Emerson and Walt Whitman."

"Fascinating." Randy leaned forward on his elbows.

"Yeah, I found it pretty interesting," Ashley said, pushing her plate aside.

"Not pantheism, I mean, that's interesting. It's you—you are fascinating."

Ashley felt herself blush. Could this be it? Could this be the one to father her child and be her partner in raising it? She took a deep breath and let it out slowly.

"You're pretty fabulous yourself," she said. "Do you want to get out of here?"

Randy signaled the server for the check. "Yes, yes I would," he said. "Let's leave the family talk for the next date."

Chapter 4

Ashley gave a contented sigh as she stretched out in the middle of her bed. The past couple of weeks were utterly amazing. She just started her period when she and Randy had their first date. Since then, she told him about her life in foster homes with Matt. He told her about him being an only child with divorced parents.

Once her period was over, she decided it was time to let him in. She told a little lie and said she was on birth control. No use risking him using a condom.

They spent most of their time at his place. Randy was a tender lover and a decent human being. He had a real job where he got to work from home and made good money. Best of all, Ashley hadn't heard one derogatory thing about women come out of his mouth. He was respectful, yet persuasive when it counted. She picked up her phone and smiled when she saw a heart emoji from Randy. Then she opened her calendar. Today was the beginning of her ovulation cycle.

"Dudley! Here kitty, kitty!" The pounced on the bed, ready for morning scritches. Ashley had been away for several nights, and he was obviously ecstatic to have her to himself.

"Guess what, Dudley? It's time. Yep, ovulation time. So, I'm going to bring Randy over here for a few nights. Gotta keep the ovulation kits handy. This could be it, Dudley. You could be a big brother in nine months. Hopefully, it's a boy so I can bring him up right."

Ashley opened her messaging app and typed a quick message.

> My place tonight, dinner is on me this time.
> I'm cooking Tuscan chicken. See you around
> 6:30?

The response was quick and short.

> YES!

She put the phone down, got out of bed to feed Dudley, and started dinner in the crock pot. "Let's see if we're rich enough to buy a farm." Ashley checked her lotto app. Despite her weekly ticket purchases, she had yet to win more than twenty dollars. With just a click of a few buttons, she bought more tickets. Maybe tonight would be lucky.

* * *

By the time Randy arrived, Ashley was in full make-a-baby mode. She styled her hair perfectly, using a subtle lavender scent that wafted away when she tossed her head. She wore a baby blue, low-cut dress with bare legs and feet. The kitchen smelled amazing. The candles flickered in their crystal holders on the tastefully set table.

"Wow," Randy said as he stepped into the kitchen. "I don't know what smells better, you or the meal."

"Sit," Ashley said, kissing him on the nose. She poured them both a glass of wine, then served the Tuscan chicken.

"This looks fantastic," Randy said, "and so do you."

Ashley spoke in her best Southern belle accent. "Why, sir, I do believe you flatter me."

"I want to know more about you, Ashley. I know a lot about your childhood but nothing about your present life. I'm curious, have you always wanted to work in a garden center?"

Ashley smiled and looked around to make sure no one was listening. Randy looked around, too, confused.

"Actually," Ashley said, lowering her voice to slightly above a whisper, "I'm an almost famous artist. I just work at the garden shop to make ends meet between paintings."

"What? No way! Where might I have seen your work?"

"Well, nowhere unless you've been in the homes of the ridiculously rich and famous."

Randy gave her a confused look and waited for an explanation.

"Finish up your dinner, and I'll show you my art studio," Ashley said. "Then we can have dessert."

"Yes, ma'am." Randy took one last bite, finished his glass of wine, and grinned. "I'm done!"

Ashley giggled and pushed her plate aside. "Fine, follow me."

* * *

Randy followed Ashley into her home art studio. When he stepped inside, his mouth dropped. He wasn't sure if this was an art studio or a medieval torture chamber. There were four sets of what looked like large fishing hooks hanging from the ceiling on chains. Thick painter's plastic covered the floor and walls, and a few streaks of red remained visible.

"Umm, what am I looking at?" Randy asked. He closed his mouth, but his eyes remained wide.

"This is where I make my art," she replied.

Randy scanned the room. It was 140 square feet at most. He didn't see an easel or anything that resembled a painter's studio.

"Umm, I still don't understand." He looked up at the ceiling, expecting to see mirrors. Randy slowly let out his breath when he saw that it, too, was covered in plastic. Only the light fixture reamined untouched.

"Stay right here. I'll be right back," Ashley called as she left the room. She returned seconds later with an iPad. She pulled up a video and handed it to Randy.

"What am I looking at?" he asked.

"Well, it's not my work, but it's the type of work I do," she answered. "It's called pendulum painting. See the large, stretched canvas on the floor." She pointed at the video. "It's about eight by ten feet. That's about as large as I can get in here and still make it work. Just watch the video."

Randy watched as the video focused on a man pouring blue paint into a bucket suspended by a hook and a rope attached to the ceiling. He stood back, pulling the bucket with him. He eyed the canvas for a moment, pulled out a stopper at the bottom of the bucket, and let it go. The bucket swung wide in an oblong motion, dribbling paint on the canvas. Once it slowed, he grabbed it and put the bucket on the ground. A few moments later, he hooked up a second bucket with purple paint and repeated the process. This bucket swung out and around and back but took a different path than the first. A few moments into the process, he retrieved the bucket and set it down beside him. Then he took a third bucket, filled it with black paint, and let it go. This paint was thinner than the first two and created eerie patterns on the white, blue, and purple canvas. When it had done all he wanted it to do, the man grabbed the bucket and set it aside. The camera focused on the painting and then faded to black.

A second later, thanks to the magic of the internet, the canvas was dry. The artist stood beside his massive creation as it hung in a place of honor in its new owners' home. Randy looked up as Ashley removed the iPad from his hands.

"That is what I do," she said matter-of-factly. "Kinda, it's that with a bit of Jackson Pollock thrown in for good measure. But tonight there'll be no painting. Tonight is all about you and me learning more about each other."

Randy took another look around the art studio and followed Ashley into the living room."Sit," she said. "I'll get the wine. Randy did as requested as Ashley went into the kitchen. This was the perfect time to ask the important questions. A few moments later, she returned and sat beside him on the couch.

"Now, it's your turn. I know about the ex-wife and your

work and some of your childhood. My parents were pretty much the shit. Tell me about your parents. Do you still keep in touch? Do you like them? I'm asking because I've never really had that, and I find it fascinating."

Randy cleared his throat. "Well, my dad left my mom when I was nineteen. It was a good thing. They fought a lot, and neither was happy. I still see him about twice a year. My mom, well, that's another story. I adore my mom, but I don't usually bring it up on dates because some women find it a bit creepy. She lives about two hours away. I call her every weekend and go visit her once a month. She's the strongest, kindest, most patient woman I've ever known."

Hearing those words, Ashley could have sworn she felt an egg drop and head down her fallopian tubes. She put down her wine glass, stood, and took Randy's hand.

"Follow me," she said, pulling him toward the bedroom.

It was baby-making time.

Chapter 5

Ashley awoke, stretched, and smiled. Last week she and Randy had made love at least ten times by her count. Ten chances over five glorious days that would give her what she so desperately wanted. She rolled over, patted Randy on the bum, and got out of bed.

"Rise and shine, sleepyhead. I'm going to have a shower." She left the room grinning from ear to ear.

Once she was in the shower, the water felt heavenly. She loved how she could wash away any tension or doubt with a nice hot shower. And right now, it was great at relieving a bit of stiffness from all the positions they'd tried. She'd told Randy it was because it helped her orgasm better. The truth was, she'd gone to a website where it showed all the different positions that produced high pregnancy results. She'd even douched with baking soda and water to ensure an alkaline environment for boy sperm to fertilize her egg. That's what the site had recommended. She'd made sure she had orgasms and continued to have sex at least twice a day until she was three days past her ovulation date. Poor Randy was a little worn out. It was time to let him rest and build up his reserves, just in case.

Randy slipped into the shower behind Ashley and kissed her back. "Good morning, my little tigress," he said into her neck. "Did you want to try a little morning delight in the shower?"

Ashley turned around and smiled at him as the water cascaded between them. "Oh, honey, aren't you worn out yet?" She grabbed the shampoo and lathered up her hair.

"Not with you around," he replied.

"Well, I'm a bit sore today." She rinsed her hair. "In fact, I think we should cool it for a bit. I haven't painted a thing in over a week, and I have a new client."

"What?" Randy said. "That's fabulous news." He grabbed the shampoo and quickly washed his hair. "This is perfect timing. I haven't seen Mom in about four weeks and was going to cancel my trip, but if you need your space, this works out perfectly."

Ashley put conditioner in her hair and smiled. He really could be the one. He would be a good father, the kind of father her child deserved. She rinsed her hair and stepped out of the shower.

"You know what, Randy?" she said. "You treat your mom so well. I think you'd make a good dad. You still want kids, right?" Ashley held her breath. She didn't want to lose this one.

"Yeah, of course, I do," he replied. "But not at this exact moment." Randy pulled back the shower curtain, grabbed a towel, and wrapped it around his waist. "We've only known each other a few weeks, so best to leave the baby-making talk for another time, eh?"

Ashley smiled. "Oh, of course, I was double-checking."

She towel-dried her hair and went back into the bedroom to get dressed. Perhaps she was rushing the baby-making talk. If she wasn't pregnant this time, she would try again next month and then bring it up.

A few moments later, Randy stepped into the bedroom. "So, how long do you need?"

"Say what?" Ashley looked confused. Was he talking about babies or something else?

"To complete your art project for your client. I assume you like to work alone. Most artists do. Plus, you have to work at the nursery, so I'm asking when you'd like to see me again?"

Ashley opened the calendar on the phone. "Well, how about you give me at least a week to ten days? That will give me two whole weekends to get my work done, plus time after work."

"Oh, okay," Randy replied, a tinge of disappointment in his voice. "I was hoping you'd tell me to come back right away, but I get it. An artiste such as yourself needs your space." He pulled on his jeans and shoved his arms into his shirt, forcing a smile. "Besides, this way, I can stay a few extra days at Mom's place. She'll like that. I can always work from there. Gotta love the internet."

Ashley grinned. "That's the spirit! And I'm not an artiste. People confuse artist and artiste. An artiste is an entertainer."

Randy winked at her "Well, I find you very entertaining."

Ashley pretended to swat him then finished getting dressed. "Before you go, would you like some coffee?"

Randy grabbed her around the waist. "What I'd like is to throw you back into bed, but I know you have to get to work, so coffee it is."

Ashley gave him a quick peck on the cheek and headed to the kitchen to make coffee and feed Dudley.

"So, this new client of yours, would I know them?" Randy asked. "I don't quite understand how you get your clients."

Ashley brought two cups of coffee to the table and set them down.

"Would I know any of them," Randy asked.

"I doubt it," she answered. "Only if you are secretly filthy rich. Most of them are new money rich and come from the west coast. They move here for a more relaxed lifestyle and better buying power for houses and toys. They buy up these big ass homes with twenty-foot-high ceilings and then realize their art doesn't quite take up enough space."

"Wait." Randy looked confused. "There were no canvases in your art room. How the hell are you going to get an eight by ten-foot canvas in your car? Do you need some help? I know a guy with a truck."

"Nope, I know a guy, too," Ashley grinned. Randy looked even more confused.

"What guy? I didn't know you had a guy." He grinned, but his face revealed he was a little concerned.

"Oh, silly, it's my brother. You know, my foster brother, Matt. I told you about him. He does odd jobs and deliveries and such. He's coming to get me today after work, and we're going to pick up the canvases at the art store.

"Canvases? Plural?"

"Yeah, the client wants a triptych with similar colors."

"A trip what?"

"Triptych, three panels placed side-by-side that form somewhat of a whole picture. Except in this case, it's abstract, so I just have to make sure I get the edge colors to be the same as the other edge colors and even have it look like they went off the canvas and onto another canvas. It's tricky because the room is small, but I've done it before."

"Oh, okay." Randy finished his coffee. "Okay, I'm going to head out, grab a suitcase and my computer from home and head up to Mom's place. I'll call when I get there, okay?" He stood, kissed Ashley on the cheek, and smiled. "You are so beautiful."

Ashley beamed. She could get used to this. "And you, dear sir, are dashing. Now get out of here. I need to get to work, too. I'll walk you out."

Ashley turned off the coffee pot, grabbed her purse and keys, and opened the door. "Hurry, I don't want the snoopy neighbors to see you. They have enough to gossip about."

Randy playfully held his arm in front of his face as they left the house. "Not to worry, they'll never ID me."

Ashley playfully swatted him but did not knock his arm away from his face. It would be better if the neighbors didn't see his face, just in case.

* * *

Matt pulled into Ashley's driveway at exactly six p.m. He walked to the back of the house and patted the side of the drum sitting there. It sounded empty. He smiled. Maybe Ashley had finally found a good one. Only time would tell. He went up to the side door and knocked.

"Be right there!" came a voice from inside. A few seconds later, Ashley emerged, grinning from ear to ear. "You checked the drum, didn't you?" she asked.

Matt nodded. "Yeah, had to. Habit."

The pair walked to his truck. Ashley noted the clean tarps and tie-downs in the back. Matt was such a sweetheart. He always made sure the bed of the truck was spotless before going to the art store. He truly was the best brother ever. She hopped into the passenger side, and the two of them drove toward the art supply store.

"So, this new guy. How long has this one lasted?" Matt asked.

"Oh, about two and a half weeks now," Ashley replied. "He loves his mom, and so far, not a bad word has fallen from his lips when it comes to women. Plus, no sign of a bad temper. I'm hopeful this is the one."

"Should I come back at the end of the month?"

"Goodness, Matt, I should just ask you about my cycle. You know it better than I do!" Ashley chided.

Matt grinned. "Habit," he said. "I need to schedule my other pickups around your cycle, just in case."

"Nah, I think I'm going to give this one a few months," she said as they parked in front of the art store. Once inside, Ashley picked out some new paint, thinners, and three eight by ten-foot canvases. She had the clerk ring it all up and let them know they'd pick it all up at the loading gate door. Once everything was loaded and safely tied down, Ashley suggested a late dinner.

"I'm starving," she said. "Let me treat you to a steak dinner. My client gave me a great advance."

"Aren't you worried someone will take this stuff?" he asked, motioning to the bed of the truck.

"Nope, I'm not. And if this past week worked, I'll need to be putting some iron in my body, so let's go."

Once they settled into the booth at the steak house, Ashley told Matt all about Randy.

"I just hope this one is a keeper. I mean, he feels and acts perfect," she said as the waiter brought them water and took their order.

Matt reached across the table and took her hand. His shirt rode up from his wrist, giving Ashley a glance at his scarred lower arm. Her mood darkened for a moment, and then she smiled.

"Thanks, Matt. Your love and support have meant so much to me over the years."

Matt patted her hand and sat back in his seat. "You too, little sis. You too." He pulled his shirt sleeve down to cover the marks.

"I love it when you call me that," she said. "Every time I see those scars, I remember how much you sacrificed for me. I'm so sorry, but I will make it up to you. You'll see. Just a few more painting commissions, and I'll have enough money, and I can buy you a new truck! One with a winch and a canopy and everything you desire."

"You don't need to do that," he said. "Save it and pay off your mortgage. Besides," Matt lowered his head, "I do things for you because I love you. You don't have to pay for picking up your fertilizer barrels."

"Yes, I do," Ashley said. "With the price of gas, it barely covers your costs."

The pair fell silent as they recalled the last foster home they'd been in together. The father figure was a real piece of work. He loved to spank the teenage girls and catch the teenage boys masturbating. If he caught one of the boys masturbating after he'd spanked one of the girls, he'd burn the inside of their wrists with a cigarette. Sometimes he'd heat a fork on the stove and press it into the flesh above the wrists. One night Ashley caught him trying to burn Matt with a big barbecue fork. She'd lunged at the man just as the hot metal hit Matt's already scarred flesh. A battle for the large fork ensued, resulting in Ashley stabbing the man in the cheek with the hot tines.

As he lay writhing on the floor, Ashley called 911 and told Matt to go pack his things. Ashley ran into her room, grabbed her essentials and a few clothes, and met Matt at the door. After that, they survived on the street together until they were able to get jobs and places of their own. When Ashley turned twenty-one, she got her dad's insurance money and bought the house. Matt got a job as a delivery driver and lived in a shared home across town.

Ashley looked up as the waiter brought their steaks.

"A toast," She lifted her water glass. "To family. I wouldn't change anything in my life if it meant I couldn't have you in it."

Matt grinned and clinked her glass. "To family."

As they ate, Ashley saw Matt looking at her when he

thought she didn't notice. This was a sure sign something was on his mind.

"Okay, enough of the glances," she said. "What's up? What's on your mind?"

"Well, I was thinking. Do you ever feel bad about what you do? You know, after they aren't the one?"

Ashley chewed thoughtfully, swallowed, and took a sip of water.

"No. I can't." She looked around, trying to figure out a way to say what was on her mind without being too obvious. "The way I see it, each one of my potential, shall we say, friends, had a major character flaw. If I kept them in my life, well, I'd be miserable." Ashley popped another bite of steak into her mouth. "Make sense?"

"Yeah," Matt replied. "It's what happens when you decide you don't want them in your life. Do you ever think that you've, I dunno, made a mistake or gone too far?"

"No, never." She pointed her steak knife at Matt. "Each one had the potential to be the same type of asshole that you and I were forced to live with. Each one had the potential to cause mental, emotional, and physical harm. So, no. I don't feel bad that they are out of my life, and I don't ever think I've made a mistake. Now, can we talk about something more pleasant?"

"Sure," Matt said and hung his head. "It's just that I don't want you to ever feel like you've made a mistake …" His voice trailed off. "You know, choosing me, having me as your brother."

Ashley's face broke into a huge grin that shone from her eyes to her chin.

"Oh, my goodness Matt! You are my protector, my guardian angel, my brother from another mother, and you hold my heart in your hands. I would never, never, ever wish you were gone from my life. We've been through too much together. Now let's order dessert. I still have room for cheesecake!"

Matt grinned at Ashley. "Okay, just checking."

"Listen up, bro. I will always have your back, and I know you will always have mine. One day you are going to be an uncle to my baby or even babies. I want them to know what a great guy their mama has on her side. I want them to know you can go through shit in life and still be a decent human being. You are twice the man of any of the so-called men in my failed relationships. You, Matt, are my hero and always will be. You're always there for me, and I love you for that."

Matt nodded as he watched Ashley wrap three tiny pieces of steak into her napkin and put it in her purse. "For Dudley," she said as the waiter came to clear their plates.

"Two cheesecakes, one strawberry for me and a blueberry for my brother," Ashley said.

The waiter nodded and left.

"And you, my dear sister, know me better than I know myself." He lifted his water glass in a toast. "To new beginnings and to this new fellow being a great man to be there for you and create a family with you."

"I'll drink to that," Ashley said. "I'll let you know in a few days if that wish comes true."

Chapter 6

Ashley was thankful to have the weekend to herself. That way, she could focus on the painting and not wonder if she was carrying the son she yearned for. It was, in her mind, the only way she could make life better for herself and all concerned.

She had the Saturday off and she planned on spending the whole day in her studio. She poured some white paint into her special bucket and stirred in a bit of water to make sure it was the right consistency. She placed her blank canvas on the floor and took a step back The client asked for a black background, and fortunately, the art store had some pre-primed, black canvas available. She decided to start with the white and see what transpired. She attached her container to the suspended chain, brought it to the center and pulled out the little plug that held the paint in. She closed one eye, pulled back the bucket, and let it go.

She sat, mesmerized, yet highly alert, as the paint drizzled out of the container and onto the once black canvas. It swayed rhythmically, creating an oval pattern. She lightly touched the container, and it began to create circular patterns within the oval. It reminded her of the Spirograph she had as a child. It was a time before the beatings started. An innocent time before she decided to kill her father.

Dudley sat at the doorway to the art room, watching. He hated the feeling of plastic beneath his paws. He also disliked the smell of paint. It was clear there'd be no more meat treats today. With a quick, disgruntled meow, he turned and left the doorway in search of a better place to contemplate cat life.

When the container of white paint created tight, small circles, Ashley grabbed it and disconnected it from the chain. She stared at the canvas. It was a good start. Now to decide if she should do white on all three canvases first or apply another color to this one. The size of the room made the choice easy. She had nowhere in the house to lay a canvas this large to dry where Dudley wouldn't walk all over it. She sighed, wishing she had a home with a huge art studio and a large garden. But this was what she was dealing with, so she would make the best of it.

Ashley grabbed the can of red paint and a new container. She poured in the flow paint, added some acrylic paint, and added water. She stirred and contemplated adding her special ingredient. She decided this one deserved a human touch.

She walked into the kitchen and pulled one last ice cube-sized chunk of frozen blood out of the freezer and put it in a bowl. She popped it into the microwave on defrost and, when it was done, returned to her art studio and mixed it in with the paint. She studied her work. The paint was still too wet to add another color. Best to leave it a few more minutes. She turned on a fan in the corner of the room, hoping to speed up the process.

Back in the kitchen, Ashley rinsed out the small bowl and placed it in the dishwasher. The water would take care of the rest. It was the final leftover of her latest failed attempt at finding a baby daddy. But that was okay because Randy was looking like a real winner. She grabbed her breakfast dishes out of the sink, put them in the dishwasher, and started it.

Dudley came into the kitchen and wound himself around her ankles, looking for a treat. "Not today, little one. All I have for you are these." She held up a bag that clearly stated they were paw-licking good. Dudley stared at her and walked away.

"Hey, you! These are good treats. You may never get the other ones again, so take what you're offered. Dudley flicked his tail in her direction, stopped, and turned around as if to say they would have to do. He walked toward Ashley and sat at her feet. She smiled, opened the bag, and tossed him three treats.

"That's all you get for now. We don't want you to get too fat."

She headed back to her art room. The white should be dry enough by now. It was time to add the red. As she stood above the painting, she contemplated the speed and arc the container would take as it dripped its delicious red onto the canvas. She lined it up, removed the plug, pulled back, and let it go. Immediately the red formed the most beautiful contrast between the white paint and the black canvas. A knock on the door interrupted her thoughts.

"Are you kidding me?" she asked of the walls.

The knock got louder. Ashley hollered out through the door. "Give me a minute! I'll be right there." She watched in anticipation as the red swirled and circled the canvas. When it had done all she needed it to do, she stopped the container and disconnected it. She put the plug back in, took it into the kitchen and placed it in the sink.

The knocking was louder now.

"I'll be right there, hold onto your panties!"

Ashley filled the bucket with water, swirled it and dumped it. She put some soap into the bucket and added hotter water. Who the hell was at the door? She wiped her hands on her painting pants and headed toward the front door.

"I'm coming!" she shouted as the knocking started again.

Ashley opened the door and was surprised to see a rather handsome middle-aged man. He was nicely built, with a little salt and pepper hair around the temples.

"Yes? Can I help you?" she asked.

"Sorry to bother you, ma'am. I'm Detective Colombo. Can I come in? I have a few questions about a missing person."

Ashley pushed some stray hair behind her ear, leaving a streak of diluted red on her temple. "Your name is Columbo? Like the weird old detective from the seventies TV show?"

"No, that was C O L U M B O. My name is C O L O M B O. It's Italian, in case you were wondering." He stared at the red streak on Ashley's temple. "Did you cut yourself, ma'am?" he asked.

Ashley shook her head no and made a face. "No, I don't think so. Am I bleeding?"

"Well, there's a streak of red by your eyebrow there."

Ashley ran into the bathroom, looked in the mirror, and burst into nervous laughter.

"Oh, that," She walked back to the waiting detective.

"Nope, that's paint. I was painting when you knocked. I must have got some of the red on my hands. Please, please, come in. Give me another minute to clean myself up."

She pointed to the couch and disappeared into the kitchen. She grabbed a paper towel, wet it, and wiped the paint mixture off her brow. She dumped the soapy water from the bucket, wiped it with the towel, the added more soap and hot water and gave it a swirl. She glanced into the living room as she scrubbed it both clean and placed it upside down in the sink. She was pretty sure they wouldn't find blood in the paint container, but it was a hard plastic, so she wasn't sure. She made a mental note to look it up on her Tor browser, to avoid tracking.

Ashley went back to the living room and sat down opposite the detective. "Okay, sorry about that. How can I help you, Detective Colombo?"

Dudley sauntered into the room and rubbed himself up against the detective's black pants, leaving little light brown hairs embedded in the material.

"I, uh, well, actually, I'm allergic to cats. Could you put him in another room for now?"

"Oh, sure, of course," she said as she scooped up Dudley. "Sorry, kiddo, it's a time out in my bedroom for you. Behave." She set the cat down on her bed and gently closed the door.

"Be right there," she called as she stepped into her art studio. The paint was setting nicely and should be ready for the blue by the time the detective left. She shut the door and returned to the living room.

"Now, how can I help?"

"Well, ma'am, as I said before," he pulled out a small notebook and pen, "I'm on a missing person's case. A man named Rodney Albright. Do you know him?"

Ashley scrunched up her nose and thought for a moment. "Ummm, I met a Roddy recently, but I didn't catch his last name."

"That's probably him. Tell me, where did you meet this, Roddy?"

"Well, it's a bit embarrassing, but I met him at a club about a month ago. We danced a bit, laughed a bit, and even kissed a bit." Ashley felt her face go red. It was more out of fear than embarrassment, but the detective didn't know that.

"And did you bring this, Roddy, home Ms. Taylor?"

Ashley sat up a bit straighter when she heard her last name fall from the detective's mouth. He'd done his research and already knew she'd left the club with a man who was now dissolving somewhere in a large barrel buried in a field.

"Please, call me Ashley," she said. "Well, please don't think bad of me, but yes, yes, I did. I wasn't thinking straight. We got home, and he was pretty demanding. He wanted to have sex, and I, well …" She let her voice trail off.

"Well, what?" The detective leaned forward.

"Well. . ." Ashley hesitated again. "Okay, I confess. I slapped him right across his face and kicked him out!" She stood and paced the room as she addressed the detective. "I mean, really. I was hoping for some conversation, or showing him my paintings, or maybe more kissing, but not sex! What is wrong with some men!"

"Well, ma'am, I can't speak for the entire male population, but some men can be a bit crude. And you did bring him home after a night of drinking and dancing." He paused and wrote something in his notebook. "What time would you say it was when you kicked him out."

"Gosh, it must have been around two in the morning. We came back here after the club. We took an Uber because neither of us was in any shape to drive. I didn't bring my car. Safety first, ya know."

Ashley hoped she sounded convincing. She'd had half of one drink that night. She liked to keep her mind alert and her body fairly clean of substances. The reason she didn't take her car that night was because she didn't want the neighbors to think she was out. It was safer that way. If they saw her car, she could say she was home all night. However, in this case, it was obvious someone at the club recognized her, so leaving the car didn't help at all. She'd have to rethink her hunting techniques.

The detective smiled at her. "Did you watch him leave? Which direction did he go?"

"Yes, I watched out the window to make sure he was gone. He stumbled off toward the street and turned left. I figured he'd catch a cab or something a few blocks up where there's more traffic."

"I see." The detective closed his notebook and stood. "So, you said you were painting. Do you mind if I look around?"

"Actually, I do," Ashley said. "I don't let people see my work before it is done. It's actually in my contract with my clients—no showing anyone what I'm doing. They get the first look when I'm done."

"Understood." The detective brushed some stray hairs off his pants.

"So, when did this Roddy guy disappear?" Ashley asked, hoping to get ahead of the questioning.

"We aren't sure. He was seen at the club leaving with you around 1:30 in the morning. Your neighbor across the street, Rocky, I believe his name is, said he saw you and the missing man, or someone that fit his description, get out of a car with you just before two and head into your house. His family and friends haven't seen him since."

"Hmmm," Ashley mused. "I didn't know Rocky was up at that time of night. Well, was he up when Roddy left? Did he see him leave?" Ashley felt a trickle of sweat escape from under her armpit.

"No, he was only up for a glass of water when he saw you two exit the vehicle. He went back to bed afterward. We've canvassed the neighborhood, and no one saw Rodney leave here. But one of your neighbors up the street saw a lone male walking toward the highway right around the time you said you kicked him out. She couldn't ID him from the photo, but the general description fit. It could have been him. So that fits with your story."

Ashley felt her entire body relax. "Well, there you have it, Detective. He probably hitchhiked or something once he got to the highway."

"It's possible." The detective turned toward the door and then stopped. "Will you be around later? Just in case we need to ask you any more questions."

"Yes, of course." Ashley reached around the detective and opened her front door. "I work up the road at the local nursery part-time. If I'm not here painting, I'm at work."

"Good to know," he said as he opened the door. "Thanks for the information."

Ashley watched him head to his car, then closed the door and slowly exhaled. She'd have to be much more careful if Randy didn't work out.

It was time to formulate a new a plan, just in case.

Chapter 7

Detective Francis Colombo tossed his notebook on his desk and headed into the break room to grab his fourth cup of coffee for the day. His nose itched, and his eyes were dry. He hated cats.

Tate Sparks was already in the room and looked up when he walked in. "Hey, Frank. How'd it go today? Any leads on the Albright case?"

Frank shook his head as he poured cream and sugar into his cup. "Nope. But I have a weird feeling about this Ashley woman. She was the last person or maybe the second last person to see him alive."

"Did you make her 'walk the Frank?'" Sparks laughed. It was a long-standing joke among Colombo's fellow officers. Francis, or Frank as he preferred to be called, was well known for pushing suspects to the brink and sitting back and relaxing while he watched them confess. A tactic known in his department as making a suspect, walk the Frank.

"Nah, I wish. There was another witness who saw someone walking down the street about the time this Ashley woman says she kicked him out, so their stories jive." Frank stopped and took a sip of coffee. Perfection. "But there's something about her, something she was hiding, and I just can't put my finger on it."

"Well, if your history is any indication, you're either going to fall in love with her, or you'll get her to confess to a shit ton of stuff."

"Knock it off, Tate. Once, one time, I dated a suspect, and that was only after she was cleared of all wrongdoing by the higher-ups and the case was closed. Let's just leave that one alone."

Frank shook his head and wandered toward his desk. He sat down, turned on the computer, and flipped open his notebook. She was an attractive woman, but there was something about her that put him on alert. He'd done a search, and the only thing he could find on her was some old records of her being in a string of foster homes. Her dad died when she was a young teen, and that was it. There was a record of home ownership, auto registration, and driver's license, but other than that, there was no information. She didn't have any social media presence, which was odd. Even Frank had a Facebook page and wandered over to Instagram now and then. TikTok was not to his liking, and he didn't see the point of X as someone was always cranky about something.

There was an email with webcam footage from the night Albright disappeared. It showed Albright and Ashley leaving the club and getting into an Uber. That was the last recorded instance of Rodney Albright being alive. Since then, there'd been no credit card transactions, no social media, nothing.

The Uber driver was only slightly helpful. He said he barely remembered the couple but he did remember the woman wasn't as eager as the man to get up close and intimate in the car. That supported Ashley's claim that she wasn't up for a one-night stand. But why take a guy home from a club at two in the morning if you aren't going to hook up? Women's reasoning baffled Frank and trying to figure out Ashley's motivation would get him nowhere. He knew no meant no, but still. Maybe she was that naïve. Maybe he'd said something about wanting to see her paintings or something. He would never know. Perhaps one of the female detectives could help. He'd ask them once he filed his reports.

"Colombo. Got another case for you." Sergeant Kay Lenz waved a manilla file folder in the air above her head. "Come into my office, and I'll fill you in."

Frank gave another brief look at his unopened emails and headed toward her office. Things had been crazy these past few years. There were more and more cases and fewer people to work them. He had ten missing person cases on his plate, and only one looked like a runaway.

"What is it this time?" Frank asked. "Runaway, missing spouse?" He sat in the chair in front of her desk and took the file from her.

"This one should be simple to solve. Missing woman, engaged, missed her bachelorette party two nights ago. The wedding is in four days. Think you can find her before that?"

"Well, that all depends, Sarge. Are you saying this one outranks the other ones?"

"Yes, and no," came the reply. "She's the daughter of a prominent politician. We'd like this wrapped up as soon as possible. He's in charge of police funding, do your best, okay?"

Frank took the file and started to leave. "Hey, Sarge, can I ask you a question? It's got to do with a case and, well, women in general."

Sergeant Lenz grinned at the detective. "Still having a hard time figuring us out?"

"Yeah, something like that." He sat back down. "This Rodney Albright case. I interviewed the woman he left the club with today. She admitted to bringing him home but kicked him out when he got handsy. She said she hoped he just wanted to talk, but he had other ideas. She claims she sent him on his way shortly after two in the morning. A neighbor across the street confirmed he saw the pair pull up in an Uber just before two a.m. He went to bed after that and didn't see the man leave. But someone a few blocks away said she saw a man, matching Albright's height and weight, walking down the road by her place toward the highway around 2:15 a.m."

"Okay, and this woman who brought the guy home, her story matches up with the other witnesses' reports, right? So, what's your question?"

"Why would a woman bring a man home from a club at two in the morning only to kick him out?" Frank sat back in the chair and waited.

"Frank? Are you really asking me this? Are you sure you want to go down this road with me?"

Frank nodded.

"Wow, you are old school, aren't you? In case you wondered, that's my way of saying you're a Luddite—a totally unaware human who thinks sex is always on the table. Would that be an accurate conclusion?"

Frank's face turned red. "No, not at all. It's just that they were at a club, dancing, and drinking, and she brings him home just to kick him out. I don't get it."

Sergeant Lenz shook her head and made tsk-tsk sounds.

"Frank, there must be a dozen reasons why she'd invite the guy back. You don't know what they talked about beforehand, so you jumped to the conclusion that the evening would automatically end in sex if she brought him home. And even if she did hint at sex, and changed her mind once she sobered up a bit, then no still means no."

"It was two in the morning, for gawd's sake!" Frank leaned forward in his chair. "I know I'm old-fashioned, and I'm not great with the ladies, but why? Can you help a guy out here? Without the sarcasm, please."

"I don't know, Frank. Maybe she invited him over to see her etchings." The sergeant let a small laugh escape her lips.

"Hmmm, that could be right."

"Excuse me?"

"The suspect, er the woman, I questioned; she's some sort of painter. Maybe that was it."

"There you have it then," Lenz said. "Now, if you don't mind, I've got a lot of work to do. Get on that new missing person's case ASAP and keep me posted."

"Yes, ma'am." Frank stood and left the office. His workday just got a little longer.

Chapter 8

Ashley stood at the doorway to her art room and admired the last of her three paintings. It took eight days to make sure everything was exactly as she wanted it and that the paint was truly dry.

She'd moved the other two into the living room and created a little tent out of plastic so Dudley wouldn't go near them. Now it was time to move the third and call the client.

She dared to touch the back of the large painting and checked to see if even the small drips had dried. It was ready. She found her phone and dialed.

"Hi, this is Ashley, the artist. Could you please tell Corbin his paintings are ready and send the installer to pick them up? Yes, that's right, I'll be here all day. Thank you."

She disconnected the call and looked around. She'd finished them in record time and made a good chunk of money in the process. After paying for materials, she netted a full $25,000. Her clients were happy to pay for work that would never be duplicated or turned into prints.

She gently picked up the painting and maneuvered it out the door and beside the other two. The triptych filled her entire living room. She was glad to have them out of her house. The sooner, the better. She hated clutter.

Her phone pinged and she glanced at the screen.

> How is the painting coming along? I miss
> you.

Ashley smiled as she read the text twice.

> Done early. Are you back from your trip?

She watched as the three little dots bounced across her screen. Part of her wanted to see him right away. Another part wanted some space. She needed time to look into cleaning up whatever bits of evidence might still be left in the house. The detective had made her realize she wasn't as careful as she'd thought.

> I'll be home tomorrow. I stayed a bit longer
> as Mom's not feeling well. Thank goodness I
> can work anywhere as long as there's Wi-Fi.
> When can I see you?

Ashley sighed. She really liked this one. What a nice guy to stay with his mom when she wasn't feeling well. She was certain this was the man to father her babies.

> I've got some cleaning up to do, so how
> about the day after tomorrow? I need to
> decompress and get back into the real
> world. Besides, I work at the nursery

> tomorrow. I don't work the day after so let's
> make a day of it. Maybe order in or eat out?

She watched as the little dots bounced around, stopped, and came back to life on her screen.

> Okay, I think I can wait that long. I'll plan
> something. My treat.

Ashley smiled. She wasn't sure if she could wait that long either.

> It's a date. See you at my place around 10
> a.m., and we'll make a fun day of it. Then
> we'll go eat!

Ashley set the phone down and went into the kitchen. She opened her laptop and logged into her Tor browser. She needed to know how long it took for blood to break down on a carpet or wood floor. The results didn't make her feel any better. Apparently, blood was pretty hard to get rid of.

"Years? Oh, that's not good," she said to Dudley. "Well, I guess we'd better figure out how to get rid of it then."

She did a few quick searches, including some scientific papers that said hydrogen peroxide was great at breaking down set-in blood stains. She had a few bottles in the bathroom, and she also had some OxiClean. She'd get rid of those stains, if there were any, once and for all.

Ashley grabbed a huge garbage bag and headed into the

art room. She was determined to get all the plastic off the floor, walls, and ceiling before her date with Randy. With a few good tugs, some scissors, and a lot of patience, she pulled it all down and stuffed it into the oversized garbage bag. One bag wasn't enough, so she grabbed a second. As she stuffed the last of the paint-stained plastic into the bag, her doorbell rang.

"Be right there!" she called as she tied a knot in the bag and headed to the door.

"Hello, ma'am. I'm here to pick up some paintings. I was told you'd be expecting me."

Ashley looked out into the driveway at the shiny Mercedes panel van. The driver had a helper, and both wore white gloves.

"Yes, of course, come on in. Please make sure they don't touch anything. Not the walls of the van and not each other. You can touch the backs but be careful of the sides. Best not to touch them either."

"Yes, ma'am," the taller of the two said and gave a side-eye glance to his helper.

"Please forgive my instructions. It's just that I worked hard to get these just right."

"No problem, ma'am," said the shorter of the two. "I've got proper transport crates behind me, and if you don't mind, we'd like to pack them up in here. Less exposure to the elements that way."

"Okay," Ashley said and stepped out of the way.

She watched closely as the men handled her paintings as if the slightest bump would destroy them. Satisfied with their commitment to the job, she headed into the kitchen and filled a bucket with hot water and OxiClean. She'd start the cleanup as soon as they were gone. Twenty-five minutes later, they were done, and the paintings were safely stored in the van.

"Oh, one other thing," Ashley said. "Is there a dumpster near where you are going? I have all this plastic that I use when I do my paintings, and I need to dump it."

The taller of the two gave the shorter one a side-eye but agreed to take the bags. "Not a problem, ma'am. We'll dispose of it for you." With that, he picked up both bags, tossed one to his helper, and left the house. Ashley breathed a sigh of relief. She hated to ask, but it was so much easier than sneaking down alleys at night to find an open dumpster. It was too much garbage for her local service to handle.

With the paintings gone and most of the garbage out of the house, Ashley set to work. She scoured any spots she found on the carpet, blotting them with paper towels after scrubbing. After she was finished with the carpet, she went to work on wiping down the walls, the chains, the light fixture, and the ceiling. Her neck throbbed from being in such an odd position on the ladder, but it was worth it.

Once everything was clean, she took another look at the room. It was obvious which parts of the carpet she'd cleaned. Maybe she should get out the carpet cleaner and go over the whole thing again. Then she had a horrible thought. What if some of her previous failed lover's blood soaked through the carpet and into the backing, or worse, into the rough wood of the floor below? She thought back to Roddy. He was a quick one.

Ashley was in a hurry to receive his sperm and hadn't taken much time between shutting the door and pulling down his pants. There was no time to lose as she was already one day into her ovulation cycle. He was pleasantly surprised and came quickly. Ashley assured him it was fine. There was plenty of time for more fun. They'd sat and chatted for a bit, and then he'd said that bit about being in touch with his feminine side and equated it with housework. The next thing Ashley remembered was him tied up in her art room, arms raised, attached to the chains in the ceiling. She hated it when she blacked out, especially when it was ovulation time.

She remembered asking him what other feminine things he considered himself in touch with. Before he could speak, Ashley backhanded him across the face, and blood flew from his mouth. The next thing she remembered was holding her favorite chef's knife. Roddy's head lolled to one side as blood dripped down his torso and legs and into the large buckets she'd placed his feet in. She'd cut him from ear to ear, but she suspected he was unconscious when he died. At least, she hoped so. She hated hurting people.

She left him there overnight until all the blood was drained. In the morning, she tossed the contents of the buckets down the kitchen drain. Then she cut off his fingers and toes. Just like the others before him, she tossed them into a crock pot for Dudley.

The rest of the early morning was a blur. She'd cut Roddy into barrel-sized pieces, sawing his legs at the knee and his arms at the elbow.

She was no surgeon, but she could spatchcock a chicken, and people were basically big chickens. Cutting him in half was fairly easy. You just needed to get through the spinal cord, and voila, done.

After he was cut into the right sizes, she'd gone out back and wheeled the 55-gallon drum inside on a dolly. She carefully placed all the pieces into the drum, making sure there was enough room for the lye and water. Then she'd wheeled it back outside, covered Roddy with lye, and went inside to put the kettle on. After pouring several kettles of boiling water over his body bits, she replaced the lid and decided it was safe to add cold water and let the lye do the rest of its work at a slower process. It wasn't perfect, but it had worked well for the last half a dozen suitors.

Ashley looked around the room, recalling all the men, all the kills, the blackouts, and all of the dismemberment. She touched her belly lightly. Maybe this time would be different. She'd know near the end of May.

The knives. She had to clean the knives. The carpet cleaning would have to wait. She'd seen shows on TV where they found blood embedded into the handle where the blade met the wood. She'd have to clean that, too, and the trap under the sink. That had to be cleaned. That damn detective spoiled her one full day off.

Ashley turned on the fan to dry the spots on the carpet and headed for the kitchen. Instead of putting the knives into the dishwasher, she filled a baking pan with hydrogen peroxide and placed them in it. Small bubbles formed around the blade where it met the wood. She'd been right. There was blood there. This was no time to get sloppy.

As the knives bubbled away, she went back into the art room and grabbed the larger buckets, the ones used to catch the blood and hold her paint. She brought them into the kitchen and filled each one almost to the top and added a cup of OxiClean to each. She'd have to get more next shopping trip, just in case.

"Oh, the rags!" Ashley ran for the cupboard, where she kept her cleaning rags. She almost tripped over Dudley as he came to see what all the fuss was about.

"Hey, watch it, Dudley. Mama is on a mission."

Ashley grabbed every one of her rags and cleaning towels and plopped them into the buckets of OxiClean. Then she went into her bedroom, pulled out the clothes she'd been wearing that night, and pushed them into the mixture as well. She was so close to realizing her dream. She couldn't be stopped now.

With the knives, buckets, rags, and clothing soaking, Ashley pulled out the carpet cleaner. It was a smaller, handheld one, mostly used for cleaning up cat puke, but it would do. She spent the next hour going over every square inch of the art room, soaking the carpet, sucking up the murky-colored water, and then dumping it down the drain. She'd clean the sink traps last.

Ashley triple-rinsed the carpet cleaner, the final rinse being a strong OxiClean solution. Then she tossed the contents of the buckets into her washing machine. Once again, water would help her erase her sins and give her a chance at a better life. She turned on the machine and went into the kitchen. The knives had long since stopped bubbling and were ready to dry. She watched the slightly bubbly mess go down the drain and waited twenty minutes. Gawd, how she loved water.

"That should do it," she said to Dudley, who by now was waiting for his dinner.

MEOWR!

"In a minute, little guy. One more thing to do. I should have done this last month, but better late than never."

She turned off the water under the sink, retrieved her tool kit, and turned on her computer. She searched YouTube until she found a video she was pretty sure she could follow. Once one of the newly cleaned buckets was under the sink, she grabbed her wrench and loosened both ends of the joint, then waited as the remaining water leaked into her bucket. She easily removed the P trap and cleaned it out with a bottle scrubber. The seals looked good, so she rinsed out the joint with more OxiClean and water and then cleaned the ends. A few minutes later, everything was back where it belonged, all nice and clean.

MEOWR!

"All right, all right, just a minute!" she hollered as she made her way out from under the sink. "I'll get your dinner now."

Ashley grabbed Dudley's dish and scooped some soft food out of a can. Then she added some dry food and stirred.

"There, enjoy."

As she looked around her kitchen, Ashley felt a wave of exhaustion wash over her. Trying to find a baby daddy was hard work. Cleaning up after they didn't work out was even harder.

The washing machine made a sing-song noise, and Ashley headed to the laundry area to put everything in the dryer. When she returned to the kitchen, she saw a message on her phone.

> Just got home. I'll see you the day after
> tomorrow. Wear something casual. I have a
> plan.

Ashley smiled at her phone. Yeah, this one was a keeper.

> I can hardly wait.

In two days, maybe three, she'd take the pregnancy test and know for sure if her future was as she planned it.

Chapter 9

Ashley pulled on a fresh pair of jeans and a T-shirt. It was a beautiful warm May day, but she grabbed a light jacket, just in case. Randy would be there any minute. She cleaned the litter box, filled up Dudley's food and water dishes, and stuffed his toy mouse with catnip. It would keep him busy for the day.

Randy showed up at exactly ten a.m. with a big grin on his face.

"Hey there, beautiful. How did you get more gorgeous in the past few days? Just stunning."

Ashley rolled her eyes and shook her head, but inside, she was beaming and blushing. This guy was the real deal.

"Well, you look pretty darn tasty yourself," she replied as she grabbed her purse and shooed Randy out the door. "Best we leave right away before Dudley knows I'm gone."

"Gotcha." Randy ran to open the car door for her.

"M'lady," he said with a swoop of his hand.

Ashley got into the car and noticed it was freshly cleaned. She commented on it once Randy was inside, and they were on their way.

"Car looks great. You must have had some extra time on your hands."

"Nah, I had to take it to the shop this morning to get the

brakes checked. They'd been squeaking a bit, and I thought it might be time to get new ones, but the shop said they're good for a little bit longer. They insisted on cleaning the car for me. Great guys, but I was worried about being late and I wanted to get over here."

"I have a phone, you know," Ashley said with a grin. "You could have let me know you were going to be late."

"Nope, no worries. The guys assured me they were good for another thousand clicks or so. I've got an appointment in the third week of June. All good. And I made it here on time. Now, for our special day out."

Ashley gave a little squeal of delight. A whole day of fun, plus tomorrow she'd find out if she was pregnant. Life was good.

"So, where are we going first?" she asked.

"Not telling," Randy replied. "When we get near, I'm going to ask you to close your eyes."

"All right, I can do that," she said.

The pair drove along the streets and headed out on the highway. Ashley was curious but didn't want to ruin the surprise. She wondered where he could be taking her. To quiet the curious part of her mind, she took in the scenery. Bright, newborn green leaves burst into the sunshine, erasing the dull browns of the spring landscape. Ashley rolled down her window and took a few deep breaths, then quickly shut it.

"Not lovin' the spring air?" Randy asked.

"Yeah, not lovin' the exhaust from that crappy truck ahead of us. But the trees are so beautiful!"

Ashley turned to look behind her at the copse they'd just

passed. As she turned back in her seat, she noticed a picnic basket on the back seat.

"A picnic! Oh, my gawd. I haven't been on a picnic in ages!" She leaned over and kissed Randy on the cheek. "I hope I didn't ruin the surprise."

Randy simply grinned. "Not at all, that's not the surprise, but we will have our picnic before the surprise."

Ashley settled back into her seat and sighed a happy sigh. This one was a keeper. A half-hour into the drive, Ashley's curiosity got the best of her. "Where are we going? Is it far?"

"Patience," Randy replied. "We've got another hour at least of highway driving and then about twenty minutes to this cute little park, I know."

"We're headed to the big city?" Ashley asked. "No, don't tell me. I want to be surprised. But are we?"

Randy laughed. "Yes, we are headed into what you so adorably called the big city."

"Oh, goody!" Ashley clapped her hands like a child. She reached over and found a radio station she liked, sat back and settled into her seat. "Don't mind me. I'll be sitting right here enjoying the scenery."

"You do just that," Randy said. "Sleep if you want. We'll be there around noon."

Ashley nodded, more to herself than to Randy. Yes, this one was a keeper.

* * *

Ashley slowly opened her eyes as she felt the car come to

a halt. They were in a parking lot somewhere near a park. She stretched and yawned.

"Gawd, what a horrible road-tripper I am. How long was I asleep?"

"I think you nodded off about five minutes after you picked that slow jazz station. I like watching you sleep."

He opened his door, then the back door, and pulled out the picnic basket.

"Where are we?" Ashley asked.

"A somewhat obscure, somewhat famous little botanical garden, miles from work and any cares you might have," he said.

Ashley got out and stretched. "Lead the way."

Randy came around to her side of the car and took her hand in his. He led her down a winding path with gorgeous peonies, irises, and pansies, nodding to them as they walked. They came around a corner, and Ashley was struck by the scent and the beauty before her. Hundreds of lilac bushes enclosed a small natural amphitheater. A gentle breeze brought the soft, powdery scent to them and wrapped them in a romantic hug.

"Oh my gawd, Randy! It's gorgeous here. Well worth the drive." Ashley looked around and noticed there were three other couples in the area, all sitting far enough from each other not to be overheard.

"Did you know lilacs were my favorite flower, well next to Lily of the Valley?" Ashley turned around slowly, arms outstretched, taking in the full experience.

The sun warmed her face as the scent of lilacs transported her back to a simpler time. A time when her mother was still with her, when her father didn't hurt her. A time when her foster parents didn't abuse her. She felt a wave of melancholy wash over her, then shook her head to rid herself of the past. Today was her day, and she was going to enjoy it.

She took another look around and realized Randy had found a spot in full sunshine to place the blanket and basket. She ran over to where he stood and pretended to tackle him. "This is fabulous! Really, it is. I don't know how to thank you."

"I'm glad you like it, Ashley. You work hard. You deserve some time just for you."

Ashley sat down on the blanket and waited patiently to find out what was for lunch. Her stomach gave a little growl, and Randy chuckled.

"Okay, I guess it's time to bring the food out," he said and opened the basket. He pulled out two plates, two napkins, two forks, and two glasses. He poured some sparkling water into the glasses and then raised his in a toast. "To us," he said. "May we have many, many more days together."

"To us," Ashley repeated and clinked his glass. "Now, what did you bring to eat? I'm starving."

"Well, it was a tough choice. There were so many choices at the market. I could have got a whole roast chicken and a salad, or some delicious sandwiches, or soups, but I didn't get any of that."

"Don't make me guess!" Ashley swatted his arm playfully.

"Well, I'm pretty sure you like spicy food, but not too spicy. Hot, but not too hot. Just before I took my car in to be checked, I saw this Jamaican Fusion food truck, and I got us ..."

Randy reached into the basket and pulled out two wraps, carefully covered in parchment paper and tinfoil. He put one on Ashley's plate and one on his. The smell snaked its way through the lilac perfume and snuck into Ashley's nostrils.

"Oh, you didn't!" Ashley squealed. "Jamaican jerk chicken wraps. Oh, I could kiss you! No, I am going to kiss you." She leaned over and grabbed Randy by the back of his head and planted an overly energetic kiss on his lips.

"Wow, I have to find out where that food truck is should we ever fight. I think I've found a way to make things up to you." He grinned and opened up Ashley's wrap and then his own. He pulled out a knife and cut them both in two and handed Ashley a napkin. "Enjoy," he said.

They spent the next ten minutes in silence as they enjoyed their meal and gazed around the natural amphitheater.

Ashley closed her eyes for most of the meal, savoring the spicy mayo and lime, letting the food sit on her tongue before chewing and swallowing. She had no idea how he knew this was one of her favorite foods. He must've been listening to everything she said. She made up her mind right then and there that she was going to keep this one. No matter what. Any minor flaws he had could never outweigh the good she saw in him. The only thing left was for her to get pregnant.

Once she'd finished every bite of the wrap, she turned to Randy. "If you keep this up, I'm going to have to keep you," she said. The smile on her face was teasing, but the look in her eyes was dead serious.

"Well," Randy said. "I've been thinking a lot about that.

I know we've only been seeing each other for a few weeks—"

Ashley interrupted him. "A month, to be exact."

"Well, yes, a calendar month, but I didn't get to see you for over a week!" he protested. "But as I was saying. I know it's only been a short time, but …" This time, his voice trailed off as he looked over at the lilacs. "But I want you to know that in that short time, I believe I've fallen head over heels for you."

Ashley blinked at him, speechless.

"What I'm trying to say is, well, it's, oh heck, I'll just say it. I love you, Ashley."

Ashley was stunned. She vaguely recalled hearing those words from her mother almost thirty years ago. She'd told her she loved her the night she left. And now, after all this time, someone else on the planet, someone good and kind and decent, said he loved her. She swallowed to clear the emotion rising in her throat.

"Oh, Randy," she said.

"You don't have to say it back," he said. "I thought you should know. I was telling my mother about you, and she told me it sounded like I was falling in love. And she was right."

Ashley reached over and took Randy's hand, then playfully licked at a spot where some of the spicy mayo had fallen. She looked back up at him, grinning from ear to ear.

"Well, I know I don't have to, but I've been thinking about you a lot over the past few days, and I think I'm in the same boat. I love you, too." She let out a little sigh and stared into his eyes. It was the strangest feeling, being loved and being in love, but she liked it. She liked it a lot.

Randy shook his head. "Okay, well, now that that's out of the way." He leaned over and kissed Ashley firmly on the lips. "It's time for part two of Ashley's day out."

"It couldn't get much better than this." She lay back on the blanket. "Just a few more minutes. I don't want this feeling to go away. Gorgeous surroundings, a full tummy, and a very handsome man just told me he loves me. Let me savor this for a while."

Randy laughed and lay down beside her. "As you wish."

* * *

Half an hour later, the pair were back on the road and headed into a busy downtown area. Ashley didn't ask where they were going. After the last two hours, she knew that wherever it was, it would be perfect.

"Okay, close your eyes," Randy said. "I trust you. Keep them closed."

Ashley complied and swayed slightly as the car took a right and then another right. It slowed and came to a halt.

"Keep them closed. I'm coming around to get you."

Ashley kept her eyes closed. She could hear horns honking, people talking, and a child laughing off in the distance. She took a deep breath, and despite the pervasive scent of exhaust fumes, she could also smell perfume, cigarette smoke, and even a hot dog.

"Okay, take my hand and step out of the car. Eyes closed now." Randy helped her out and onto the sidewalk. "Just a few more steps. Okay, wait, I need to open the door."

Ashley stood still, anticipating what was to come.

"Eyes still closed? Good. Three small steps up. I've got you. Take your time."

Ashley felt the first step with her toe and stepped up. She gingerly climbed the next two steps and waited.

"Almost there," he said. "Just a bit longer." He took Ashley by the elbow and led her into the building.

Ashley closed her eyes and took a deep breath. It smelled like old-fashioned floor wax and laundry. She could feel the texture of the old floor beneath her as she slowly followed along with Randy.

"So close, just five more steps," he said. Then he stopped and turned her at a forty-five-degree angle from where she'd stopped.

"Okay, open them."

Ashley opened her eyes, and her mouth fell open.

Before her stood an original Jackson Pollock painting. Tears threatened to spill over onto her cheeks, and her throat felt dry and tight. This man, this fabulous man, had heard her. He'd listened and deduced what she loved in life and delivered it.

She swallowed and was finally able to speak. "I don't know what to say. Wait, yes, I do. Thank you." She continued to stare at the painting.

Randy stepped in closer and put an arm around her shoulder. With his other hand, he wiped a stray tear. "You're welcome." He kissed her on the cheek.

She turned and looked up at him. "I'm the luckiest woman in the world," she said. "I mean, holy hell, a Jackson Pollock."

Ashley continued to stare at the painting, then realized there were more great abstract paintings in the gallery. She wandered over and gasped.

"This is a Tom Shannon! Are you kidding me? Jackson Pollock and Tom Shannon are in the same gallery! Have I died and gone to heaven?"

Randy shrugged. "I just wanted to find somewhere to see some artists that may or may not have influenced your work. I think I did a good job."

Ashley playfully whacked him on the shoulder. "You think! I feel like I've walked into a Hallmark movie, and I'm the leading lady. Randy, if I ever doubted if you were right for me, this day, these gestures have sealed the deal. You're stuck with me now."

Randy smiled. "I was hoping you'd say that. Now let's go see what else they have on display here."

Chapter 10

Ashley stretched, yawned, and rolled out of bed. Randy was sound asleep beside her, and she didn't want to disturb him. It was time to take the test.

She padded into the bathroom and Dudley stopped her mid-step. He was about to protest about his empty food dish, but Ashley shushed him and told him to follow her into the kitchen.

"You are such a brat," she said as she poured kibble into his dish.

Dudley glared at her, then at the fridge.

"Right, soft food, gotcha." She put a heaping tablespoon of tuna into his dry food and mixed it up. "Now, I really have to pee!" She gave Dudley a quick pat and ran to the bathroom.

She didn't dare sit down yet. Instead, she opened the vanity cupboard, pulled out the box, and ripped it open. She got the test out just in time, sat, peed a bit, stopped, then peed on the stick. She pulled the stick away and gave a sigh of relief as she finished her morning pee. If nothing else, at least her Kegel exercises came in handy. Now to wait. She finished up in the bathroom and tucked the pee stick into the waistband of her panties. Fully awake now, she headed to the kitchen to make some coffee and wait.

Before she had a chance to look at the test results, Ashley felt a familiar cramp.

"No!" she moaned, just loud enough for Dudley to be curious but not concerned.

Ashley headed into the bathroom, sat, and gave a gentle wipe. Sure enough, a small pink dot appeared on the toilet paper.

"Dammit!" Ashley went back under the sink and, this time, pulled out the fiendish box of tampons. She hated that box, hated it with a burning fire that made her wish she had something or someone to stab. But now was not the time. She did what she had to do and went into the kitchen. Her test result was ready, but she already knew the answer. Not pregnant by a mile. She picked up the pee stick and put it in the trash, being careful to place it under something so Randy wouldn't see it. She wanted it to be a surprise when she got pregnant. She'd tell a little white lie and say her contraception failed. It was for the greater good.

"Good morning," a voice whispered in her ear and grabbed her from behind.

"Oh goodness, you startled me," Ashley said as she turned away from the garbage. "Coffee is ready." She faced Randy and gave him a quick peck on the lips. "Breakfast?"

"Not for me, thanks. Coffee though. I have a Zoom meeting at ten a.m., and I need to go home and prepare for it. Are you okay?" He went over to the counter and poured himself a cup of coffee.

"Yeah, I guess," she said. She wanted to tell him why she was disappointed but knew it could strain things between them.

"I got my period, so I'm feeling a bit off."

"Okay, so how about tonight we just watch a movie, and I'll give you a back rub."

"Sounds like a plan," she said. "Excuse me. I need to get some pants on." Ashley left the kitchen, barely holding back tears. She went into the bedroom, screamed into her pillow, then pulled on a pair of sweatpants. She would try again next month.

Chapter 11

May turned into June, and things got busy at the nursery. Ashley picked up some extra shifts to boost her bank account. She didn't feel like painting anymore. The depression she felt from not being pregnant lasted right up until her period ended. Her mood picked up as she ticked off the days before she ovulated. She daydreamed of a future with Randy and their son. She knew it was going to be a son because she was doing everything right. When she did get pregnant, it would be a boy. And even if it was a girl, there were still some special skills she could teach her.

Randy was busy as well. Something about online marketing and new products. Ashley didn't listen very closely to the work part of his life. She much preferred to know the man outside of his work interests. All she knew was that she was in love, and he loved her. After all the false starts and men with shitty attitudes, at least there was something good in her life.

Ashley headed into the kitchen as soon as she got home from work. She quickly fed Dudley and then checked the crock pot for her latest creation. She lifted the lid and inhaled deeply.

"Oh my gawd," She stood for a moment savoring the aroma. "He's going to love this chicken tortilla soup." She went into the small pantry and pulled out some tortilla chips to break up and sprinkle on the top when served. She glanced at the clock, then opened a bottle of Malbec to go with the meal. It was simple, but when she placed the good napkins on the table and the candles, it became a romantic dinner for two. And maybe, just maybe, she'd get pregnant tonight or the next. It didn't matter, she had five days to get pregnant, and she was sure this time was it.

Dudley wove his way between her legs, his way of begging for some of the chicken tortilla soup. Ashley shooed him away and got his kibble and tuna ready.

"Knock, knock!"

Ashley looked up as Randy stepped into the kitchen.

"It was open. I hope you don't mind. I just let myself in."

Ashley ran to meet him, put her arms around his neck, and gave him a lingering kiss.

"You can ring my bell and knock on my door anytime," she said playfully.

"Well, you certainly are in a good mood. It smells great in here, too." Randy stepped farther into the kitchen area and took in the candles and wine.

"Special occasion?" he asked.

"Nope, just you and me enjoying each other," she replied.

"Well, it certainly smells amazing. I'll go wash up."

Ashley patted his bum as he left the room. She chose white, shallow soup bowls and ladled up a serving for each of them. She placed the broken tortilla chips on the table. He could add what he wanted. Finally, she poured the wine, straightened her hair, and waited for him to return.

"Gawd, this smells so good," he said. "I'm starving!"

"Then sit, eat." She pointed to his chair and sat in hers.

The rest of the meal transpired with small talk about work, his and hers, and a discussion about visiting his mother.

"It's been a month or so. I really should head up there to see her," he said. "I was thinking about going up next weekend. Head up on Friday and come back on Monday. Would you like to join me? I'd love for you to meet her."

Ashley tried to hide her surprise. It had only been two months, and he wanted her to meet his mother. Maybe things were further along than she realized.

"I can't," she said. "I signed up to work from Friday to Monday next week. But I would love to meet her. Does this mean we're officially a couple?" she jokingly asked.

"Oh, I'd say that would be an accurate label." He smiled and finished the last of his soup. "That was delicious. You sit, pour some more wine, and I'll clear the table."

Ashley watched him as he took away their bowls, napkins, and cutlery, leaving the flickering candles and the half-finished bottle of wine on the table. She rarely drank, but she'd read an article online that said that women who drank red wine had a better chance with planned pregnancies. She wasn't sure if it was true, but she was willing to try it.

Randy sat back down and raised his glass in a toast. "To a bright future together," he said as he clinked her glass. "Look, Ash, there's something I've been meaning to tell you, and I think you should know before this, before we go any further."

Ashley straightened up in her chair. This didn't sound good.

He put his glass down and continued. "Remember when I said I got divorced because I wanted kids and my wife didn't."

Ashley nodded, waiting for the blow she was sure was about to happen.

"Well, we did try to stay together for a time. But she insisted I get a vasectomy."

Ashley finished the rest of her wine in one big gulp, then emptied the bottle into her glass and took another drink. She was trying very hard not to get upset.

"Go on."

"Well, I agreed."

Ashley held her breath.

"But I did something first. I got a few vials of sperm frozen just in case she changed her mind. Plus, there's a seventy percent chance that a reverse vasectomy would work. Results only really start showing up after a year or two after the operation."

"I see." Ashley took another big gulp of wine. She was furious, but at the same time, she'd come to love the man in front of her. She wasn't sure if a secret like a vasectomy was worthy of her disposing of him. Then again, he lied. She hated liars.

"I'm telling you this because, well, because I'm done with dating. You can go off your birth control, and when the time is right, if you want them, we can plan for children."

Ashley stared at him blankly. True, she had lied about being on birth control, and he was now being completely honest, but she wasn't about to tell him she was trying to get pregnant. She wasn't sure she even wanted to have his baby any more.

"What exactly do you mean, you're done dating?" She held her breath.

"I mean, I want to spend the rest of my life with you. I want to have a family with you. I know it's only been a few months, but I'm so crazy in love with you. I don't want to waste any more time."

Ashley finished her wine, scowled, and pushed her chair back from the table.

"Wait," Randy said. "There's more."

Ashley stayed seated and waited.

Randy stood and walked around to her side of the table and got down on one knee. Ashley didn't know if she should laugh, cry, or stab him. There were no knives left on the table, so she opted to sit and see what happened.

"Ashley, I think I've loved you since I first saw you at the plant store. After our first date, if you can call it that, I haven't stopped thinking about you. You are the perfect woman for me and the perfect woman to have our children." Randy pulled a ring out of his pocket. "I know this is sudden, but we aren't getting any younger, and I need to know."

Ashley looked at the ring and then at Randy. Could this be happening? No baby-making now but babies for certain in the very near future. Her lips turned upward.

Randy smiled up at her. "Ashley, would you do me the honor of marrying me?"

Ashley stared at him for a moment. Not once, in all her planning and scheming, did she think about marriage. Not once had she considered any of the men she brought home, husband material. It had always been about having a baby. Marriage was immaterial. She could raise a child on her own if necessary. And you didn't have to be married to have a child. She had Uncle Matt to be there for her and her baby.

"Ashley?" Randy interrupted her thoughts and held out the respectably sized diamond ring.

"Yes," she whispered.

"Yes?" he asked.

"Yes!" she shouted. She watched him put the ring on her finger, then stood up, pulling him with her. She threw her arms around his neck.

"Yes, yes, yes! The sooner, the better. I want to fill our house with babies and laughter and love."

Randy held her at arm's length. "I'm going to make you so happy, and our future children, of course."

"Of course!" Ashley giggled and winked.

"What?" Randy looked at her intensely.

"Let's practice making babies right now." She took Randy by the hand and headed into the bedroom. "After all, practice makes perfect."

Chapter 12

Ashley felt she was the luckiest woman alive. It took her a few moments to let the whole vasectomy/frozen sperm thing sink in. Once it had, she was okay with it. To be able to plan for a future with lots of babies was a relief. She and Randy even talked about having some of her eggs harvested, just in case. Better to get it done sooner than later. In the meantime, they practiced.

She knew women who had babies in their mid to late forties. Secretly, she hoped for at least three boys, but she didn't want to tell Randy and jinx it.

She called Matt a few days later when she felt comfortable talking to him about her upcoming nuptials. She and Randy hadn't decided on a date yet, but they'd hoped for a fall wedding, with baby plans immediately after that.

"What do you mean he froze his sperm?" Matt asked. "And a vasectomy? Ashley, this isn't like you. You normally wouldn't allow that kind of secrecy. It was dishonest!"

"Oh, Matt," she replied. "He's worth it. He really is. Randy has a great job, and he even wants me to harvest some eggs so we get the best chance and great kids. I'm in love. You should be happy for me."

"I am happy for you," he replied. "I just don't like that

he lied to you."

"He didn't lie. He just left out some information until he was sure. I'm the one who lied about using contraception. But it's all good, Matt. Really, it is. He's heading up to see his mom in a few days. He'll tell her then, and the following weekend I'll go up with him to meet her. Can you believe it, Matt? I'm going to have a proper family."

"A proper family, huh?"

Ashley could hear the disappointment in his voice.

"Matt, c'mon now. You'll always be my brother, no matter what. I want you to walk me down the aisle."

The line was silent for a moment. Ashley could hear Matt let out a long sigh. "You want me to walk you down the aisle?" he asked. "For real. Like a real big brother."

"Yes, Matt." She let out a gentle laugh. "Like the real big brother that you are. I love you, you're my family, and now it's going to get bigger. You're going to have nephews and maybe even a niece, who knows! So, will you? Will you do me the honor of walking me down the aisle?" She waited impatiently for his answer.

"You know what, yeah, I will. I would be honored to walk you down the aisle."

"Oh, Matt! That's wonderful. I'll even get you a new suit!"

"Hey, where's Randy now?" Matt asked.

"Oh, he's got some work meeting. After that he's going to get his brakes done at the local shop before he heads up to his mom's place tomorrow."

"Safety first, right? Sounds like you have a keeper there, sis."

"I think so. Thank you for doing this for me. It means a lot."

"For you, anything. So, he's leaving from your place tomorrow then? Should I pop over tonight so I can give you both my congratulations in person?"

"Not tonight, Matt. I'm working until six, and he's not coming over until later. Then he leaves for his mom's place in the morning. Come over on Tuesday once he's seen her and broken the news. Then we'll all celebrate."

"Sounds like a plan. I love you, sis, and congratulations. I'll see you on Tuesday for dinner."

"You bet. I love you, bro."

* * *

Matt stared at his phone. Ashley was getting married. His gut twisted at the thought of her permanently replacing him as the number one man in her life.

"Oh, Ashley," he whispered to no one. "I don't know if I can let you do that."

* * *

The next morning, Ashley kissed Randy goodbye as she walked him to his car.

"Give your mom my love and tell her I can't wait to meet her." Ashley opened his car door. "Matt is coming over Tuesday night for dinner to celebrate our engagement. Oh my goodness,

I just realized I have a fiancé!" Ashley giggled as Randy shook his head.

"Have a great day at work and relax on the weekend." He leaned over and kissed her. "When I get back, I want to plan the where and when of our wedding."

"Absolutely," Ashley replied as Randy got in his car and drove away. She noticed some scuff marks by where Randy parked his car but thought nothing more of it as she headed to work. Tuesday couldn't come soon enough.

.

Chapter 13

Ashley headed straight to her garden when she got off work. There were some overages shipped to the nursery, and she wanted to get them into the ground as soon as possible.

She and Randy hadn't discussed where they'd live once they got married, but she assumed her house would be the best choice. It had a fenced yard, a nice patch for vegetables, and a prolific flower garden. Although the house was smaller than Randy's townhouse, it would be perfect for raising at least their first child. They could decide where to go after that.

She loved the idea of planting things on the summer solstice. There would be plenty of sunshine, so she could work well past dinnertime. She returned to her car and retrieved the rest of the seedlings and brought them into the backyard. After retrieving a clean pair of gardening gloves and her trowel from the shed she surveyed the area. Then she remembered the compost under the sink in the house and her container of dried vegetable peels. She brought them back outside and tossed them into the empty rain barrel.

Dudley followed her outside and rubbed up against the barrel.

"Sorry, Dudley, no special treats for you. Probably never again. Besides, you're getting fat!" She gave the cat a scratch down his body and went to get the hose. "Now add water and stir," she said to Dudley, who watched her from a distance, flicking his tail.

Once she'd filled the rain barrel halfway, she returned to the task at hand. Green peppers, green beans, cucumbers, kale, and lettuce were soon snug in their new home. There was also a pile of weeds to dispose of. She tossed those into the barrel and looked around the yard. She wasn't hungry, and the sun was out, so she decided to do a thorough weeding of her gardens. She chuckled when she thought of the old saying about the shoemaker's children having no shoes. By the looks of her garden today, it was true. The woman who worked with plants all day long had a weed-filled yard!

Half an hour later, all the weeds floated atop the mixture in the rain barrel. She stirred it and put the lid back on just as her neighbor, Rocky, peeked over the top of the gate.

"Hey, neighbor, how's the garden coming?"

Ashley jumped at the interruption. "You scared me, Rocky! It's going well. All planted for the year now, I think. Flowers are doing great, and I've got all my vegetables planted."

Rocky opened the gate and strolled into the yard. "Looks great. The reason I ask is that I think my garden is in trouble. The plants look wilted, but I'm watering them, and the edges of the leaves are brown. I came over to ask you for professional advice."

Ashley started to answer him when she heard her phone ring in the house. It could wait. She didn't want Rocky snooping around her garden or shed.

"Sounds like a calcium deficiency. Did you add wood ash like I told you earlier?"

"Yes and no. I repeated the recipe all the way home and then promptly forgot it when I started to empty the wood stove. I did remember ashes, though." Rocky turned, went out the gate, and brought back a huge bucket of ashes. "Can you help?"

Ashley laughed despite her annoyance at her too-friendly neighbor. "Yes, of course. What would you like?"

"Well, I'll supply the wood ash if you supply the rest." He grinned sheepishly.

Ashley considered his request. "Well, Rocky, I just started a batch of compost and veggie waste, so we could add that ash and let it sit for a few days. Or you could just sprinkle the ash around your plants. Not on them, around them."

Rocky stared at her for a moment and then responded. "Nope, I think I like the compost and ash combo—sounds more nutritiony. Is that even a word?"

"It is now," she said. "Bring that bucket over here." She headed toward the barrel. It felt odd to have someone this close to one of her barrels, even if there wasn't a body in it.

She opened the lid and motioned for Rocky to toss the ashes in. "Slowly, though. I don't want the wind to blow it all over my yard."

Rocky did as he was told and slowly transferred the wood ash from his bucket to her barrel.

"So, what happens now?" he asked.

"Well, when the ash hits the water, it reacts and becomes sodium hydroxide. Then we have to add some sugar and a bit of calcium to make a great mix."

Randy shook his head. "For a woman, you sure know a lot about chemistry."

The hair on the back of Ashley's neck stood up. What she wouldn't do for a cleaver right now. She'd shut her misogynistic neighbor up in a hurry with one quick slash to his neck. She shook her head to remove the image and pasted a smile on her face. Then she had a thought. She had a container of ground-up bones in the shed. They would make a great addition to the fertilizer. Then that would be the last of any evidence that might be of use should that detective come around again.

"How about I go get the calcium, and you pour it in and stir?" Ashley walked toward her shed. She returned a moment later with a large container.

"Woah!" Randy said, taken aback by the sight. "When you said calcium, I didn't think you meant real bones. What are those? You didn't kill someone, did you?"

Ashley shook her head. "Yeah, right, Rocky. I kill people and break up their bones to put in my garden."

Rocky laughed as she handed the container to him.

"Just pour it in slowly, don't spill any, and then give it a stir with the pole there."

Rocky did as he was told and then stared at the mixture. "Hey, do you think Bone China ever had real bones in it?"

"I'm sure it did, Rocky," she replied as she took the container from him. She'd wash it out later. "This should be ready by Sunday, so get yourself a plastic bucket, and come on over and get some. You'll have to dilute it still, but it should make your garden much happier."

"Thanks, Ashley. You are a great gal, almost like one of the guys."

"Ummm, thanks?" Ashley replied. "I'll see you in a few days then."

Rocky exited through the gate, latched it, and headed home. Ashley could hear him whistling all the way down the driveway and across the street. Now she could see who had called. She hoped it wasn't Randy. She'd hate to have missed a call from him.

Once inside, Dudley followed and zig-zagged in and out between her legs.

MEOWR!

"Oh crap, right, you need to be fed." Ashley fed the cat and then went to get her phone. The missed call was from an unknown number. She was glad she didn't rush in to pick it up. She hated phone scammers. If she could figure out where they were calling from, and if, of course, they were local, she'd teach them a lesson. She looked at the phone again and noticed they'd left a message.

She logged into her voicemail and listened. All she heard was someone breathing heavily and maybe softly crying. She deleted the message before it got to the end. Some people were plain old sick.

Despite wearing gardening gloves, her fingers were still dirt stained. She took out a pizza from the freezer and set the box on the counter to defrost it. A nice shower before dinner would be the perfect way to end her day.

No sooner had she stepped into the shower when she heard what sounded like a doorbell, followed by a loud knocking at the door.

"I'm busy. Come back later!" she hollered through the sound of the water and the closed door. The doorbell and knocking became more insistent.

"Geez Louise! Hold onto your panties, would ya!" Ashley rinsed herself off, grabbed a towel, and opened the door to the bathroom.

"Who is it?" she hollered.

"Police," came the reply.

"Fuck," she hissed as she wrapped a towel around her head and pulled on her dirty clothes. She was annoyed and also relieved the last of the evidence was now pretty much destroyed. She opened the door to see a uniformed female police officer on her doorstep.

"Ashley Taylor?" the officer asked.

"Yes, that's me," she replied as she removed the towel and started to finger-comb her hair.

"Can I come in?"

"Can I see some ID?" Ashley asked. "What's this all about anyway?"

The officer pointed to her badge on her belt, opposite her gun.

"Please, ma'am, can I come in? I'd rather discuss this inside."

Ashley stepped aside and pointed to the couch. "Give me a sec. I need to put this away." She went back into the bathroom and hung up the towel. She returned to the living room and sat on the overstuffed chair. "So, now what?" she asked.

"It's about Randall Hicks."

Ashley felt the blood rush out of her head and into her heart. She thought the officer could hear it pounding.

"What? Is he okay? He just left here this morning to go visit his mom. We got engaged!" Ashley stood to pace the room. "No, don't tell me. If you don't tell me anything, it didn't happen. Police never come knocking if it's good news."

Ashley's knees buckled, and the officer stood to help her sit back in the chair. She recalled the day the police came to her home to take her away. The day she finally rid herself of her evil father. But this—this was worse. This was her future baby daddy. And he would make a good daddy.

Dudley slowly made his way into the living room and jumped on the chair, sensing his roommate's anxiety. Ashley absent-mindedly stroked his fur.

"At approximately ten this morning, a car driven by one Randall Hicks failed to negotiate a turn and crashed into a concrete barrier."

"No!" Ashley screamed. "He's in the hospital, isn't he? Which one? I need to go to him." She stood and made a mental note of what she needed to bring with her. "I'll get my purse," she said. Before she reached her purse, the officer stood and gently held her by the arm.

"I'm sorry, ma'am. He didn't make it."

Ashley's knees gave out. The officer led her to the chair.

"I'll get you a drink of water."

"Water! You think water can erase this! Water can get rid of a lot of things, but it won't bring Randy back, will it!" Ashley sobbed.

She tried to catch her breath by doing some deep breathing. She stopped mid-breath. She was making the exact sound of the message on her voicemail.

The officer returned with a glass of water. Ashley took a sip and put the glass down.

"His mom, he was just going to see his mom. Does she know? Where did it happen? Where's his body? I need to see him!"

"His mother has been informed. She tried to call you earlier. You were one of his emergency contacts on his phone. When she couldn't reach you, she asked us to let you know. I'm so sorry for your loss."

"You're sorry! You. Are Sorry! What the hell? You don't know him. You don't know me. Why are you sorry?" Ashley looked at the officer and imagined her hanging from the hooks in her art room. She'd never killed a woman before, but she could make an exception. The realization that she hadn't put fresh plastic down snapped her back to reality.

"Sorry, Officer. It's not your fault. Where is he? I want to see him."

"His body is still at the hospital near his mother's home. The car has been towed to the police lot to be checked out."

Ashley shuddered. This was way too real. She wanted it to be a dream. After all this time, she found the perfect man, and now he was dead. It couldn't be real. It was the stuff of late-night TV, not her life.

"I should go somewhere, shouldn't I?" Ashley sat back down in the chair. "I mean, what should I do? His family knows. You know, I never met his mom. Did I tell you we got engaged? I was supposed to meet her next week." She showed the officer her ring and then cradled her hand close to her heart.

"Can I call anyone for you?" the officer asked. "Anyone who can come be with you?"

Ashley stared at the officer blankly, then closed her eyes. When she opened them, she looked directly at the officer.

"No, thank you. I can do that." She paused. "Did you know today is the longest day of the year? Well, not really the longest. I wonder why we say that. It's the day with the most sunlight. I mean, all days are twenty-four hours, right? Huh, I never thought of it that way before. How strange that the solstice, a time of rebirth and growth, is the day my future ended."

The officer nodded. "Are you sure there's nothing I can do, no one to call?"

Ashley stood and shook her head. "No, no, thank you. I, uh, I need to finish my shower now."

The officer nodded, gently touched Ashley on the shoulder, and left.

Ashley stared at the closed door. It was only a few hours ago that Randy left through that door, and now he would never be come back.

"Huh," she said aloud and went into the bathroom.

* * *

Ashley stayed in the shower until the hot water turned warm. Only then did she notice a faint trickle of pink running down her legs and into the drain. Another failed attempt at conceiving a baby. Of course, now she knew why.

A shiver ran down her spine as the water turned cold and she stepped out of the shower. She wrapped a towel around her, found a tampon, and dealt with her period. A few minutes later, she found herself fully dressed and standing in the kitchen, putting food into Dudley's dish.

"Huh," she said aloud for the second time that day. She had no idea how she'd got there and had no recollection of getting dressed.

Dudley happily ate up his meal and then sauntered away to do cat things. Ashley stood in the kitchen, a smelly spoon in her hand. She blinked twice, then put the spoon into the dishwasher. She glanced at Randy's morning coffee cup, sitting innocently in the dishwasher. The dishwasher was full, but if she turned it on, the water would wash away any remnants of Randy. It would be like he'd never existed.

She hesitated, reached under the sink, and grabbed a dishwasher pod. Without thinking she put in a dishwasher pod and closed the door. When she looked out the window, it was dark.

"Well, best get it over with." She hit the start button. Tears flowed freely as she heard the water enter the dishwasher, moments away from washing the last traces of Randy from her kitchen. She turned her back on the window, leaned against the cupboard, and slowly sank to the floor.

There was still the bedroom, though. And his toothbrush in the bathroom. There were still tiny pieces of him with her. She might wake up alone tomorrow, but she still had little pieces of him today. But today would end, and she'd wake up in the morning alone.

"Well, Ashley," she said to herself as she stood and made her way to the bedroom. "It's time to find a new baby daddy."

A few seconds later, she replied, "Yes, but not today."

She undressed and crawled into bed. She held Randy's pillow in her arms and inhaled his scent. Before long, she fell into a blissful sleep where no one or nothing could harm her.

Chapter 14

Ashley called in sick and spent the next three days walking around her house and yard. She'd start something, get distracted and go start something new. Nothing got finished. Finally, she emptied the dishwasher. She stared at Randy's favorite mug, kissed the rim where his lips once were, and put it in the cupboard.

She wondered if she could use the DNA from Randy's toothbrush and mix it with her egg to grow a baby. But she didn't want to make a baby that way. It was probably fake news that she read anyway. Besides, she wanted Randy, in person, in the flesh. That was not going to happen. She wanted to be left alone. Life was better alone. But you couldn't make a baby alone.

The phone rang, and it was Randy's mother, extending an invitation for the funeral on the upcoming weekend. Ashley thanked her, and the two shared a few tears. Ashley said she would consider coming, but the thought of meeting all of Randy's family and friends after he'd died didn't seem right. His mother understood and told her she was welcome at any time.

No sooner had she hung up when the phone rang again. This time it was Matt.

"Hey, sis, what time is dinner? Should I bring anything?" The cheerful voice on the other end asked.

"Oh, Matt." Ashley paused. She'd been so deep in her grief that she hadn't even called her brother.

"What's wrong?" he asked.

"It's Randy." She didn't want to say the words. "He's dead. Car accident. Friday morning. I should have called, but I …" Ashley's voice trailed off as she tried to swallow her tears.

"I'll be right over," Matt said. But before he could hang up, Ashley spoke.

"No, don't. Please. I need to be alone. I need to get myself together. I've got work tomorrow, and . . ." She didn't know what else to say. "Can you come over on the weekend? I've got Saturday and Sunday off this week. Let's do lunch on Saturday. Come over. I'll make grilled cheese."

"Yeah, sure, sis. But are you sure? I don't want you to be alone at a time like this."

"Yes. Yes, I'm sure. I think I'll have a nice hot soak in the tub and let the water wash my grief away. I'll talk to you on the weekend, Matt." And with that, Ashley hung up.

* * *

Matt stared at the phone. He wondered all weekend if Randy had died. The fact she'd known since Friday made him uneasy. He thought she would call him right away. He would have run over, taken her into his arms, and comforted her. He would have spent the whole weekend looking after her. Grief was funny. He knew it affected different people in different ways. He made a mental note of her response and opened his phone. He typed in four words and hit send.

Mission accomplished. Debt paid.

* * *

Ashley went to work on Wednesday and tried to concentrate on her job, but it was impossible. The plants were all in the wrong spot. The hose didn't reach. And the customers had the strangest questions. On top of that, she couldn't remember the price of anything. One of her workmates asked her what was wrong.

"I got engaged on Thursday night," Ashley said, her voice monotone.

"That's fabulous, Ashley! Is that why you've been so absentminded today? I guess that would make me a bit unfocused, too."

"He's dead now," Ashley said in the same monotone voice. "Car accident. Friday. So unfair."

Her workmate moved to hug her, but Ashley pulled away. "No, no hugs. I'm fine," she said and walked away.

A few minutes later, her boss was by her side. "Ashley?"

She didn't respond, only stared into space.

"Honey, I'm so sorry. Look, I want you to take the rest of the week off and don't come in until you feel you're ready. You get two weeks bereavement leave, with pay, so don't worry about coming in. Okay?"

Ashley stared at her boss. "With pay?" She looked around the fruit and vegetable section and to realized where she was.

"Yes, with pay. Here, let me help you get your things and

take you home. We can have one of the girls drive your car home. Does that sound good?"

"Yeah, yeah, sure." Ashley nodded. "My keys are in my purse."

"Good, okay, let's do that then." The manager motioned for one of the employees to come with him as they got Ashley out to his car. She handed her keys to the employee and got in like a child doing exactly as she was told.

Thirty minutes later, she was alone in her home wondering what to do with herself. Dudley weaved in and out of her legs as she stood inside her living room. He was happy to have her home, but she didn't react. A few seconds later, he left and went back to napping in the living room window.

Ashley dropped her purse on the floor and leaned against the door.

"What am I supposed to do now?" she asked the empty room. "What the actual fuck am I supposed to do!" She walked around her living room, screaming at the ceiling.

"What the ACTUAL fuck! You, yes, you God! You give me a shitty crazy mother and an even shittier father. Then you punish me for killing my shitty father by torturing me in those horrible foster homes. What the hell! What is this big plan of yours? Are you testing me!"

Ashley sobbed, taking in big heaving breaths as she walked from the living room to the kitchen and back, berating a God she wasn't sure she believed in.

"Who the hell are you to do this to me? I finally find a good guy I can make a great life with and raise beautiful babies who will be decent human beings, and you kill him! What is wrong with you? Are you just going to keep punishing me forever? Well, screw that! I'm going to have a baby. I'm going to make a great life for it, and I will never leave it. Do you hear me!" Ashley's voice was becoming hoarse, but she didn't care.

"And you know what else? I don't believe in you anymore. I doubted you existed before, but now I know for sure it's all a big hoax. Some men, somewhere a long time ago, told this great story and called it the Bible, and everyone believed it. Liars and storytellers who fooled the world. Well, not me. Not anymore. You don't exist because if you did, none of this would have happened!" She punctuated the last sentence with a soul-ripping scream that stretched her vocal cords to their limit.

She was about to punch the wall when the doorbell rang.

"Now what!" she screamed.

Ashley ripped open the door and screamed at the man standing there. "What do you want!" A second later, she realized it was the cop from before, Callahan or Colombo or something.

"Are you okay, ma'am?" he asked. "I heard you scream as I was coming up to the door."

"Yeah, I'm just great," she said and turned to go back into the house.

"Not sure if you remember me. The name's Frank Colombo. We met a few months ago after a guy you'd dated disappeared."

"Yeah, I remember," she said and sunk into her chair. "Did you finally find him? Or are you here to find out if any of my other boyfriends have disappeared." Ashley glared at him, exhausted from her rant, but her eyes were full of fire.

"No. I thought since we'd already met, I should be the one to tell you what happened to your friend, Randy."

"Friend? Are you kidding me? He was my fiancé. Yeah, that's right, I finally found a good one, and guess what. Now he's dead. So if you've come to tell me he's dead, you're too late." Ashley wiped her arm across her nose and then swiped away the tears from her eyes. "So? Why are you here?"

The detective took a deep breath. "We, well, I, wanted to tell you we found out why your boy–er fiancé drove into the divider. It was his brakes. They failed."

"Wait? So you're here to question me about his brakes? Do I look like I know how to mess up someone's brakes!" Ashley stood, hands on hips. "Get out! Get out right now!" She'd had it with men and their accusations and their holier-than-thou attitude. "OUT!"

"No, that's not why I'm here," the detective said in a quiet voice, hoping to calm the ruined woman in front of him. "I came to tell you we've investigated and have come to the conclusion that it was an accident."

Ashley sat back down in the chair. "How? He just got the brakes fixed, like the day before or something." She calmed herself and tried to focus on her breathing.

"The kid at the brake shop wasn't supervised when he worked on Randy's car. Now we can't prove it was him, but there's no other real explanation." He paused and waited as Ashley's breathing slowed.

"The forensic team determined that some bolts weren't

tightened properly. Every time Randy stepped on the brakes, the bolt loosened a bit until finally, it fell out."

Ashley leaned forward in her chair. "I don't understand. How could something like that happen?"

"Well, with the design of Randy's car, the caliper would have stayed in place for a short time, but eventually, and unfortunately, right around the time he had a tight corner to take, the caliper stopped working because it wasn't attached to anything. In other words, the brakes failed due to mechanical error."

"Who was the mechanic?" Ashley asked.

"I'm not at liberty to tell you that, ma'am. He's been let go. He no longer works at the mechanic's shop."

"So, Detective, that's it?" Ashley asked. "Some kid gets lazy, and my Randy is dead. My future is shattered. That's it, so long, farewell?"

"I'm afraid so, ma'am. It wasn't on purpose. It was dumb luck and a preventable accident. When I saw your name on the report, I thought it might be easier if someone you knew told you the news."

"Seriously? You came here a few months ago, sniffing around, asking about my sex life, making subtle accusations, and that, somehow, made you think it would be okay for you to come to my home and tell me some schmuck didn't tighten some bolts. Do I have that right?"

Detective Colombo stood up. "Yes, ma'am. I see now I was wrong. I'll leave you alone." He reached into his breast pocket and pulled out a card. "But if you have any more questions, please, call me."

Ashley stood, took the card, and flicked it in his face. "Just leave," she said as the detective opened the door. "And don't come back!"

Chapter 15

Matt knocked quietly on Ashley's door. A moment later, she opened it. What he saw, shocked him. She hadn't washed or even brushed her hair for days. He stepped inside to a noticeable odor of an unchanged litter box. He watched as Ashley made her way to the big chair and curled into it. Matt closed the door and knelt in front of her.

"Oh, Ashley, I'm so, so sorry. I should have come over sooner."

Ashley just stared into space.

Dudley came out of the bedroom and wound his way around Matt, mewling and rubbing up against him.

"Tell you what, I'll feed Dudley and deal with his litter box and then make us something to eat. Or better yet, I'll order in." Matt pulled out his phone, pulled up a meal delivery service, picked out a few items, and hit send. "Dinner will be here in about thirty minutes. I'll get Dudley his dinner now."

Matt headed toward the kitchen. The sink was full of water glasses and coffee cups. It looked like Ashley hadn't eaten in days. He sighed, opened the fridge, and found an open can of cat food. He put it in a clean bowl, put down a freshwater bowl, and set Dudley's dirty dishes in the sink. Dudley gave him a quick meow and then dug into his meal.

Ten minutes later, all the dishes were in the dishwasher, the counter wiped, and Dudley's litter box cleaned. Matt took the garbage outside and returned to the living room. Ashley hadn't moved.

"Let's get you cleaned up before dinner. You'll feel better with a shower and some clean clothes."

Matt went into the bathroom and turned on the shower. Then he stepped into the bedroom and picked out some clean undergarments, an oversized T-shirt, and some sweatpants. He went back into the living room, helped Ashley up out of the chair, and steered her toward the bathroom.

"C'mon now, sis. Get in the shower, please."

Ashley stared blankly at him.

"Okay, how about we pretend we're thirteen again, and I'll help you like I used to."

He gently lifted Ashley's shirt over her head and removed her bra. He turned away so as not to embarrass her. Then he undid her jeans and slid them and her panties down to the floor. "Okay, that wasn't so bad. Now hop into the shower, okay?"

Ashley did as she was told and stood under the water. Matt put his arm into the shower and gently moved her head under the water. He had no idea she was this bad. "Please, Ashley, don't make me get in there with you." He opened up a shampoo bottle. "Open your hand. Here's some shampoo." Ashley did as she was told and appeared to understand. She stepped out of the flow and slowly lathered up her hair.

"The water," she said. "The water will make everything better. It will, won't it, Matt?"

"Yes, it will help," Matt said, relieved that she was at least speaking. "Now, let's put some conditioner in. Your hair is a bit matted. This will help." He poured some conditioner into Ashley's upturned hand.

She rubbed her palms together and distributed the conditioner through her hair. Matt handed her a bar of soap, and she slowly lathered up her body while staring at Matt.

"Water is amazing, isn't it? It can wash away so many sins. I'm being punished, I think, for the things I did to the others. I think that's what this is." She stepped back under the flow of water and rinsed her body and hair clean of any soap and conditioner.

Matt waited until she was done, then turned off the shower and wrapped a towel around her. "I put some clothes on the bed for you. Go get dressed, and I'll set the table for dinner. I'll come to check on you in a bit." With that, he left the bathroom and headed into the kitchen.

He knew she'd be upset by Randy's death—he just didn't think it would be this bad. She was broken, and it was his responsibility to help put her back together. That's what family was for. To be there through good or bad times and to help out when needed. Ashley was the closest thing he had to a real family, and he was determined to make things right again.

The doorbell rang as Matt finished setting plates, glasses, and cutlery on the table. Once he'd thanked the driver he put the food in the kitchen. He found Ashley dressed and sitting on the edge of her bed, absently brushing her hair.

"That's much better," he said with a smile. "Now, let's get

some food into you." He took Ashley by the arm, led her into the kitchen, and sat her down at the table. "I'll serve, okay?"

One by one, he opened the containers and placed a small portion on Ashley's plate. She gave him a weak smile and picked up her fork.

"Thanks, Matt. I'm sorry I didn't ask you to come earlier. I needed time to grieve, you know. I needed to feel this. I've never felt so much joy or so much sorrow in my life. Not when Mom left, not when Dad, well, you know, died."

Ashley pushed her fork into something that looked like meat and took a bite. Her stomach growled loudly in anticipation.

"Hmmm, I guess I was hungry." She took another bite and looked at Matt. A solitary tear made its way down her cheek and splattered onto her plate. "I, I mean we, yes, we can get through this, right?"

"Of course, sis," Matt replied. "You'll find a good sperm donor out there, I'm sure of it. And if you just want him for his baby-making juice, that's cool. You know, I'd love to be a dad or an uncle. So, when you do get pregnant, if you don't like the guy, I'd be happy to step up and be its dad. I'd be a good dad, I think. I know what not to do."

Matt watched Ashley's face as she considered the option.

"You don't care if it's, you know, biologically yours?" She stabbed a piece of broccoli and put it in her mouth.

"Well, don't you think it would feel weird to make a baby with me? Being that you're my sister and all. I know we aren't blood-related, but still. Yeah, I'd be happy with whatever role

Cleansing Water

you want me to play. Uncle Matt, Dad, whatever works for you. I'd do anything to make you happy. You know that."

"Yeah, I do," she said. "You know, I was thinking about asking Randy's mom if I could have his sperm. That's pretty crazy, isn't it? I mean, we were only engaged for a day before he . . ." Ashley's voice trailed off, and she swallowed to fight back tears. "Yeah, never mind. It would be crazy, even for me." She gave a small laugh.

"Well, how about we just take this one day at a time? You cry and scream and sleep as much as you need to. I'll stay on the couch until you kick me out. Sound like a deal?"

"Yeah, that sounds good, Matt. I am really tired. Oh shit, does Dudley have enough food? I haven't been to the store since, well, the accident."

"I'll go to the store, get him more food, and stock up your fridge while I'm at it. You just do what you've got to do, okay?"

"Okay." Ashley pushed away her plate. She'd eaten about half her meal. "I think I want to lie down."

"Good idea," Matt said. "I'll find a funny movie and get you a blanket. Why don't you curl up on the couch, and I'll put some fresh sheets on the bed."

"You're so good to me, Matt." Ashley smiled at him as she made her way to the living room. "Whatever would I do without you."

Matt turned on the TV, found a comedy special, and tucked Ashley in on the couch. He went back to her bedroom, stripped the bed, and tossed it all in the wash. He looked around and found a man's T-shirt and tossed that in the wash, too. It wouldn't do her any good to have his scent still around. He knew how powerful memories were when linked to a smell. Best to get rid of him completely—for Ashley's sake.

He returned to the living room, where Ashley was asleep on the couch. He kissed her softly on her forehead and left to get groceries.

Chapter 16

It took another week for Ashley to start feeling normal again. She'd called her boss and told him she'd be back to work the following Monday. She thanked him for his understanding and contemplated her next move. She had anywhere from four to seven days before she could even try to get pregnant again. She decided to spend the weekend hunting for a new prospect. It would do her good to get out. She'd spoken to Randy's mom on the phone once since the funeral but decided it was time to put that behind her as well.

Matt was over almost every day and night that week. She loved him but seeing him every single day was starting to put a strain on their relationship, or so she thought. Best that she went out, had some fun, and got back on track with the pregnancy plans. She picked up her phone and called him.

"Hey, Matt," she said when he answered. "Look, I'm doing so much better, so I'm going out with some girls from work tonight. Friday night is ladies' night at clubs, so I might as well take advantage of the no cover charge."

The line was quiet for a bit.

"Yeah, sure, sis. I totally get it. I'm glad you're feeling better. Call me when you want to hang out. I've got some rush jobs to do this weekend, so I'm glad you have things to do."

"Great, how about we connect on Sunday? I may even make you brunch."

"That'd be great," Matt said. "I'll call you Sunday morning, but not too early."

"Perfect. It's a date." She hung up and went to look in her closet for some appropriate hunting attire.

She opted for a pair of tight skinny jeans and a low-cut top that showed just the right amount of flesh. She stood in front of the mirror in her bathroom and decided it was time to disguise herself a bit. Some dark brows, deep purple eye shadow, and dark-winged eyeliner. She put on her deepest red lipstick and stared at herself in the mirror. The hair was next. Although she looked young for her thirties, so she opted for a high pony which allowed her hair to fall around her face.

She returned to her bedroom and rummaged around in a bottom drawer for a pair of lightly tinted glasses. They were just enough to change her appearance. She looked at the finished product in the mirror and shrugged. The jeans weren't cutting it.

Ashley checked her closet and dug out an old mini skirt. She never wore short skirts, so this would help a bit. She finished her ensemble with a pair of thigh-high patterned socks and white sneakers.

"That will do it." She admired herself in the mirror. "I don't look like me at all."

Dudley came into the room, hopped on the bed, and meowed.

"You're right, Dudley. I shouldn't wear my engagement ring if I'm out hunting." Ashley put the ring on the side table. "I also need a disguise. You know how those neighbors are."

It was early July, so a long coat or sweater was out of the question. She rummaged around the closet again and came out with a simple calf-length dress with short sleeves. "Yep, this will do," she said to the cat.

She'd lost a bit of weight over the past couple of weeks, so the dress fit perfectly over her outfit. She pulled a baseball cap onto her head, pulled the ponytail out the back, and admired the finished product. She put the glasses and a smaller purse into a larger handbag and admired yet another transformation. From a distance, she looked like regular Ashley.

"I can't go hunting in town anymore," she said to Dudley. "So, I'll be a bit later tonight. It's an hour or so to the city, but with any luck, I'll be home before sunrise." She headed into the kitchen, put some dry food into Dudley's dish, filled up the water, and checked the litter box. "You're all set. Wish me luck!"

The sun was still shining when Ashley stepped outside. She pulled on her sunglasses and headed to her car. As she closed the door, she saw her neighbor, Rocky, wave to her. She waved back, then ignored him as he walked toward her car. She pulled away, pretending she didn't see he was approaching and wanting to talk. There was no need for that, not tonight.

* * *

Ashley pulled into the transit parking lot about fifteen minutes from the club. She was being extra cautious, but that cop had been around twice now, and she wasn't taking any chances. She removed her sunglasses and hat. She pulled the dress over her head and stuffed everything into her larger bag. She tossed her keys in the smaller purse, put on the tinted glasses, checked her lipstick, and headed toward the rapid transit platform. Twenty minutes later, the sun had set, and she was standing at the doorway to the club, smiling at the bouncer. He let her in with a nod and an appreciative once-over.

Once inside, Ashley searched for potential mates. There were several college types playfully shoving each other in the chest over by the bar. In a back corner were some bad boys with face tattoos, open leather jackets, and bright white sneakers. Farther down the bar were what Ashley assumed to be two business types. Dark pants, shirt open at the collar, but no suit jacket. She assumed they'd left them at the office. She pondered her choices for a moment. College boys were too easy, and their friends would remember her. The bad boys probably weren't that bad after all. They just had some not-so-pleasant things happen in their life, so they played tough. She glanced over at the two men near the end of the bar. One looked over and raised a glass of something in a toast to her. She nodded and decided to circulate.

There were the usuals in the club. Women who showed as much skin as possible without looking cheap, and others who just looked easy.

"Might as well have 'come and get me' written on their foreheads." Ashley surveyed the crowd.

"Agreed." It was the business guy. He stood beside her and handed her a glass of something.

"Ummm, thanks, but I don't take drinks from guys at

clubs." Ashley smiled and sized up her prey.

"Oh, right, of course. Sorry, I never thought about that. How about we head over to the bar, and I'll buy you whatever you want? You can even watch the bartender make it."

"Yeah, that sounds nice. Thank you." Ashley made her way toward the bar. She smiled at the bartender and leaned in close to give her order. He nodded and filled a glass with ice and club soda.

"My name's Michael," came a voice from behind. "My friends call me Mike, and I'd like it if you called me that, too."

Ashley turned and gave her target a slow look up and down. He would do. He looked healthy, around twenty-eight to thirty, with no obvious signs of drug use.

"Thanks, Mike. You can call me Jessie." Ashley smiled and sipped her drink.

Just then, the DJ came out and hollered. "Let's make some noise!" The crowd cheered, and within seconds the bass thrummed out over the crowd, and most of the partiers were on their feet.

"Would you like to go to one of the private rooms?" Mike asked.

"Just the two of us?"

"Yeah, why not," Mike said as he took her hand. "It's a bit quieter, and we can get to know each other better without shouting."

Ashley shrugged and nodded.

The couple made their way past the bad boys and up three steps into a private room with glass windows. Inside were two couches, pushed together in an L shape with a small glass table in front of them. They could see out onto the dance floor and the rest of the club. It was still noisy, but only to the point where you had to speak loudly, not shout.

"I've never been in a private room before." Ashley clinked glasses with Mike. "You do this often? Rent a private room and bring women in here?"

Mike shook his head. "Ummm, not all the time, but sometimes when you see a gorgeous woman, you want to spring for a little private space. We can always go dancing if you prefer. I've got some E if you like."

"E?" Ashley looked confused.

"Ecstasy, Molly, you know, MDMA, make you feel good and dance all night." Mike flashed her a smile and pulled out two small tablets. So much for him not looking like a drug user.

"Yeah, no." Ashley didn't want someone who was able to go all night. She needed someone who was less lively. "I prefer a more relaxed night." She gave him her best smile. "You have anything to relax a girl?"

Mike grinned and put away the Ecstasy. "Ah, you're looking for something more like Special K than E. Something a bit further up the alphabet." Mike laughed at his joke and reached into his other pocket and pulled out a tiny baggie with white powder inside. "This stuff is great. It'll knock you back and make you relaxed as hell."

Ashley gave him a questioning look, then nodded. "Sure, let's try that."

Mike took a drink napkin and wiped down a section of

the glass table. He motioned for Ashley to sit down. He sat beside her, opened up the packet, and shook out some of the powder. "I usually save this until the end of the night, but what the lady wants, the lady gets." He pulled out a credit card and carefully made two short lines on the table. Then he pulled out a bill and rolled it up. "Ladies first," he said.

"No, I want to watch you do it first." She cocked her head to the side. "I've never snorted anything before. Show me how it's done. Please?" She gave him her best smile.

"Wow, a K virgin. No problem," he replied. "You stick the rolled-up bill up against your nostril, close the other nostril with your finger, and inhale quickly. The powder goes up, stings a bit, and then, nirvana. It's a bit bitter, so keep your drink handy."

"Sounds good," Ashley said. "This should be fun."

Mike nodded and bent over, bill in position. He inhaled sharply, and the small line disappeared. He sat back and gave Ashley a lopsided grin. "Your turn," he said and passed her the bill. He sat back on the couch and tilted his head back, waiting for the drug to kick in.

Ashley took the bill and stared at him. His eyes were closed. This was going to be easy. She quickly swept the rest of the ketamine into his drink. She inhaled sharply and pretended to cough.

Mike sat upright and smiled at her. "First time is going to be a rush," he said, then laid his head back gain.

Ashley pocketed his credit card, with a plan to use it later to show he'd been at the club all night. She'd ditch it and wipe the prints off later.

"So," she said as she held out Mike's drink for him. "How long does it take? You know, to make me feel all dreamy and laid back."

Mike sat up, took his drink, and downed it in two gulps. "For some people, it takes five minutes, but most likely ten to twenty.

"And how long does it last?" she asked.

"Anywhere from a half hour to an hour. It's your first time, so maybe an hour. Just sit back, relax, and let it happen."

Ashley sidled up beside him and started tracing her finger on his chest. She didn't know how Special K affected sexual performance. All she needed was a bit of sperm, and she'd be on her way. She reached her hand down into his pants and felt his erection spring to life.

"Hey now, Jessie," Mike said. "I'm not that kind of guy."

"Oh, oh, I'm so sorry." Ashley had never encountered a man in a club who didn't want sex. She removed her hand and sat back.

"Hey, I'm kidding." He grabbed her hand and put it back into his pants. "There's a switch over there. Turns the glass opaque so no one can see in."

"Really?" Ashley was liking this room more and more.

"Yeah, it's like those public bathrooms you see online or in big cities. You know, the kind where the glass is see-through when no one is inside, and then when someone goes in, the glass darkens. Privacy glass." Mike inhaled deeply and exhaled slowly. "Oh yeah, feeling it now."

Ashley removed her hand and went over to the switch.

Sure enough, the glass changed from see-through to dark. A corner light turned on, bathing the room in a purple haze. She mentally calculated her ovulation date for the third time and figured it might be early, but if his swimmers were strong, they might survive a day or so up there. She returned to the couch, pulled up her skirt, and straddled him. He grinned up at her, starting to feel the full effects of the double dose.

"I knew it. I knew when I saw you that you were a naughty girl." He slipped inside her.

Ashley buried her head into his neck so he couldn't see the disgust on her face. She wasn't naughty. That's what one of her foster dads had called her just before he raped her. He was the naughty one, not her. She was a child then.

She tried to think of more pleasant things and thought about Dudley and her garden while Mike kept pumping. Five minutes later, there was still no end in sight, and Ashley was getting bored. She stopped him from moving and looked at him.

"Are you going to cum?" she asked.

"Yeah, well, that's one of the side effects of Special K, sometimes it's hard to cum, but I so love the feeling."

He tried moving again, but she stopped him. "Are you kidding me?"

"Don't worry, babe. We can do this all night long or at least the next hour."

Ashley wanted to slap his face or slash it with a knife. She lifted herself off him, straightened out her skirt, and pulled up her thigh highs.

"No thanks, I'm good," she said.

Mike put himself away and then lay his head back on the couch. The drugs were taking full effect now. His eyes were closed, and his breathing was shallow but regular.

Ashley had to figure out what to do with him. She should never have agreed to this Special K crap. She wondered what else it did. She glanced over at Mike, who didn't seem to notice she no longer enjoyed his company.

She pulled out her phone and googled the sexual side effects of Special K. She read through a few articles and learned that while it made men horny, they had a hard time finishing the job. It also affected the motility of the sperm.

"Damn it!" Ashley shouted. "Can't come, and the boys can't swim. What a waste of time this was."

She stared at the semi-conscious man before her. He had to pay. There was no other way. She'd wasted an entire night on this loser, and now he would face the consequences. Ashley stood and paced the small room. Too many people had seen her come in here with him. It was doubtful, but they might recognize her if asked. She went over to Mike and poked him in the chest.

"Hey, get up. Let's go get a drink."

Mike lifted his head and rapidly blinked. "Hey there, beautiful. Was it good for you, too?"

Ashley shrugged.

"C'mon, I want a drink." She helped Mike up and led him toward the door. She flicked off the privacy glass so people in the club would see her leaving the room with him. She walked Mike back to his friend, keeping her head down.

"I think he's had a bit much." She deposited Mike on a bar stool next to his buddy.

"Damn, that was fast," his friend said. "He's no use as a wingman in this state. I'll get him out to the car."

"Yeah, you do that." Ashley followed a few steps behind and watched as Mike maneuvered toward the door and out into the parking lot. Ashley made a note of which car it was. His friend opened the back door, pushed Mike in, and rolled down the window.

"Sleep it off, buddy," he said as he shut the door. "I'll check on you later."

Ashley quickly headed back into the club and made sure Mike's friend saw her dancing with some other women. He nodded at her and then went back to chatting up a rather buxom brunette.

Now what? Ashley thought. She glanced around the room. She didn't feel like hunting anymore. She wanted revenge, though. She wanted Mike to hurt for being so stupid. She smiled at the women she danced with, sidled up to a few men, and danced her way back to the ladies' room. At least ten people had seen her there after Mike left.

Instead of entering the washroom, she snuck out the back door and headed toward the parking lot. The window was still open, and Mike was half reclined on the back seat with a stupid grin on his face. His credit card was useless now. So much for her great plans. She wiped off her prints with her skirt, picked up Mike's hand, and squeezed his fingers on the card. Then she tossed it on the floor of the back seat and put Mike's foot on it.

That should make it look less suspicious. She didn't dare try and put it back into his wallet.

Ashley looked up to make sure she was still alone. There wasn't another soul in sight. She only had a few minutes, but this jerk had to pay. The question was, how? She had nothing to stab him with. There was nothing in the car to smother him with. She looked around and saw a fist-sized rock behind the car next to the bushes. Problem solved. Ashley picked up the rock and leaned through the open window again. She wasn't worried about DNA. After all, people had seen them together, just not in the car.

She stopped and thought over her plan. She wasn't sure she wanted him dead, but he did have to pay for being an idiot. Head wounds bled a lot, and she couldn't afford to get blood on her clothing. Perhaps a broken nose would bleed less.

She hesitated. There was no way to guarantee she or the rock wouldn't get splattered. She tossed the rock back into the bushes behind the car. Time was running out, so she had to do something quickly. She rummaged around in her purse and found a Bic pen. Not the best weapon, but it could do some harm.

Ashley held her breath and leaned into the car. She slowly pushed the pen into Mike's nostril and waited until it hit something solid. She held onto the pen with her left hand and then smacked the bottom of it with her right. Mike barely flinched. Ashley quickly pulled herself out of the window and looked at the pen. In the light dim light, she could see it was moist, but she didn't know with what. Was it snot? Blood? She didn't care as long as it hurt tomorrow or whenever the Special K wore off. She wrapped the pen in tissue and re-entered the club. Once in the washroom, she examined it. A little bit of blood, but mostly snot.

"Damn it!" she said aloud for the second time that night. "I'm not having any luck. I might as well go home." Ashley thoroughly cleaned the pen with soap and water, rewrapped it in clean toilet paper, and stuffed it in her purse. She'd dispose of it later.

A toilet flushed, and a young blonde came out of the stall. "You too?" she said.

"Excuse me?" Ashley adjusted her glasses and pretended to tighten her ponytail.

"No luck. Me too. The guys here aren't worth the time. Not a single rich guy either. Oh wait, aren't you the girl who went into the swanky private room?"

Ashley applied a fresh coat of lipstick. "Yeah, that was me, but he got stoned on Special K and was useless. His friend took him away about fifteen minutes ago."

"Damn." The blonde adjusted her breasts in her bra. "What's a girl to do?"

"Right." Ashley put away her lipstick. "But who knows, maybe someone new will come in."

"Good luck," the blonde called as Ashley left the ladies' room.

If her disguise wasn't enough, at least she had a good alibi for the night. She wandered over to the bad boys' group and asked if she could join them. An hour later, she was bored. It was time to go home.

As she left the club, she saw Mike's friend walking him around the parking lot. He was whining about how much his nose hurt. Ashley waved as his friend looked up, making sure he saw her walk toward the street. A half-hour later, she was in her car. She scrubbed her face clean with some wet wipes, put on the baseball cap and dress, and drove home. If anyone asked, she'd just say she drove up to the lookout to watch the stars.

Tomorrow she would try again.

Chapter 17

Ashley woke with the sun. She rolled over and stared at the engagement ring on the nightstand. A small tear formed in the corner of her eye. She swiped it away and got up to face the day. Perhaps a little daylight hunting would do.

She fed Dudley and poured herself a hot cup of coffee. She was determined to find a baby daddy, and soon. And if not a keeper daddy, then at least a sperm donor.

"What is it they say, Dudley? If at first you don't succeed, try, try, again."

Dudley gave an appreciative meow as if agreeing and then went to find a sunbeam to bask in. Ashley took a sip of coffee and said, "Hey, Google, antique stores within one hundred miles of here."

There was no response. Ashley tried again. "Hey, Google, are there any antique stores within one hundred miles of here."

Again, no answer. "Stupid machine." She got up and realized she hadn't plugged it back in. She hadn't used it since she'd met Randy. Ashley winced, remembering she'd never see him again. Life had been so simple before she'd fallen in love. Find a man, get his baby makers, and done. It was simple, even if it hadn't been effective so far.

"Hey, Google. Find me an antique store within a hundred

miles radius of home."

"I found five antique stores in a one-hundred-mile radius. One is ten miles away. One is thirty miles away. Three are ninety-eight miles away."

"Thanks, Google, that's enough." She opened up her phone, found the three were ninety-eight miles away. They were in the exact opposite direction of the city she'd been hunting in the night before. Best to keep herself seen as little as possible. There was also a farmers' market today, right next to an antique store. That would work.

Ashley double-checked to make sure the litter box was clean. She headed into the bedroom, pulled on shorts and a tank top, and filled her water bottle in the kitchen.

"I'm outta here, Dudley!" she called to the cat, who did what most cats do when told their servant was leaving. He ignored her.

Ashley grabbed a couple of reusable shopping bags and headed out the door. She was barely at the car when Rocky came up to her. This time she couldn't escape.

"There you are," he said as he blocked her from opening the car door. "How are you doing? Beth and I have been worried about you. We see that other fellow over here, the one with the pickup, and we hope you're doing okay. We found out from the folks at the nursery what happened. We're so sorry for your loss." Rocky leaned against the car door, ensuring Ashley couldn't leave.

She opened the back door and tossed her shopping bags and purse in the back. "Thanks, Rocky, but I'm doing okay now.

And that *fellow with the pickup truck* is my brother."

Rocky cocked his head to the side. "You don't say. We've been neighbors for three years now, and I never knew he was your brother."

"I'm a pretty private person," Ashley responded. "Now, if you don't mind, I want to go shopping." She nodded toward her car door.

"Oh yes, of course." He stopped leaning on the car but stood just close enough so she couldn't open the door without hitting him. "I was coming over last night to see if you needed anything. Well, Beth sent me over to see if you wanted to come for dinner or whatever."

Ashley tried not to glare at the man. "I appreciate your concern and your offer; however, between my brother and my garden, I'm doing just fine."

"Yes, that's another thing I wanted to talk to you about. I think I got that recipe wrong. Did I tell you that already? Anyway, if you could come over sometime this weekend and have a look at our plants, we'd appreciate it. The folks at the nursery said you're the best at figuring out what plants need when they aren't doing well."

"Okay, sure, yeah." Ashley opened the door a bit too forcefully, causing Rocky to jump back. "I can come over on Sunday after lunch if that works."

"Yes, that'd be great." Rocky grinned and gave Ashley's legs a once over. When he realized his gaze lingered a bit too long, he cleared his throat and took another step back. "So, we'll see you around one in the afternoon. I'll have Beth make up some iced tea or something."

"Sure, fine." Ashley got in and started her car. "See you then."

Once she was clear of the driveway she let out a little scream. "What a frickin' pain that man is! Oh, how I'd love to see him in pieces."

Ashley thought about her neighbors as she merged onto the highway and headed to her destination. Beth was nice enough, not pushy like Rocky. They were older than her, maybe mid-forties, and had no kids. Rocky was a jerk, as far as Ashley could tell. He mansplained. He was overconfident and plain old annoying. Plus, he couldn't take a hint. She'd never killed for pleasure before, but if she ever did, it would be Rocky.

One of her favorite tunes came on the radio, and Ashley sang at the top of her lungs as the trees and hills whisked past her. She felt lighter than she had in days. Today was going to be a good day. Even snoopy Rocky couldn't change that.

* * *

Ashley pulled into the parking lot off a side street. The city cordoned off four blocks for the market and everyone from hobby farmers to crafters to book and antique sellers lined the street. She put on her sunglasses, pulled her hair into a ponytail, and tucked it up under her baseball cap. Not the most ingenious of disguises, but it would do.

She picked through some large bunches of kale and lettuce and chose a nice iceberg for her dinner that night. The next stall had fresh berries and asparagus. She picked out and paid for a few items and put them with the others in her cloth bag.

She walked up one side of the four-block area and didn't see a single prospect. Most of the men were over fifty, and half of the vendors were women. She reached the barricade and made her way back toward her car on the opposite side of the street. Halfway there, she noticed a younger man about her height, not too good-looking, but enough to make a nice-looking baby. She walked over to his stall and admired his woodwork. There were small wooden toys, some signs with names on them, and a few wooden puzzles. Way back in the corner, she saw some cute little wooden stakes with vegetable names on them. She turned to look for the wood carver and bumped right into him.

"Oh, I'm so sorry." He put his hands on her shoulders to steady her. "I hope I didn't scare you. I was just coming to talk to you."

"I'm good," Ashley said. "I was looking at those garden stakes, but I didn't see a price."

"Well, for pretty ladies, they are three dollars each."

Ashley almost walked away, but she remembered why she came. She put on a smile and looked into a set of hazel eyes. "And how much for someone who isn't a lady?"

The man gave her an approving glance. "Oh, well, we could seriously arrange something if you want."

Ashley's skin crawled. Gawd, how she hated this cat-and-mouse game, especially when the mouse thought it was the cat.

"Well, I'm feeling a bit dirty," she said. "You know, from working in the garden." Ashley winked.

"I'm done here around one o'clock if you'd like to get a

bite to eat," the man said. "My name's Martin, and you are?"

Ashley hesitated. Who did she want to be today? "I'm someone you just might get lucky with," she said. "So, you can call me Lucky. Is there somewhere nearby where we could meet up?" She glanced at her watch. There was still an hour or so before this Martin fellow was done. He probably had to grab all his stuff and haul it somewhere, so she had time to do a secondary hunt and perhaps set another trap.

"Umm, well, my van is parked a few blocks away down the alley over there. We could meet up there if you're saying what I think you're saying."

"I am," Ashley replied. "I have some shopping to do, so I'll meet you back here at one o'clock." There was still time to do some antiquing.

* * *

Ashley found some long, colorful beach coverups at a stall near the end of the street. She slipped it over her shorts and top and made her way back to the car. She deposited her produce in the trunk in a cooler bag and headed toward the antique store. Once inside, she started her search for old artist tools. She didn't care what they were; brushes, palettes, easels, as long as they were antiques.

At the end of a corner aisle, she hit the jackpot. There was a box of vintage Laurentien colored pencils, never used, in an unopened box. Beside them was a set of three sable brushes, obviously well-loved and used but still in great condition. Her mouth formed into a grin as she ran her hand over the handle of the largest brush.

"Can I help you?" A tall, bearded man with a slight accent stood beside her.

"Oh, hello," she said. "I was admiring these brushes and the pencil crayons. I usually do large abstracts, but I've been thinking about going smaller recently. What can you tell me about these?"

"Well, the pencil crayons, I don't know about. But, the brushes, well, they belonged to a frustrated artist who turned his back on art and took a sales job to feed his family. Quite tragic. His wife left him ten years later, taking their three teenage sons with her. He died penniless and an unknown."

"How sad," Ashley said, putting the brush down. "You don't think they have negative energy or bad luck attached to them, do you?"

The man laughed. "No, I don't. I made that up. I bought them at an estate sale of an old woman who dabbled in acrylic painting, but she wasn't very good."

Ashley picked up the brushes. "Well, in that case, I'll take them." She looked at the pencil crayons. "But not those. I'd hate to open them and never use them."

"Great," the man said. "I'll ring you up at the counter."

* * *

Ashley headed back to the wood carver's stall just as he was packing up.

"Well, hello there," he said with a smirk. "I didn't think you'd be back. Thought you were just a tease."

It took everything in Ashley's power not to grab one of his tools and stab him right there. She calmed herself and put on a fake smile.

"Yeah, I came back. Do you know of anywhere private you can park your van?" She cocked her head slightly. She knew it looked like she was being flirtatious, but in her mind, she was wondering which one of his tools she'd use on him if he couldn't get his swimmers into her.

"Actually, yes. There's an old campsite not far from here, and it doesn't fill up until late July. Some end stalls are quite, um, secluded for private moments."

"Great," Ashley said. "I'm parked down at the end of the street. I'll walk you to your van so I know what it looks like, then follow me to my car, and I'll follow you to the spot."

"Or," he said, still with a smirk on his face, "I could just take you there."

"That's not going to happen," Ashley said with a plastered-on smile. "I don't have a lot of time. I have to get home."

"Oh, you have a husband?"

Ashley pondered that for a moment. She could have a husband, but Randy was dead. And this jerkoff in front of her was alive. The universe truly was in a state of constant chaos.

"Yes, you got me. I have a husband, and he sucks in bed. So I'm hoping you can scratch my itch if you get my meaning."

"Hell yes, I do!" Martin haphazardly tossed his carving tools into a satchel. He closed it and handed it to Ashley. "It'll go quicker if you help me haul this stuff out."

"What about this tent thingy and the tables?" she asked.

"Are they yours, too?"

"Nope, the city provides them for a fee. I just have to pack up my stuff and go." Martin turned and continued to pack up his carvings. When he got to the garden stakes, he passed the one that said, Dill, to Ashley. "A present for you."

Ashley took the ten-inch T-shaped stake and tried to bend it. The wood was solid, about a half-inch thick and an inch wide. The upper part of the T displayed the word "Dill" in large lettering. She smiled and put it into her carryall bag.

"Thanks."

She continued to watch as he loaded up all his wooden wares, tablecloths, and cash box.

"Normally, I'd go get my van and wait for people to clear out, but if you could put the satchel straps over your shoulder and carry a box, we could just go now."

"Sure. No problem," Ashley said, hoisting the satchel over her shoulder. She readjusted her carry-all and took the offered box.

"Okay, let's go," Martin said, easily lifting the last three stacked boxes. "Hope I don't bump into anyone."

He laughed, and for one split second, Ashley felt almost normal. Like they were a team, and she was in a relationship. But that feeling was fleeting.

"Lead the way," she said.

A short walk later, they were at Martin's van. He put away all the boxes and the satchel. Ashley noticed he had a makeshift bed, a hot plate, and a mini bar in the back. She figured this was where he slept when he was doing market garden stuff.

"You live in here?" she asked.

"No, not all the time. I'm actually from up north a bit. Markets start earlier down here. I've been here a month or so, and I'll stick around another couple weeks and then head back home."

"Sounds like a fun life," she said. It really didn't. It sounded horrible, but at least he wouldn't be missed if things went wrong. "Okay, follow me with your van. I'm about a block away."

Ten minutes later, they were in a secluded part of a campground ten parked RVs. She followed Martin to the back part of the campground, sheltered by old trees. She watched him park in the farthest possible spot. Ashley backed up her car and parked a good fifty yards away, near a vacant tent trailer. She grabbed her carryall and walked toward Martin's van.

"Hey! Why'd ya park so far away?" he yelled as she came closer.

"Habit," she replied as she approached. When she got to the van, she smiled at him. "I don't want anyone to see me, if you know what I mean."

"Right, the lady has another life." Martin went around to the sliding door of the van and opened it up. "After you, Lucky."

Ashley ducked as she stepped into the van. She wasn't sure where to sit. Did she sit in the passenger seat and chit-chat until the mood hit them, or was she to go to the makeshift bed? She felt very much out of her comfort zone, but she couldn't risk bringing men back to her place. What with her snoopy neighbor, her brother's drop-in visits, and the nosey cop, it wasn't safe anymore.

"Where do you want me?" she asked.

"Well, darlin', I think the bed is our final destination, so why not head there now."

Ashley grabbed her carryall and placed it on the floor beside the foam mattress covered in an old quilt. "Here?" she asked coyly.

"Yeah, that's perfect." He shut the van door.

It was warm outside, but with the shade of the trees, the van wasn't too hot. Ashley turned to Martin before he got comfortable. "Can you please shut the window up front? I'm a bit of a screamer, and we don't want to garner attention, do we?"

Martin gave a half laugh, half snort, and did as he was asked. He returned, still laugh-snorting, and sat down on the mattress. He reached for Ashley and went in for a kiss.

"Ah, nope," she said. "No kissing. Just sex."

Martin shook his head and stared at her. "You are a strange one, but what the lady wants, the lady gets." He took off his shirt, shorts, and underwear and tossed them to the foot of the bed.

Ashley stared at his semi-erect penis. If she hadn't been sure she was ovulating, she would have fled the van in that instant. Her biological clock ticked mercilessly in her head, and she removed her shorts and panties, bunching the beach coverup around her waist.

"No breasts either," she said and laid down on the mattress. "Just an orgasm if it's not too much bother." Ashley checked to make sure her ponytail was still tucked up tightly under her baseball cap.

Martin shook his head, grinned, and climbed on top of her. "Whatever you say, Lucky. Whatever you say. Do I need a condom?"

"No, I'm on the pill, and you look like a clean guy." She just wanted to get this over with, get the sperm, and go.

"Yes, ma'am," he said as she spread her legs.

Ashley's mind went elsewhere. She closed her eyes and thought of Randy and their tender lovemaking. She pictured his smile, his face, his hand holding her as they became one on her bed.

Above her, Martin rutted away, but it didn't feel good. It didn't feel right. He was too small, and her body wasn't responding. Before she could shift her weight, she felt him give one last pump and collapse atop her.

"Wow, sorry about that," he said, not bothering to move. "You are such a hot piece. I couldn't help it."

Ashley froze inside when he called her a piece. She hated that phrase. To him, she was just something to use and throw away, just like all those men from her childhood. At her last foster home, the foster dad always called her a piece of tail, like she was an appendage on a dog or something. Ashley knew what she had to do.

Martin started to move off of her, but Ashley stopped him. "Let's lie like this for a bit." She reached out for her carryall. "It's nice."

"Whatever you want, but I might fall asleep on you."

Ashley stroked his hair and felt him slowly lose

consciousness. She knew it was because of the hormones produced with male orgasms, and in this case, it was perfect timing. She found the garden stake and slowly pulled it out of her bag. Then she put her shorts and panties into the bag and awkwardly tossed her bag onto the front seat.

Martin moved a little but stayed asleep. She carefully slid out from under him, being careful not to wake him. He lay there, gently snoring.

She looked at the garden stake and decided she needed something sharper. His satchel of tools was within reach. She quietly pulled it over and opened it up. She hadn't thought about gloves, and there was no way she wanted to leave her fingerprints anywhere. And her hair was well-contained, so she wouldn't leave any DNA. There might be some skin cells on the blanket, but she figured Martin had taken several women into his van, and hers would just be one of dozens. Besides, her DNA wasn't in the system, and she planned on keeping it that way. After some mild hesitation, she grabbed Martin's underwear and gingerly used them as a makeshift glove.

The first tool she took out had two edges, like a continuous V shape. It looked dull. She preferred knives. Her second attempt at finding the right tool was a success. The knife was sheathed in leather and, once out of its protective cover, looked perfect for the job. There were no buckets to collect blood here, so she'd have to improvise. She gently placed his shirt around his neck area. It would stop most of the blood, and her beach coverup should absorb the rest.

Ashley picked up the knife and sighed. She used to love

this part—ridding the world of bad men. Now it felt like work, like a job she had to do, but her heart wasn't in it. Randy had done that to her. Randy had found a part of her that wasn't irreversibly damaged, a part that needed, wanted, and deserved love. Now he was gone, and she was alone again. Maybe this time, if she was lucky, she'd be pregnant from this little adventure.

She stared at Martin. The neck was the best place to cut. His head was turned away from her, exposing his carotid artery. She got into position. With the precision of a well-practiced surgeon, she slit through the flesh, into the carotid, and toward his vocal cords. Blood spurted out, most of it caught by the underwear.

Martin jerked awake. His hand went to his neck, trying to stop the flow. But it was too late.

Ashley dodged a few blood sprays and watched as the life drained out of his eyes. She managed to leave the van with only a few splatters on her beach coverup. Once outside, she slouched down behind the van and put her panties and shorts back on. She rummaged through her purse and found her alcohol wipes. She went back inside the van, being careful to stay away from the blood. She picked up his limp member and wiped it down with the wipe. A girl couldn't be too careful.

Back outside she took the wipe and the garden stake and wrapped them in her slightly stained beach coverup. There was a small area for a campfire beside the van. It was set up and ready to go. She assumed Martin was going to cook his dinner there that night, but there would be no dinner for Martin that night or any night.

All she needed was paper and a light. She returned to the van and found a lighter sitting in the console between the seats. Next to that was an empty fast-food bag and some napkins. Perfect.

Within moments she had the fire roaring. She tossed the coverup, the garden stake and wipes onto the flames. They smoked a bit, then caught and disappeared into ash.

Just like water, Ashley thought. Fire cleanses everything too.

Chapter 18

On Sunday, Ashley awoke eager to face the day. She could be pregnant, and that was all she needed to put a smile on her face. Then she remembered she promised to go look at Rocky and Beth's plants. At least the plants would be enjoyable.

"Hey, Dudley, how's my boy?" Ashley asked as Dudley ran into the kitchen, awaiting his breakfast. She was so glad she had a cat. Dogs were too much trouble. So needy and always wanting to go places with you. She liked cats. They were indifferent and had no problem killing things, even for sport. Cats were the best.

She poured his kibble into a bowl, checked to make sure her Google Home was on, and sat down to a fresh cup of coffee. "Hey, Google, what's the weather like today?"

"Today's high temperature will be seventy-five degrees Fahrenheit or twenty-four degrees Celsius with minimal cloud cover and a three percent chance of rain."

"Well, Dudley, it looks like we have plenty of time in the garden today. Care to join me?"

Dudley rarely went outside. He didn't like the outdoors and only ventured as far as the fence when he did go out.

She headed into the bedroom, scooped up the clothes from two nights of hunting, and tossed them in the wash. She added an extra scoop of OxiClean to make sure any blood stains were removed. There couldn't be any trace of the weekend left. Except, of course, for a possible baby.

Once outside, Ashley poured some of her fertilizer mixture into a bottle and attached it to the dispenser on her hose. She hummed a quiet tune to herself while the water mixed with the liquid fertilizer and soaked into the earth.

Dudley poked his head out the door and came over to stand beside her. "As a cat, I know you don't like water," she said to the feline, who was on the lookout for prey. "But I think it's magical. Add it to the right amount of fertilizer, and your plants produce like crazy. Too much water, and it's watered down. Too little water, and you burn them."

"Maybe that's what I did," a voice from the other side of the fence said.

Dudley bolted for the door, and Ashley turned off the water. "Excuse me?" she said.

Rocky came into the yard. "Maybe that's what I did. Maybe I didn't add enough water."

"What are you doing here, Rocky?" Ashley tried to hide the irritation in her voice, but she was too annoyed to do a good job.

"Just wanted to remind you of our afternoon plans." He grinned and gave Ashley an appreciative up-and-down glance.

"I'll be there at one o'clock. Now, if you'll excuse me, I have my own garden to attend to."

"Sure is pretty back here," he said, not trying to hide the double meaning.

"Rocky. Go away." Ashley had enough. It was time for serious boundaries.

Rocky looked shocked and slightly hurt.

"Seriously. This is my morning off, and I just want to be alone. Please, go home to your wife, and I'll see you both this afternoon."

"Oh, okay," he said.

"And Rocky . . ."

He stopped and looked back at her before going through the gate.

"Don't come back. I've tried not to be rude, but you've been coming over here a lot, and I need my space."

"Uh, okay. I didn't mean any harm. I'm sorry." He hung his head like a dejected puppy and closed the gate behind him.

Dudley poked his head out the door. "See that, Dudley, that's how you deal with snoopy neighbors. I should have done that a long time ago."

Ashley finished her watering and pulled a few weeds in her flower and vegetable gardens. She thought of the garden stake Martin gave her. She was glad she'd burned it. She had her own already in the ground for the dill.

"Hey, Dudley," she said as the cat came closer. "I don't think that fellow knew what a pickle he'd be in when he gave me the dill garden stake." Ashley laughed at her joke, while Dudley looked disinterested. "You're right. I wouldn't make it as a stand-up comic."

Once finished in the garden, Ashley headed inside to clean up. She transferred the clothes into the dryer and had a shower. One final step was to remove all traces of where she'd been. Before she knew it, it was lunchtime and then the dreaded visit to the neighbors. She put together a chicken and cheese sandwich and washed it down with a glass of water.

"There, now I'm fortified and ready to face the snoops. Well, one snoop anyway. I'm not sure about Beth."

Dudley meowed in agreement. Or so Ashley liked to think that's what it was. She grabbed her keys and headed out the door to see Rocky and Beth's sad garden.

* * *

Beth brought them all some iced tea with a lemon wedge as Ashley surveyed the garden.

"So, what do you think it is?" Beth asked. Rocky was appropriately quiet, considering their last interaction.

"It looks like you either overwater or underwater them," Ashley said.

"So both things cause yellow leaves? How on earth can we figure it out then?" Beth sighed and shook her head. "I thought it needed more nutrients, that's why Rocky got your recipe, but that didn't seem to work."

"Depends on how often and how much you water," Ashley added. "Do you have a trowel? We can take a look right now."

"I'll get it," Rocky offered. He returned with two small garden trowels and handed them to Ashley and Beth. "If you ladies don't mind, I have some things to do in the RV. I'll leave you be." He nodded to Ashley and went into the garage.

Ashley headed over to a tomato plant. "See the small

fruits on here?" she asked Beth. "Most plants need more water once the fruit is growing." Ashley dug her trowel into the dirt and gently removed some. Then she brushed aside more dirt to expose the roots. "See this here. The dirt is really wet. Once the ground gets this much moisture into it, the roots shut down, just like when they don't get enough. The best way to know if you are over or under-watering is to dig down a few inches and see how moist the soil is. If it's powder dry, you need more water. If it's damp, less water."

Beth nodded and dug a few inches away from another plant. "Wow, there's a lot of water down there," she said. "That Rocky. I swear he only comes out here to use up that fertilizer recipe so he can get more from you."

Ashley raised an eyebrow. Could it be that Beth wasn't as clueless as she thought? Did she know Rocky was a lech?

Beth motioned for Ashley to follow her to the very back of the garden. There were flowers everywhere. Many looked bright and happy, while others looked sad and at death's door.

"What can you tell me about this area," Beth asked with one eye on the garage door.

Ashley inhaled deeply. The smell of freshly watered earth and a slight fragrance filled the air.

"This one is easy to diagnose, but we should still check the soil. It looks like your Lily of the Valley and Daylily and Irises are doing great. They love lots of water. The rest, not so much. In the fall, I suggest moving all the bulb flowers into their own area, and you can add some ferns for more greenery. Then you can give them the extra water they need."

"You're so helpful, Ashley. I appreciate it," Beth said, then lowered her voice. "I'm so sorry about Rocky. I think he's going through male menopause or something. He's become almost obsessed with what happens at your house, always looking over there."

Beth's disclosure shook Ashely to the core. She knew Rocky spied on her but didn't realize to what degree. She was extra thankful she'd stopped bringing men home.

"I, uh, don't know what to say," Ashley said. "But to be honest, he's been rather snoopy lately, and he looks at me differently."

Beth pulled Ashley closer. "I'm divorcing him. He just doesn't know yet. I can't take much more of his wandering eyes. I know, given the time and circumstances, more than his eyes will wander. I've talked to him about it, but . . ." Beth's voice trailed off as she watched the garage door for signs of Rocky.

"Oh, Beth," Ashley lowered her voice to a whisper. "I'm so sorry. I didn't know."

Beth took her arm and led her to another part of the garden, even farther from the garage.

"It's okay. I wanted you to know, just in case, well, you know, he tried anything, and you didn't know what to do."

"I appreciate that, Beth. Really, I do. Is there anything I can do to help?" Ashley didn't mention how lately his stares lingered on the wrong parts of her body.

"No, thank you." Beth sighed. "It's been a hard decision to make. Please don't tell anyone. Everything's in Rocky's name, and if I leave, well, you know the rules. Possession is nine-tenths of the law. And I know this may sound terrible, but I'd be better off if he died."

Ashley looked directly at Beth. "Oh, you don't mean that, Beth. You loved him once."

"I do mean it," Beth said, her voice getting louder. "There's more. I might as well tell you. I've seen him down the street, about a block and a half over, talking to that big-breasted older gal that moved into the Scotts' old place. You know the one on the corner?"

Ashley did know the one. She assumed it was the woman who told the cops she'd seen someone resembling Rodney walking toward the highway. She'd have to thank her someday.

"You don't think Rocky is, well, you know . . ." Ashley couldn't think of a polite way to say it.

"Yes, I do," Beth was close to tears now. "He gets up and goes for walks late at night. Says he can't sleep. But he comes home smelling like chamomile tea. And he always notices if your lights are on or if your car is in the driveway."

Ashley nodded. Things would be better if Rocky simply disappeared.

"Look, Beth, don't do anything yet. I mean about the divorce. You know, sometimes these things work themselves out. Maybe Rocky will leave you for her. Or maybe the universe will take care of him for you. I know that sounds cold, but if my Randy can be taken away from me—"

Beth cut her off mid-sentence. "I'm so sorry about that. I'm being inconsiderate, putting my burdens on you when you so recently lost someone you loved. Goodness, you barely know us, and here I am babbling away. Forgive me?"

Ashley smiled. She was beginning to like this woman. "You're forgiven. Think nothing of it. To be honest, it takes my mind off my own troubles. I'll keep an eye out for Rocky if I'm ever up late, and maybe between the two of us, we can get enough evidence against him to ensure you get everything in a divorce, or at least a good portion."

"You'd do that for me?" Beth bent down and pulled a yellow leaf off one of her flowers. "Part of me is grateful, and another part of me feels like I'm being a total fool."

"Well, I won't make it a full-time job, but yes, if I see anything, I'll tell you and record it."

Beth leaned in and hugged Ashley. "I think I should've gotten to know you better earlier. You really are a great neighbor."

Just then, Rocky came into view. "Hey Ashley, your, um, brother, just pulled into your driveway. Thought you should know."

Ashley waved and said thanks, then turned to Beth. "I should get going. If you ever want to talk or need a shoulder, I'm available."

Beth squeezed Ashley's hand. "Thank you, Ashley. That means a lot. I'll see you around the neighborhood."

"You bet," Ashley said and headed toward the walkway between the garage and the house. "Don't forget to dig up those bulbs and transplant them this fall!"

* * *

Matt helped Ashley clean up the dinner dishes and place

them in the dishwasher. She turned it on and stood transfixed as the water flowed into the machine, ready to wipe away all traces of their dinner. Some nights, when alone, she would stand there and just listen to the dishes being washed and rinsed. She always air-dried them, flicking little pools of water off the top of the mugs and glasses before leaving the door slightly ajar.

"So, what were you doing at the neighbor's earlier today? I thought you didn't like them."

Ashley followed Matt into the living room. "Well, it turns out she's an okay person. I wasn't imagining that her creep of a husband was watching me. He has been and will continue to do so. Beth is gathering information so she can divorce him and not be left penniless because of his wandering eye."

"Is he having an affair?" Matt asked.

"I'm not sure, but if ever I'm up and see him walking down the street, I just may follow him. I kinda like the idea of being a spy, and thanks to my smartphone, I can even take pictures!"

"You could google how to spy on someone," Matt said with a chuckle.

"Did you want me to search for how to spy on someone?" Google Home asked.

"No, thanks, Google," Ashley said. She walked back toward the kitchen counter and unplugged the machine. "Damn thing listens to everything!"

She motioned toward the couch and sat in the big comfy chair. Matt took a seat.

"Matt, I wanted you to know I won't be needing you to

take away any more barrels. It's too risky, what with Rocky being so snoopy and now Beth striking up a friendship. Plus, that cop is still snooping around. I'll figure something else out."

"Oh, okay." Matt looked hurt by her pronouncement.

"I can find you other odd jobs if you need the money," she said.

"No, no, it's not that. It feels like the end of an era, you know. We were a team, and now, that's over."

Ashley got up from her chair and sat beside Matt on the couch. She put her hand in his.

"Sweetie, you'll always be my brother. We are a team." She hated it when he got moody like this. He was such a sensitive soul when it came to her.

"I know, sis, really I do. It's just that, well, I liked protecting you by taking out the trash. And now, that's done. What are you going to do?"

Ashley smiled and patted Matt's hand. "Oh, I have some thoughts. I'm going to watch some YouTube tutorials on contouring and shading and such and change my look. It'll be like painting, only on my face. I'm also going to shop at a few consignment stores, find some clothes that aren't my style, and wear them. Easy peasy. Just wash my face and toss the clothing later. What do you think?"

Matt beamed at her. "I think you are the most beautiful, smartest, sneakiest, bravest woman I know, and I'm glad you're on my team. I'd hate to think what would happen if you weren't."

Ashley laughed and stood up. "Well, you are on my team, now and forever. Tea? Coffee? Perhaps a splash of sherry for the ole digestive system?"

Matt stood as well. "No, I think I should be going. I need to connect with some people tomorrow and let them know I'll have time for some extra work." He gently pushed a few hairs behind Ashley's ear. "Are you okay, I mean, really, okay? I know the whole Randy thing is messed up. I just want to make sure you're going to be okay."

"I'm sad but fine." Ashley leaned over and kissed Matt on the cheek. "I love that you care so much about me. It will take time, but as the saying goes, good things come to those who wait."

"Yeah, sure." Matt gave a quick snort. "Like you've ever waited around. You go get 'em, sis. Do what you need to do, and someday I'll be an uncle, and we'll get an acreage, and you can grow whatever you want. And me, well, I'll build a big garage and start a little home car repair shop. It'll be perfect. Just wait and see."

"Sounds like a great plan." Ashley opened the door to let Matt out. "I'm working all week, so maybe see you next Sunday?"

"I'll give you a call," Matt said as he stepped out the door. "Thanks again for dinner."

Ashley closed the door, locked it, and went to find Dudley. He was sound asleep on her bed, curled up in a ball around his felt mouse.

"Hey, Dudley," she called before entering the room.

Dudley opened one eye, yawned, and stretched himself into the perfect petting position. Ashley obliged and gave him a tummy rub.

"What do you think, Dudley? Is it time to shake things up a bit? I've been thinking about moving. An acreage sure sounds nice. I've got almost $650,000 saved up from my paintings and investments, and I could sell this place easily for another $550,000. I wonder if that's enough for an acreage with a big ole garden and a big shop for Matt."

Dudley gently nipped at Ashley's finger, letting her know that was enough tummy rubs.

"Okay, I get the hint." She pulled out her phone and searched for local realtors. Maybe now was a good time to start planning for the future.

New baby, new home, new life.

Chapter 19

By Wednesday morning, Ashley had narrowed it down to two realtors with great online reviews. She sent them both emails with times they could meet with her on the weekend and let each know she was deciding between the two of them. She closed her email, grabbed her purse, and headed off to work.

The July weather was glorious, and Ashley was excited to help out the mid-summer clientele. She liked helping the slow starters, the indecisive ones. They were the folks who couldn't decide what to plant in spring and were now desperate to have a garden that would produce something edible or beautiful before summer was over.

Ashley parked, stored her purse in her locker, and headed to the fruit and veggie section. There were pretty slim pickings there now. Mostly herbs and the odd everbearing strawberry plants. She picked little weeds out of the discounted corn pots and the now two feet tall tomato plants. She hummed a little tune as she worked and didn't notice a customer come up from behind.

"Um, excuse me?" a female voice said.

Ashley jumped, knocking over a tomato plant. "Oh my gosh, you frightened me!"

"I'm so sorry. I didn't want to interrupt, you look so

content here, but I could use some help."

Ashley took a look at the woman. She seemed familiar but couldn't figure out how. "Do I know you?" Ashley asked.

"No, I don't think so. My name is Kate. Kate Johnson. I have an older home I'm selling for a client and wanted to grab some plants to put in the garden. My client needs to sell quickly, and I thought a flower and vegetable garden would be a nice touch. Gardens are a big seller for homes this time of year."

Ashley cocked her head to the side. "Now I know why you look familiar. You were one of the realtors I looked at online."

"Oh? Were you going to call me?" Kate asked.

Ashley set the tomato plant upright, patted down the soil, and stared at the woman. "Well, honestly, no. You weren't on my shortlist, but it appears you do love to help your clients out. I think I should reconsider. In fact, what the heck? Would you like to meet me at my house after work and let me know what you think?"

"I'd like that," Kate said. "But I can't until tomorrow. I need to get this garden in today and take photos and upload everything. I'll be working until at least nine tonight. Can we do it after work tomorrow? Say 6:30 p.m.?"

Ashley liked the fact this woman couldn't spare the time to get a new client that night because she had made a promise to an existing client. It showed character.

"You know what? I think that would be perfect. I'll text the other realtors and let them know I've changed my mind."

"Perfect." Kate handed Ashley her card. "Now, I know there's not a lot of seedlings left, and some of these look full-grown, so can you help me pick out which ones would work in a partially shaded garden?"

Ashley smiled. "Sure thing." She took out a notepad from her apron pocket and wrote down her phone number and address. "Here's my number and address. I'll see you around 6:30 p.m. tomorrow. Now let's go get your client some great plants for their mid-summer garden. Wait here."

Ashley went to find a trolley. She returned and started putting tomato and corn plants on the cart. Then she found some string beans, with beans already on them, and a couple of squash plants in full bloom.

"Plant the tomatoes on their own. They'll need more water than these others. Plant the corn with lots of space in between. Plant the beans between each corn plant, then the squash just in front of it all. The beans will climb the corn and nourish the soil. The squash will kill out weeds, too. Would there be room for an herb garden?"

"Absolutely," Kate said with a smile. "You are good at this. If your garden is as great as I think it is, we shouldn't have any problem selling."

Twenty minutes later, the cart was full, and Kate was at the till getting checked out.

"Thanks again, Ashley. I'll see you tomorrow around 6:30."

"Anytime, Kate. See you then." Ashley smiled as she watched Kate pay and maneuver the cart to her car.

"I should be on commission," she muttered and went back to work.

* * *

Ashley noticed a strange blue SUV parked on the street as she pulled into her driveway. As soon as she got out, a man exited the car and waved.

"Hey Ashley, I'm Dave Miller. The realtor you emailed today. I thought I'd pop by, see the house, and introduce myself. I know you said you wanted to meet this weekend, but I happen to have a client in the area. I, um, looked you up on the property tax website and found you. May I come in?"

Ashley felt the hairs on the back of her neck bristle. "David, is it? Well, David or Dave, I specifically said I wanted to meet on the weekend. I just got home from work, and it's not a good time."

She turned her back and headed to her front door. She couldn't believe he was being so pushy. She turned and found him almost nose-to-nose with her. Now she was mad.

"And, since you've come all this way, I'm letting you know I've already decided. I met another realtor today and was impressed with how she cared about her clients, so I won't be needing your services. Have a nice day, Dave."

Ashley put the key in the front door and opened it. She felt a hand on her arm as she was shoved inside. Dave shut the door quickly behind her and locked it.

"Now, you're a smart woman, I can tell that, but I don't like being spoken to like that. It's not very polite."

Ashley shook free of his grip. "Get out! Get out now!" She reached in her purse for her phone and dialed 911.

Before she could hit send, Dave knocked the phone out

of her hand and, in the next instance, backhanded her so hard she landed with a thud on the floor. He picked up the phone, turned it off, and tossed it on the couch.

Ashley got up and was on him in a flash. She jumped on his back and held onto his hair with one hand while she reached around front to gouge out an eye with her other hand. Dave calmly turned away and threw himself back into a wall. Ashley's head snapped back, hit the wall, and she slumped to the floor.

"Now, as I was saying." Dave leaned down and lifted her chin with his index finger. "I came all this way. It wouldn't hurt you to be nice to me." He brushed some imaginary lint off his shirt, stood, and put his hands on his hips.

"I have the perfect solution. You and I will go into the bedroom. Once there, we'll undress and have sex. Once I'm done, you are going to see me to the door, wave politely goodbye, and never, ever tell anyone of this. I will find out, and when I do, your life won't be worth much."

Dudley came out of the bedroom to see what all the commotion was about. He meowed at Ashley and rubbed up against her bruised body.

"Oh, you have a cat. How cute." Dave grabbed Dudley by the scruff and threw him through the bathroom door and into the bathtub. Dudley howled as his little kitty body hit the inside of the tub. Then he was quiet. Dave calmly shut the bathroom door. "I don't like being watched," he said matter-of-factly.

Ashley's head hurt, and she felt dizzy. This wasn't right. This wasn't right at all. She was the predator, not the prey. Her mind raced. If only she could get to the kitchen and grab a knife. Where was her snoopy neighbor when she needed him? She put her hand to the back of her head, and it came back bloody. This was not good, not good at all.

"So," Dave squatted down in front of her. "This is how it's going to be. You are going to be quiet, or I'll gag you. Try to hurt me again, and I'll tie you up. Fight me, and I'll keep you here all night long. Do you understand?"

Ashley gave a quick nod. She knew this kind of man. She'd dealt with others like him her entire teenage and young adult life. They were bullies with no respect for women. They took what they wanted, when they wanted, and then used threats to keep their victims quiet. No wonder he had such great ratings. They were probably written under duress.

"So, let's go in here and see what we can find." Dave jerked Ashley up by the arm and pushed her into her bedroom. "Sit on the bed and don't move," he commanded. "Besides, I know you want this."

Ashley felt her pulse quicken as adrenaline surged through her body. That was the same thing her rapists had said to her over and over again—that she wanted it. She didn't want it, never wanted it that way, and was always made to feel it was her fault. Years later, she understood and knew it wasn't her fault at all. It was their fault, and she was not a willing participant. She wasn't a kid anymore. There had to be something she could do.

"I want to see my cat," she said defiantly. "I have to make sure he's okay."

Dave let out a bone-chilling laugh. "Nope, kitty might be dead, and I can't have you crying your eyes out while I give you the best time of your life. It will ruin the mood." He opened a dresser drawer and found Ashley's socks, an old pair of pantyhose, and some blue tights.

"This will work just fine." He yanked Ashley up on her feet, spun her around and tied her wrists with the pantyhose. "Lie down, face down," he commanded.

Ashley complied. In her mind, she was kicking him in the head and screaming, but she couldn't get her body to move.

She felt the tights being tied around her ankles. Then nothing. She held her breath, trying to listen to what was happening. Had he left the room? She rolled over and found herself alone. She could scream, but none of the windows were open. She heard the quiet hum of the air conditioner and the sound of someone rummaging around in her kitchen. He was probably looking for knives. How funny would it be if he killed her with the same knife she'd used so many times to drain her unworthy lovers of their blood? She couldn't think of that now. She had to see if Dudley was okay and figure out a way to escape. She rolled herself into an upright position and put her ear against her bedroom wall. She could faintly hear Dudley in the bathroom, but she couldn't tell if he was okay. At least he was alive.

"What are you doing!"

Ashley jumped as Dave appeared in the doorway with two glasses and a bottle of port. "I couldn't find any wine, but this will do. Sit down. Let's get to know each other a little."

Ashley hopped back over to the bed and did as she was told. Dave poured the port and put a glass up to her lips. "Go ahead," he said with a smirk. "Drink up. I want you nice and loose for later."

Ashley took a sip and then turned her head. If she was pregnant, she did not want to drink alcohol. A little bit shouldn't hurt the fetus at this stage, but the thought of possibly jeopardizing her baby made her reluctant to drink.

Dave set the bottle and his glass down. He yanked Ashley's head back and poured an entire glassful into her mouth. Ashley sputtered and coughed. There was nothing she could do but swallow.

"That's my girl. I knew you could do it."

"The port's too sweet," she said, trying to buy some time. "I think I have a bottle of single malt way in the back of the cat food cupboard. Wouldn't you like that instead?"

"Oh, a scotch drinker. Aren't you the perfect little hostess? Yes, I'd like that very much. Don't go away now." Dave shoved Ashley onto her back as he left the room in search of a stronger drink.

Ashley listened to the cupboard doors being opened and closed. Then a pause. Another cupboard opened and closed, and she heard glasses clink. Gawd, she hoped he didn't make her drink scotch. She'd probably puke, but maybe she could keep him talking and get him drunk enough so she could escape. Where was that nosy neighbor now that she needed him?

He returned a few moments later with a bottle of scotch in one hand and two clean glasses in the other.

"Now, this is more like it." He poured himself three fingers of scotch. He poured two fingers into her glass and held it to her lips.

"I can't," she blurted. "I'm allergic to wheat. It'll make me sick! But you go ahead. You drink all you want. I don't mind."

"Well, we can't have you throwing up while I make sweet love to you, now, can we?" He tossed back her scotch and set the glass on the bedside table.

Ashley eyed the glass, a plan formulating in her head. If she could somehow break the glass, she could cut herself loose or cut him, whichever was easiest.

"Let me tell you what I'm going to do to you." He sipped on his scotch and licked his lips. "First, I'm going to undress you. The best part is your clothes will be around your wrists and ankles, making it even harder to move. Then I'm going to give you what you want—what you all want but can't bring yourself to ask for."

This man was a psychopath. She would know, having spent many of her younger years in therapy after her dad died. At first, they thought she might be a sociopath or even a psychopath, but it was obvious her feelings were real and not put on to impress the psychologist. In the end, their report said she had trouble with authority figures and probably had oppositional defiant disorder.

This man, this psychopath in her bedroom, had no feelings that she could tell. And right now, he was the authority figure she needed to be rid of.

Ashley wracked her brain, trying to think of what else she could do. Then it hit her. The windows may not be open, but her Google Home was on, and she could holler at it to call 911.

"Hey, Google!" she called out. "Call 911!" There was no response.

"What the hell do you think you're doing?" Dave put his glass down and backhanded her. He dragged her body into the middle of the bed so her head was on a pillow. He grabbed the socks and unceremoniously stuffed one of them in her mouth.

"That ought to shut you up. Geez, you try and be nice to a lady, and she wants to call the cops on you."

Ashley tasted blood as her tongue stuck to the dry sock in her mouth. She forgot she'd turned off Google Home when Matt was over and hadn't turned it back on. Where was big brother when she needed him?

Dave poured himself a full tumbler of scotch and set it on the bedside table. He moved Ashley over a bit and sat beside her with his back up against the headboard and his feet stretched out in front of him.

"Ah, that's more like it," he said as he kicked off his shoes. "Hi honey, I'm home!" He let out a childish chuckle and picked up his glass. "I think I'll take my time with you. You are a feisty one. I like feisty." He took a big gulp of the scotch, swirled it around in his mouth, and swallowed.

"It's not the best I've ever had, but it is tasty." Dave ran his index finger from Ashley's collarbone to her belly button. "You have such a cute little body for an older woman. I like that." He took another drink of his scotch.

Ashley tried to speak, but the sock muffled her.

"What's that? Are you trying to tell me how much you will love this? I hope you don't mind, but I do love to take my time."

Ashley glared at him and tried to sit up. He pushed her back down but took the sock out of her mouth.

"I don't think Google can hear you from here," he said. "So, what shall we talk about?"

Ashley could tell Dave was getting way too comfortable. She needed to trick him somehow.

"You know, my boyfriend will be home any moment. Just leave, and I won't tell anyone you were here." She gave him her best puppy dog eyes. Dave only laughed.

"Oh, you stupid woman." He shook his head. "Don't you think I researched you before coming over? You're Ashley Taylor. You've owned this house for ten years, and just recently, your fiancé was killed in a car crash. No one is coming to save you, darlin', so just relax and enjoy your time with me."

Ashley glared at the man. "I know my fiancé is dead, but I have a new boyfriend, and he'll be here soon. Go, and I won't tell anyone you were here."

"Yeah, that's not how this works." He finished his scotch. "This is how it's going down. I'm going to get pleasantly buzzed on this mediocre scotch. Then I'm going take your shirt off over your head and down your arms. Then I'll take off your bra. I'll probably just stare at you for a time. I love how nervous you stupid women get when a man does nothing but stare. I love how you get all uncomfortable like you've never teased a man before, never hoped they'd look at your breasts. I know you feel the power when you wear those low-cut tops. You're all the same. Just a bunch of cock teasers."

"I'm not like that, I promise!" Ashley pleaded. "Just let me go. I'll let you list the house. You can have a cut of the sale on top of your commission. Just let me go."

Dave laughed a poured another drink. "Nope. Not going to happen." He took a large gulp and unbuttoned Ashley's shirt. He shoved it roughly over her shoulders and down to her wrists. "See how great that works. Now it's all bunched up back there, and I get to see you. I bet you don't feel powerful now."

There was a slight slur to his words, and Ashley hoped she could somehow keep him talking until he passed out. With her luck, this guy was a big drinker and could hold his liquor.

"So, what do you want me to do?" Ashley asked, trying another tactic. She looked out the bedroom window and realized the sun was going down soon. Something had to work. Somehow she had to get away.

"Oh, nothin' darlin', nothin' at all." He ran a finger across the top of her breasts. "I'll do all the work. You just lie back and relax. It's a pity you don't drink scotch. You'd like it better with a bit of a buzz goin' on."

Dave finished his third glass of scotch and poured himself another one.

"Drink up," Ashley commanded. "I want to taste your mouth."

Dave's eyebrows shot up. "Oh, you want to get the party started?" he asked, throwing back half a glass of scotch. "Absolutely baby, abso-frickin-lutely."

He placed the almost empty glass on the side table and leaned in for a kiss. Ashley tilted her head back into the pillow as if ready for his kiss. Before he could touch her lips, she quickly raised her head and head-butted him.

"Ow, what the f—"

Ashley head-butted him again, this time getting the delicate bones under his left eye.

"Jezzus lady!"

Ashley twisted her body around, raised her legs and hips, opened her legs as much as possible, and caught Dave's neck between her thighs. His hands went immediately to his neck as he tried to pry her thighs off of him. Blood trickled down into his right eye, and his left eye was beginning to swell shut.

"You stupid bi—"

Ashley squeezed tighter. "Never, ever underestimate the power of a survivor, you little prick!"

Dave's hands clawed at her outer thighs, then reached for her face and missed. He shoved his left hand between his neck and her thigh and tried to gouge her inner thigh with his fingers. His right hand shot up, aiming for her face again. This time she caught his index finger in her mouth and bit down as hard as she could between the bone and the knuckle.

Dave let out a blood-curdling scream and tried to pull his hand away. They both heard a distinctive popping sound, signaling she'd dislocated his finger.

"Stop it!" He let out a guttural scream of pain. Ashley bit down harder, holding his finger tightly between her teeth. She squeezed her thighs tighter, knowing her life depended on it. There was no coming back from this if she couldn't make him pass out.

Dave pulled his hand out from between his neck and her thigh and punched her in the face.

Ashley felt his finger slip out of her mouth as her thighs loosened their grip. This couldn't be happening. There was no way he could win. Was this her punishment for trying to find a good guy and raise a son properly?

"You are going to regret this, you slut." Dave had his hands free now. He scrambled to get the fingers of his good hand around her neck. "I hate you!" he screamed. "You're all alike. You think you're better than us! I'll show you who's the boss."

Ashley barely heard a knock at her door over Dave's ranting. She shook her head and hollered. "Help! Help! I'm in here. Help me, please!"

Dave's fist connected with her temple, causing her to lose her grip on his neck. He pulled his head out and stuffed the sock back in her mouth.

"You've been a very naughty girl, and now you're going to pay for it."

Ashley heard the wood around her front door frame give way, and in the next moment, Detective Frank Colombo was aiming a gun at Dave's head.

"Freeze, asshole!" he demanded. "Stand up slowly, hands behind your back."

"Wait, no, you don't understand." Dave showed the detective his hand. "She bit me. The bitch dislocated my damn finger and tried to kill me!"

"Stand up and turn around, now!"

The last thing Ashley remembered was the blood running down Dave's face as the detective called for backup and an ambulance.

Chapter 20

Ashley opened her eyes, even though it was painful. Her head hurt, her teeth hurt, and she had no idea where she was. It took her a moment to focus, and when she did, she saw a nurse smiling down at her.

"Welcome back, Ashley," she said. "How are you feeling?"

"Like I got hit by a truck. How'd I get here?"

"There was an incident, and you were brought here."

"What kind of incident?" Ashley gasped as a cramp ripped through her belly. "Oh, gawd. The baby, did I lose it?"

"I'll go get the doctor. I'll be right back."

Ashley looked around the room. It was bright, too bright. She didn't even know if she was pregnant, but if she was and lost the baby, she'd kill the bastard that did this to her. The sound of monitors beeping filled her head. She looked at her arms and saw an IV poking out of her right arm. A pulse oximeter was on her left index finger. She touched her face and winced.

"Hey now, don't you go messing up my great work, young lady."

Ashley squinted as she tried to focus on the new voice in the room.

"I'm Doctor Hanlon. Do you know where you are?"

"Yeah, obviously, I'm in the hospital."

"That's right. Do you know why you're here?"

The doctor shone a small flashlight into each of her eyes and smiled.

"Why? Yes, there was a man, a realtor. He came to my home unannounced and tried—" Ashley cut herself off. If she didn't speak of it, it never happened.

"You were brought in a couple of hours ago via ambulance. Do you remember what happened?"

"Detective Frank. He saved me." Ashley looked around the room. "Was I," her voice trailed off. Then she squared her shoulders and looked at the doctor. "Was I pregnant? Did I lose the baby?"

"No, you weren't," he said matter of factly. "We did a few blood tests when you came in. It was negative for pregnancy."

"Oh." Ashley felt her hopes dashed once again. She looked toward the door and saw a figure standing outside. "Who is that?" She felt her panic rise. It was like being fifteen all over again.

The doctor looked toward the door. "That's a police officer. He wants to ask you a few questions. Are you up for it?"

"Did they arrest the guy? Is he still alive? What's going on?"

"I'll let the officer fill you in, Ashley. But only if you feel up to talking to him."

"Yes, yes, please. Let him come in. I want to talk to him."

"Okay, but only for five minutes. After that, we're going to take you for a CT scan. You've probably got a concussion. I'll let CT know you're coming and send a porter to get you. I'll be

172   Cleansing Water

back after the scan."

Doctor Hanlon left and spoke to someone outside the door. A few seconds later, Colombo stepped into the room.

"How are you feeling, Ashley?" he asked.

"Like shit," Ashley replied. "But I suspect I'd feel a lot worse if you hadn't come by when you did. How did you know I was in trouble?"

"I didn't. I was coming to speak to you on an entirely different matter. I knocked and heard you cry for help, and well, here we are."

"Is he in jail? Did you get him? That prick tried to rape me!" Ashley's voice rose as the reality of the past few hours set in. "Please tell me you got him."

"Yes, we got him," the detective said. "But I need to ask. Did he succeed? Did that man rape you?"

"No, no. He tied me up and took off my shirt, and then, well, we got into a bit of a fight."

The detective couldn't hold in a belly laugh. "A bit of a fight? Young lady, you beat the crap out of that man with your hands tied behind your back. He has a dislocated finger, a busted eye socket, and probably a concussion. What'd you do, head butt him?"

Ashley let out a weak laugh. "Yeah, Yeah. I did do that, didn't I? Maybe a couple of times. I was trying to choke him with my thighs, but I couldn't hold on. He kept punching me, and the next thing I knew, you were there."

The cop smiled down at her and shook his head. "Here's what I can tell you. His finger has been put back in place, his head stitched up, and he'll be back later for surgery around his eye. In the meantime, we are charging him with attempted rape, aggravated assault, and kidnapping."

"Why me?" Ashley asked. "Why was he trying to hurt me? I've never met the man before."

"Well, we think he may be a serial rapist, targeting single women who are selling their homes, but we could never get a witness to speak out against him. I'm hoping you will."

"Absolutely!" Ashley tried to sit up and fell back on the pillow. "Gawd, I feel like crap."

"You rest up, and we'll talk more later."

"Why were you coming to see me?" Ashley asked.

"Let's talk about that when you get out of here. I think we'll have more information by then. You rest up and get better."

The detective turned to leave as a porter came into the room. "Ready for your CT?" he asked. Ashley nodded and let him help her into the wheelchair.

"My cat! Wait! My cat! Detective Colombo!"

The detective stepped back into the room. "What is it, Ashley? Are you okay?"

"Yeah, I think. My cat, Dudley. Was he there? Is he okay?"

"I believe so, yes. Your brother, Matt, is it? He showed up as we were putting you into the ambulance. You asked him about the cat. From what I gather, Dudley has a broken leg, and Matt is with him at the vet right now. He should be okay, though."

"Thank you, Detective," Ashley said as she was wheeled out of the room. "Oh, and Detective—"

"Yes, Ashley?"

"Charge that bastard with animal cruelty, too."

* * *

When Ashley returned from her CT scan, Matt was waiting in her room.

"Matt! How's Dudley? Is he okay? Where is he?" The porter raised the back of the bed, adjusted her blankets, and left the room.

Matt took his place at the side of the bed. "Oh gawd, Ashley. I can't believe that bastard did this to you! The police have him, and he will be charged. From what I hear, you did quite a number on him."

"Not bad for a girl, huh?" Ashley forced a weak smile. "Where's Dudley?"

"He's still at the vet. I asked them to keep him overnight for you. He has a broken leg, but the vet said it was a clean break. They'll let him go home when you do. Or I could go stay at your place tomorrow if they don't let you out."

"Oh, Matt. Thank you so much. Poor Dudley." A tear escaped and ran down her cheek. "Why me, Matt? Do you think God's punishing me?"

"No! Absolutely not, Ashley. From what I understand, they suspected him months ago, but no one will press charges. Luckily, this time he was caught in the act by a cop. No chance of him getting away with this."

Ashley nodded and winced. It still hurt. Headbutting looked so easy in the movies. Easy, but very painful in real life.

Dr. Hanlon knocked softly and entered the room. "Good news, Ashley, it's only a mild concussion, and you have some swelling. So, we'd like to keep you overnight for observation."

"Oh, okay." Ashley touched her forehead. "Any idea how long it's going to hurt?"

"Oh, it'll hurt for a bit. I'm more concerned about dizziness or major headaches. Have you felt dizzy at all?"

"No, not dizzy, but my head does hurt. Can I get a painkiller, nothing big, just to take the edge off?"

"Certainly, I'll have the nurse bring you some acetaminophen with codeine. It'll help you sleep, too. Are you hungry? I can get a plate brought up from the kitchen. It's late, but I think they may have some soup or something."

"No, that's okay. I just want to rest up and get home to my cat."

"All right then. The nurses will be in every few hours to check on you. Then if you're symptom-free by morning, we'll let you go home."

"Thanks Dr. Hanlon." Ashley gave him a weak smile.

He turned to leave and then stopped as if remembering something. "Oh, and Ashley."

"Yes?"

"Don't head butt anyone anytime soon. Give your head a chance to heal."

Ashley's weak smile turned into a full-blown grin. "Yes, sir."

Dr. Hanlon gave her a nod and left the room.

"Hey, Ash," Matt said. "Do you want me to go get you a

burger or something? It's no problem."

"Thanks, Matt, but I think I just want to sleep. Can you lower the bed and turn out the lights for me?"

Matt grabbed the remote for the bed and put it in a fully horizontal position. "How's that?"

"Good, thanks." Ashley closed her eyes. "I'll call as soon as they tell me I can go home."

"You bet, sis." Matt walked to the door and turned off the lights. "Sweet dreams."

Chapter 21

The next morning Ashley was cleared to go home. Matt picked her up, and they went to the vet to get Dudley. He was groggy but happy to see Ashley. Once they got him home, he limped over to a sunbeam, curled up, and fell asleep.

"That's what I feel like doing." Ashley looked around her home. "But I'm selling this place. It's time to get us that place in the country with a shop for you and an art studio for me."

"Really, Ashley? You sure you want to do that?" Matt couldn't help but hide his excitement.

"Yep. It's time to create a new life for both of us. There's been too much drama, too much pain. I need to start fresh." Ashley walked into the bedroom and saw the scrunched-up bedspread and blood splatters. She picked up the scotch glass and the bottle and took them to the kitchen. Without thinking, she threw them both in the trash.

When she returned to the bedroom, Matt had stripped the sheets and bedspread and was putting a fresh set of sheets on the bed.

"You don't have to do that, Matt." She touched him on the arm. "You are such a good brother. What I need is for you to fix the casing around the door. It's pretty beat up. I won't be able to sleep tonight if I can't lock my door properly."

"You got it, sis. One handyman special coming up." Matt left the bedroom and headed out to Ashley's shed for tools and supplies. He returned with a hammer, circular saw, measuring tape, and nails, but no wood.

"Hey, Ashley." He put the tools on the counter. "I need to head over to the hardware store and get some supplies. It looks like you need a new piece for the door frame and a piece of casing. I'll be back in a bit. Don't do too much!"

Ashley finished making the bed and threw the sheets and bedcover into the wash. She walked into the living room and looked out her window over to Rocky and Beth's home. She wondered if Rocky was sleeping around. If he was, she'd be happy to make him stop—forever. She shook the thought from her mind and prepared a small bowl of soft food for Dudley. She checked the pills they'd sent her home with. "Take one immediately and then one every twelve hours for seven days." She could do that.

She brought Dudley his bowl with a pill hidden in a ball of soft food. He was so hungry he ate it all up and promptly fell asleep.

Ashley scratched him softly behind the ears. "You get better now. I can't lose you, buddy. You're one of the only things in life I can count on."

Ashley moved into the bathroom and pulled the shower curtain back. The tub had cat fur scattered all over the bottom. She wiped it up with her hand and tossed the hair into the garbage. She turned on the shower, undressed, and got in.

As the water hit her head and neck, she imagined all the

tensions of the past few days oozing out of every pore and hair follicle. The song "What's Up?" by 4 Non Blondes ran through her head. She softly sang some of the words aloud.

She looked down and realized there was blood trickling down her thigh, mixing in with the dried blood from her head.

"Damn it!" She shook her head and ignored the blood. She'd deal with that after the shower. Once again, she closed her eyes and imagined all the stresses, all the tensions, all the negativity in her life being pulled out of her pores. She visualized every shitty thing that happened to her being washed away with the shower water. After a few minutes, she grabbed the shampoo and repeated the visualization. She massaged gently around the back of her head, then rinsed. She applied the conditioner and, finally, the body wash. Each time she visualized all the crappy parts of her life going down the drain, she felt a bit lighter. Water was the great equalizer. She quickly rinsed off her groin area and said a silent request to whoever was in charge that she would be pregnant soon.

She stepped out of the shower and grabbed a tampon. Hopefully, she wouldn't have to use these much longer. Once she dried off, she put on a robe and headed to the laundry. She transferred the bedding to the dryer and went back to her room to get dressed. It was barely ten in the morning, and she was exhausted.

"Shit!" She picked up her cell phone. "I'm supposed to start at ten a.m.!" Ashley found the number, hit send, and waited for her boss to pick it up. "Hello. Yes, this is Ashley. I am so sorry, but I can't make it in today. There's been an incident, and I'm supposed to take it easy for a week or so."

She listened as her boss explained they already knew about the break-in. Some detective was there earlier that morning asking questions and letting them know she'd be out of commission for a few days. Ashley hung up, wondering what the detective had been asking about.

She found her purse and dug out the other realtor's business card. She dialed and waited.

"Hello, Kate Johnson speaking. How can I help you?"

"Hi Kate, it's Ashley. Ashley from the plant store. I'm calling to let you know I'm open all day now. I had an incident. I'm okay, but I'm also not at work for the rest of the week. Could you come over earlier?"

"Hi, Ashley! I'm so glad you called. I got all the plants in, and it looks great. Thank you so much for your help. I could come over after lunch if you like. Say, one o'clock?"

"Yeah, that'd be great, Kate. I need to know what has to be done to spruce the place up and get it sold as quickly as possible. Plus, I'm looking for an acreage, at least three acres, anywhere between here and, say, two hundred miles in any direction, preferably within a ten-minute car ride of a city limit or at least a small town for shopping and such."

"Oh, I just had one come on the market yesterday. We'll talk when I get there. I'll text you the link."

"Great, see you then!" Ashley hung up and looked around the place she'd called home for over ten years. "It's time for us to break up," she said to the walls. "But first, I'll spruce you up a bit."

She walked to the door of the spare room and took a deep breath. She hoped it smelled okay in there and that all her cleaning hadn't been in vain. Ashley turned the knob and pushed the door open. Nothing. No smells. No bad memories. No trace of anything except a few splashes of acrylic paint from before she'd wrapped the room in plastic. She noticed a corner of the carpet was loose. Curious, she went over and gave it a little tug. It came away easily.

She stood there looking at the wood underneath. It was an older house, and someone had covered gorgeous cherry wood floors with carpet.

"Idiot!" she said to herself. "But hey, natural wood floors are popular now. No time like the present."

Ashley went into the kitchen junk drawer, found her utility knife, and grabbed two hefty garbage bags. Her head hurt, but she was on a mission. By the time Matt returned, she'd pulled up half the carpet in the now-empty room.

"What the heck are you doing?" he asked as he brought the wood into the living room.

"It looks like cherry wood, Matt. It'd be perfect once it's refinished, and I'll get more for the house!" Ashley grinned at him as she stuffed the second bag full of old carpet. "Our new place, it'll have wood floors everywhere," Ashley said enthusiastically.

"You're ready to get an acreage?" Matt asked. "Are you pregnant?"

Ashley sighed. "No, but I will be someday soon. Maybe if we get ready for a baby now, I'll have better luck getting pregnant. Get away from the memories of this place."

"Okay then, I'll make sure I do a good job fixing the door. Want some help with the rest of the carpet?"

Ashley started to say no, but a wave of exhaustion washed over her, and she leaned against the wall. "You know what, Matt; I'm going to say yes and go lie down for a bit. The realtor will be here in an hour or so. Think you can get it done by then?"

She headed out of the spare room and toward her bedroom.

"How about I fix the door first? Then I'll start on the carpet." Matt went into the kitchen and grabbed the tools.

"Yeah, sounds good." Ashley walked into the living room and picked up Dudley. She took him into the bedroom and lay him down on her bed, curling up beside him. She spooned his warm, furry body and was asleep in minutes.

Chapter 22

Ashley slept right through the sounds of sawing and hammering. She opened her eyes when Matt touched her gently on the shoulder.

"Someone named Kate is here. She said the door looks great. I'll go work on the carpet while you two talk."

Ashley rubbed her eyes and ran her hand down Dudley's body. "Thanks, Matt. I'll be right out." She ran a finger along the sleeping cat's leg cast. "I'll never let anyone hurt you again, little man."

Ashley went to the washroom, splashed cold water on her face, and found Kate in the backyard.

"This place is fabulous," Kate said, admiring the deck and the gardens. "We could easily get you $600,000 for it. In this neighborhood, in this market, it shouldn't be a problem."

"Wow, that's more than I thought," Ashley said as she joined Kate in the yard.

The pair toured the gardens and deck, Ashley pointing out various plants and their uses as they went along. She showed Kate the rain barrel, now used only for creating fertilizer. They ended their tour at the back door.

"Okay, this looks great," Kate said. "Now, the inside."

Ashley gave her a tour of the house, stopping at the spare

room last. Matt was leaving the room with two hefty bags filled with carpet and underlay.

"You've met Matt," Ashley said. "He's helping me pull up the rest of the carpet. It looks like it could be cherry wood floors underneath."

Kate nodded, squatted, and inspected the floor. "You have a good eye. This is cherry wood, and it's in pretty good shape. Shouldn't take more than two grand to bring it to its former glory. Are you able to put some money into upgrades?" Kate took out a small notebook and made some notes.

"Yes, of course. If you think we can get 600K for this place, I can easily throw a few thousand at it to fix it up. Just show me where, and we can get it done."

"Is the home in your name or you and your husband's name?" Kate asked.

Ashley laughed. "Oh, no. Matt is my brother, not my husband. But I will be looking for a nice big place we can share without being in each other's space."

"Oh, sorry, my mistake." Kate motioned for Ashley to follow her to the kitchen.

She and Ashley sat at the table. Kate pulled out her tablet and pulled up the acreage she'd told Ashley about. "Did you get a chance to look at the listing?"

"No, sorry, I got busy and needed a nap." Ashley looked over the particulars. Four fenced-in acres with three buildings. One large 2,400 sq. foot house, a barn with six stalls and room for at least a dozen chickens, and the best part, a 1,400 sq. foot shop with a two-bedroom apartment above the shop.

Ashley looked over at Kate. "Wow, this would be perfect. How much is it, and when can I move in!"

"Well, it's almost two million dollars. But that's because it's close to the city. Everyone wants to live in this area."

"Two million?" Ashley's expression went from excitement to sadness. "Even if we get what you said for this place, I'm still a million short. Damn, it! This place is perfect." Ashley handed Kate her tablet.

"I've got about $650,000 saved, mostly from selling paintings, plus selling this place. I could almost buy a new place for cash at a million. But nothing more. Plus, I'd need money for moving and upgrades to the new place and money to live off until I found a job or did more paintings."

"Okay, well, now that I know your price range and what you're looking for, let's talk possession dates for this place as well as what areas you want to live in."

Ashley pondered for a moment. "Well, I would need at least three months to pack up, give my notice, and such. Plus, I don't want to move in the winter, so that puts us into next spring. That's too long, isn't it." Ashley took a deep breath and slowly exhaled.

"It's a pretty long time, yes. But since I haven't done much research on acreages, it may take that long to find what you want. You said a 200-mile radius of here. Would you be willing to move a bit farther? The farther north you go, the less expensive the properties. People, in general, don't like the cold."

"Yes, of course, we don't get much snow here, and it'd be nice to have a snow day or two, but not too much snow. And, as long as there's a fireplace, a real one, in the new home. As I said earlier, it should be within a ten or fifteen-minute drive from civilization. It could be a small town. As long as it has a grocery store, a school, and a doctor, I'm happy."

"How about we do this then." Kate put away her tablet and gathered up her things. "You get this place into top selling shape. Take your time, and I'll look for the perfect home for you. Think about it and then text me your wish list. Fireplaces, what kind, how many bedrooms, the shop, the separate living quarters, if you want a barn, etc. Anything and everything from walk-in closets to type of flooring and cupboards. From there, I'll put some feelers out. I won't list your place today, but I trust you'll use me as your realtor when it's ready. When you're done, we list it, sell it, and get you and your brother into your dream home. You have a good budget, so we should be able to find you something pretty close to your dream home on an acreage."

Ashley thought for a moment. "Okay, let's look at something for a cool million and let them know I could manage a cash payment, no need to qualify for a mortgage. I should be able to pay this place off and still do that."

Kate stood and smiled. "That is an excellent point to tell prospective buyers. The fewer conditions, the better. I'll see what I can find for you."

Ashley walked her to the door just as Matt returned. "I need to get some paint for the door casing and molding. What color do you want?"

Kate spoke up. "Doors that are black or slate blue get on average, an extra six or seven thousand dollars. Same for the fencing. That'll get you more, too."

Ashley looked at her and laughed. "All right then. You heard the woman, Matt. Black is a bit drab, so slate blue it is. Get enough for both doors, oh, and enough stain for the fence, too."

Matt gave her a small salute and headed out to buy paint.

Ashley walked Kate to her car just as Detective Colombo pulled up. He let Kate drive out first, then pulled up to where Ashley stood.

He got out and nodded to Ashley. "Wow, you've got the door fixed already. Good job. Brother do that?"

Ashley nodded. "Yeah, he's been a big help. What can I do for you, Detective?"

"Just a few questions, if you're up for it," he said.

"Sure, it's nice out. Let's go sit on the deck near the garden. Can I get you anything to drink?"

"Just a water, please." The detective headed toward the deck while Ashley went inside. She emerged a minute later with two tall glasses of ice water.

"Here you go." She set them both down on a small table between the two patio chairs. "I told you everything about the other night already, Detective. What's this about? Is he still in jail?"

"Yes, due to the violent nature of the case, he's been remanded without bail. That, plus we contacted someone we thought was also a victim, and when she heard he was in jail, she offered to testify as well. We are looking for other victims. He won't be hurting anyone anymore, that's for sure."

"Well, that's a relief. Is that what you came to tell me?"

"No, there's the matter I initially came to talk to you about when I interrupted the scum bag who assaulted you."

"Oh?" Ashley took a sip of her water. What else could he want? Rodney's body hadn't shown up, and it never would. None of her failed attempts at pregnancy would show up. "Did you find the guy that screwed up Randy's brakes?" Ashley felt a surge of hope coupled with a twinge of pain when she thought about the future she could have had.

"Ah, no. I'm sorry, but we've closed the case on that. It was ruled an accident due to mechanical error. The kid who did the brakes is long gone by now, I'm afraid." The detective paused, then added. "It's about your neighbor, Rocky."

Ashley cocked her head and scrutinized the detective. "Rocky? What's he done? Don't tell me he hurt Beth. What's going on?"

"That's what we are trying to figure out. He went for a walk a couple of nights ago. I believe it was the day after you were over there telling Beth how to save her garden. He hasn't been seen since."

Ashley held her breath. Was there nothing this man didn't know? She made a mental note to be extra, extra careful the next time she found a possible baby daddy.

"Oh, poor Beth. Have you talked to that woman up the street?" Ashley tried to look shaken up, but inside, she was happy Rocky was gone. The last thing she needed was him hanging around her house. Especially now that she was fixing up the place, she imagined him popping over to help and gave a little shudder.

"You okay?" Colombo asked.

"Yeah, there's just been so much drama lately, so much sadness. That man that disappeared, Randy's accident, my attack, and now Rocky is missing. I'm glad I'm moving."

"You're moving?" the detective pulled out his notebook. "When?"

"Oh, no time soon. I want to fix the place up a bit. I found hardwood floors in the spare room. There might be some in the main bedroom, too. Plus, you know, the front door has to be made pretty, and we're going to fix up the fence, and who knows, maybe some new cupboards, or at least paint."

"I see." The detective made a quick note. "How much do you know about this neighbor up the street?"

"There are a lot of neighbors up the street, Detective. Can you be more specific?" Ashley didn't like where the questioning was going. Did the woman give them more info on the man she saw, and it didn't match Rodney? She hated not knowing.

"About a block and a half up. I believe she's fairly new to the neighborhood." He flipped a few pages over in his notebook. "Moved into the Scotts' place about six months ago." He paused. "She's the one who saw your date leaving that night."

"Ugh, okay. Um, I don't know much. I've only seen her as I drive by. She's about fortyish and well, um, big-breasted. She waves at me now and then, but I don't know anything about her. Why don't you talk to her?"

"Well, that's the thing." The detective paused again. "She's missing, too. Well, maybe not missing. Her next-door neighbor heard her car leave around one in the morning, just after Rocky disappeared. By the time she looked out the window, all she saw were the taillights of the car. It turned right toward the highway and hasn't been seen since. She had told the neighbor she was planning a vacation, so she could just be on holiday. But it's suspicious that two of them disappeared within hours of each other."

Ashley let out a short chuckle. "Really? Detective Colombo, maybe they ran off together."

"Just call me Frank. I've been over here so much I think we can drop the formalities. And yes, we thought about that. But neither her credit card nor his has been used, and no one has seen them or the car."

"Huh." Ashley let his words sink in. Rocky was gone, and the woman was gone but no credit card info or sightings. Maybe there was a God, and Beth's prayers were answered.

"But—" Ashley stopped herself.

"But what?" Frank asked.

"But, if they don't want to be found, wouldn't they have just used cash?"

"Yeah, we thought about that. Rocky did withdraw about two thousand dollars the morning he disappeared. But that's not enough to get very far."

"But, maybe, that's the limit he has on his account. I bet there'll be more withdrawals." Ashley smiled. She liked playing detective. As long as she wasn't a suspect, this could be fun.

"Well, so far, nothing. Both Rocky Houston and Maria Wilson will be listed as missing if we can't track them down in the next twenty-four hours." He closed his notebook and stood. "Thanks for the water."

Ashley walked him to the gate. "I'll go check on Beth later. Maybe he'll turn up. Goodbye Detec— er, um, Frank."

Ashley needed another nap. Her phone rang just as she got comfortable on her bed. It was Matt.

"Hey, sis. Look, it's been a long day. The door is fixed, and the carpet is gone. How about I come back tomorrow and start painting and staining things? See you about nine a.m.?"

"Sure, that sounds good, Matt. See you then."

She put her phone on the bedside table and curled into the still-sleeping Dudley. As she stroked his fur, she couldn't help but think what a mentally and physically exhausting day it had been. With any luck, she'd sleep until the morning.

Chapter 23

Frank Colombo thumbed through his notes. He didn't know what was going on, but he was certain this Ashley woman was involved somehow. If it hadn't been for her assault, he would have been convinced she'd had something to do with Rocky's disappearance.

Part of him wished she wasn't involved. She was a beautiful woman, and there was something about her vulnerability that made him want to protect her.

"Hey Frank, whatcha daydreaming about?" His partner, Tate Sparks, stood in front of him with two takeaway coffees. "I got you one, too. Looks like you could use it."

"Thanks, Tate. It's that Taylor woman, Ashley. Between her date disappearing months ago and her fiancé's death, and now her neighbor's disappearance, I can't help but think she's tied into all of this."

Sparks shook his head. "Oh, really? So, the woman fends off her attacker, and you arrive just in time to save her, and you think because she fought back, she's done something to these men? What's that saying? Me thinks you doth protest too much."

"It's 'the lady doth protest too much, methinks,' you Neanderthal. It's from MacBeth, and I'm no lady. Now, hear me out. Her date disappears in April. No one has seen him since. Three and a half months later, the only person who might have seen him, this Maria Wilson woman, is missing. Add to that, she gets engaged to some guy two months after the date disappeared. Then her fiancé gets killed in a car accident due to a mechanical error. A bit more than a month after he dies, her neighbor disappears. It's too much to be a coincidence. Isn't it?"

Sparks finished his coffee and tossed the paper cup into the garbage can beside Colombo's desk.

"Are you serious? Do you think this woman faked her attack to cover up her neighbor's disappearance? I saw the report. She was pretty badly beaten. Mind you, she gave that Miller guy what he deserved, and good thing she did." He paused as if remembering something. "Did the boss tell ya? They have two more women coming in today to give statements. We should be able to lock this guy up until he's too old to get it up."

Colombo smiled. "Well, that is something to be happy about. Just that this Ashley woman appears to be in the middle of things. I'm not sure, but somehow, I think she's involved."

Sparks looked at his partner. "Do you want to know what I think?"

Colombo drank the last of his coffee and tossed it in the can with Spark's cup. "Sure, what do you think?"

"I think you're sweet on this woman. When you heard about the neighbor's disappearance, you asked for the case. I think you just want to be near her again. And why not? She's a nice-looking lady. She's been through a lot in the past few months, and you, despite being a tough guy detective, have a soft spot for vulnerable people and animals. You've found homes for more than a dozen strays you've found, and I know you donate to the women's shelter on a regular basis. Face it, Frank, you're a softie, and this woman has gotten under your skin. The missing persons case of her one-time date is now cold. She's no longer a suspect or a person of interest. Wrap up the case of the missing neighbor, wait for that scum bag rapists' trial to be over, and then ask her out. You have no reason not to."

Colombo smiled. His partner knew him almost too well. "Yeah, I don't think so. It'll take months, maybe years, for that scumbag's case to go to court. And until we get proof that her neighbor ran off with the other neighbor, it's an open case."

"Suit yourself." Tate's phone rang, and he walked over to his desk. "Hello. Yeah. You're kidding me? Really. Yeah, great, I'll let him know." He hung up and walked back toward Colombo's desk.

"That was Lenz. That rapist guy—he won't be going to trial. They found him half an hour ago. He's dead. Possible autoerotic asphyxiation. Idiots left him alone in his cell, still wearing what he was arrested in. They found him with his tie around his neck, tied to the bars, and his willy hanging out."

"Holy shit," was all Colombo could mutter. "I didn't see that coming."

"Yeah. But the good news is, he's dead. No trial, no dragging those women, including Ashley, through telling every detail of his debauchery. Now, all you need to do is find the missing neighbor, and you can ask her out!" He slapped Colombo on the back and whistled a tune as he walked away.

Colombo certainly wasn't going to ask her out. But perhaps an in-person visit to let her know her attacker was dead would be a good idea.

Chapter 24

Ashley stirred when she heard a knock at the door. It was still light outside as she made her way out of the bedroom to the front door. She rubbed her eyes as she opened it, surprised to see Detective Colombo standing there.

"Detective, er, ah, Frank. What are you doing here again?" Ashley looked at the sky and guessed she must have slept for at least three hours. Her stomach rumbled.

"Come on in. Just give me a moment." She left the open door and headed for the bathroom. After she relieved herself and splashed cold water on her face, she picked up Dudley and took him to his litter box. While he was doing his business, she added a painkiller to his soft food. Dudley hobbled out of his litter box and slowly ate his meal, medication and all. When he was done, he hobbled away toward the living room, straight for the detective.

"Oh, no, Dudley, no. I'll put you back into bed." She picked up the dozy cat and placed him back on her bed. She'd check on him a bit later.

"Sorry about that, Detective, um, Frank. Dudley doesn't care that you're allergic." She sat down across from the detective and gathered her legs underneath her. Still groggy, she asked again, "What are you doing here?"

"It's about Dave Miller, the man who attacked you."

"Oh. But we've been over everything. If I didn't know any better, I'd say you were looking for reasons to come and see me." Ashley gave him a small but genuine smile.

"Well, that's not the case." He stared at her without emotion.

Ashley's face fell. Maybe she was losing her ability to flirt. Then again, her hair was a mess, she had no makeup on, and she'd just woken up and probably had pillow lines across her face. While waiting for the detective to tell her why he woke her up, she pulled out her phone. It was just past 6:30 p.m.

The detective cleared his throat. "Mr. Miller was found dead in his cell about two hours ago. We don't suspect foul play. It appears he accidentally hung himself."

Ashley's eyes opened wide. She was awake now. "Accidentally? How do you accidentally hang yourself? It's only been twenty-four hours, and he's dead?"

"Yes, ma'am." The detective shifted uncomfortably on the sofa.

"But I don't . . ." Ashley's voice trailed off. She stared at the detective. "So, he didn't hang himself out of remorse for being caught? I'm confused."

Colombo looked around the room. He wasn't comfortable telling her, but it would probably get leaked to the news outlets anyway. "He died of autoerotic asphyxiation."

Ashley stared at him. A small smile tugged at the corners of her mouth. She covered it with her hands, but it was too late. A giggle escaped her, then turned into a full blow laugh.

"He died masturbating?" She stifled her laughter, but the grin on her face was harder to control.

"Ah, yeah, that's what happened." The detective lowered his head, trying not to smile. It was poetic justice at its finest, or karma, or something. When he raised his head, the smile was gone. "I wanted you to hear it from me and not on the news."

"Oh. My. Gawd!" Ashley stood and paced the room, hands on her hips. "So, he's spent the past how many months or years preying on women, raping them and threatening them, and he accidentally kills himself getting his rocks off? Maybe there is a God after all."

She walked into the kitchen and rummaged around in the garbage can. She returned five minutes later with two clean glasses, an ice cube in each, and a mostly finished bottle of scotch. She placed it all on the coffee table in front of Colombo.

"Shall we toast the poor bastard?" Ashley didn't even try to hide her smile. This was the best outcome ever. She wouldn't have to come back for a trial, and people would finally stop poking their noses into her business. She had a few more days before ovulation, and she simply wanted to put the past behind her and make a baby.

Colombo picked up the bottle and opened it. He poured two fingers into each glass and reached over to hand Ashley hers.

"I'm officially off duty now, so I suppose a private toast would be okay."

Ashley raised her glass. "To disgusting, misogynistic assholes. May they all meet the same fate as dickwad Dave." She clicked her glass to the detective's.

"Agreed," he said. "May all rapists and murderers meet their fate like dickwad Dave."

Ashley stopped mid-sip. "Not all murderers, Detective. Sometimes murder is all you've got to preserve the life you want."

The detective tensed and set his glass down. "That's a pretty strange thing to say. Care to explain?"

Ashley's face drained of color. She shouldn't have let her guard down. She thought quickly. "What I meant is that if I'd killed that man by strangling him, I would be a murderer."

Colombo gave an audible sigh of relief, and his shoulders relaxed. "Technically, that would be self-defense in the eyes of the law."

"What about in the eyes of God?" She tossed back the rest of her drink. She wasn't sure she should be drinking, but she wasn't pregnant and hadn't taken any painkillers in a few hours.

"God? Hmmm. Well, I think God would probably let you slide on that one. When you are fighting for your life, it's okay to stop someone from killing you." He finished his drink and stood to leave. "Now, if you'll excuse me, I need to go."

Ashley stood up. "Wait. I, um, well, I'm kinda hungry. I haven't eaten since I left the hospital. I don't feel like being alone. Wanna grab a burger or something?"

He stared at the woman. Ashley couldn't tell if he was attracted to her or disgusted by her. The man had the best poker face she'd ever seen.

"Sure," he finally said. "There's a place up the road I like to go to. It's called Frankie's. And no, it's not named after me. Take my car?"

"Yeah, I'd like that," she said. "Give me five minutes to freshen up, okay?"

"Sure, I'll be in the car."

Ashley stared at the door as he shut it behind him. She wasn't sure if it was a good idea to be getting close to the detective, but there were more reasons to stay close than to keep him away. She went into the bathroom and brushed her hair. She stared at herself in the mirror as she put on some makeup.

She was still a good-looking woman, and the detective was handsome for a middle-aged cop. At least he didn't have a seventies porn mustache. He'd probably make a good baby daddy. He was single, and if she could seduce him, that would taint any testimony that might happen down the line. Besides, she was hungry. It was still a week or so before she would be fertile again. Might as well see if this cop was as straight and narrow as he acted.

* * *

To anyone looking, the couple in the booth at the back of Frankie's could have been on a date. Frank had no idea why he agreed to the meal except they were both hungry.

When she burst out laughing at her assailant's fate, he couldn't help but smile, too. It was a fitting end for that scumbag. He saved the taxpayers a lot of money and his victims a lot of time in court. He'd seen reactions like that before. It was nothing out of the ordinary. Many a victim had burst out laughing when hearing of their attackers' untimely demise. It appeared that Ashley was simply one of them.

"So, what's good here?" she asked, breaking him out of his thoughts.

"Pretty much everything. My favorite is the Frank burger, and not just because it's my name. It's loaded with lots of pickles, tomatoes, and lettuce and seasoned just right. Their fries are good, too."

The waitress appeared and asked for their order. Ashley spoke up. "I do believe we are having two orders of the Frank burger and two orders of your house fries. I'll have water and—" she stopped mid-sentence and pointed at the detective.

"Oh, and I'll have a Coke or Pepsi. Either is good."

The waitress nodded and headed to the kitchen to place their order.

"What? You don't prefer Coke or Pepsi?" Ashley asked. "You aren't like all the other guys, are you."

Colombo smiled. "They taste the same depending on the day," he replied. "I've done the Coke and Pepsi challenge a dozen times. Every time the one I like most is different. I might pick Coke ten times and Pepsi nine, but it's pretty even depending on if it's from a can, a bottle, or from one of those fountain drink machines. It also makes a difference if you add ice or drink from a metal, plastic, or cardboard straw."

Ashley stared at him and smiled. "Yeah, you aren't like other guys at all."

The waitress returned with their drinks. "Food will be up in five," she said, then walked away.

"So, Frank, are you married? Any kids?"

"Nope. I'm married to the job. Although some days it

would be nice to have someone to come home to. I guess I just couldn't put anyone through the hours that I keep. But let's not talk about me. Tell me about you. Why is such a talented painter like yourself working in a garden shop?"

He had to change the subject. Getting close to a potential suspect was not a good idea. Until they found her neighbor, she was still on the list. Besides, the more he learned about her, the more he could piece together this mystery woman who appeared naïve and worldly at the same time.

"Oh, I've been drawing and painting since I was a kid. It helped me forget my life was shit."

The waitress returned with their meals, placed them on the table, and left.

"How so?" he asked as he took a big bite of his burger.

"Come on, Frank. You know my history. Let's not bring that up." She reached for the ketchup and poured a glob onto her plate.

"Okay, fair enough. How'd you get to be making the big bucks as a painter? Did you know someone who knew someone?"

Ashley took a bite of her burger and took her time answering. She swallowed, took a sip of water, and responded.

"It was luck. Pure, unadulterated luck. I went to a gallery opening with some guy about nine years ago. I was looking at one of the abstracts and said I could do better with my eyes closed. A patron heard me and made me an offer. He said if I could paint an abstract on an oversized canvas that looked better than the one before us, he'd give me five thousand dollars." She paused and took another bite of her burger.

"So what? You just went home and painted it, and that was that?" He salted his fries, picked up five of them, and stuffed them in his mouth.

"Well, kinda, yeah. I got his name and number, waited for my paycheck from the nursery, and went out and spent a crazy amount of money on some high-grade acrylic pouring paint and a canvas. I think it cost me about fifteen hundred for a 120" x 84" canvas and paint, more with tax. I was pretty damn scared I would mess it up." She took another bite of her burger. "This is so yummy!"

"Told you so." He smiled as he watched her devour the burger. "So, did you? Screw it up?"

"Hell no!" she said. "I went home and watched videos for a dozen days or so, then I rigged up the buckets, covered the walls and floor in plastic, and let 'er rip." She dipped more fries into her ketchup and poked them into her mouth.

"And I'm assuming it turned out well?"

"You assume correctly, sir." Ashley took the last bite of her burger.

"Did he pay you the five thousand?"

Ashley swallowed and took a sip of water. "Yep, he sure did. He liked it so much that he gave me an additional thousand for getting it done so quickly. I tripled my prices after that and got even more business. That first year he ordered six more and introduced me to several other art buyers. My specialty is making triptychs.

"A trip tick?"

"It's three paintings that, when placed slightly apart on a

wall, form an entire painting. Anyway, he liked my work, sent some of his friends my way, and I've been stashing the money away ever since. I've got enough saved up now to buy myself a nice house on an acreage where I can just go and paint to my heart's content."

The detective finished his burger and washed it down with his soft drink. "I see, and that's why you're selling your house? To buy an acreage?"

"Yeah, I mean, Randy and I, we were going to be a family. Kids, dogs, the whole enchilada, maybe even a chicken or two. Well, kids, anyway. He was gone before we could figure out the rest." Ashley hung her head and pushed the last of her fries through a smudge of ketchup. "But that's not gonna happen now."

"I'm sorry." Colombo wished he'd never brought it up. He was insensitive at times. It came from years of interrogating perps. But this woman had lost her fiancé and her dreams. He had no right to pry.

"It's okay. It's still kinda raw, but hey. A girl can dream. Who knows, someday, and hopefully soon, I'll find my prince. We'll live happily ever after in the boonies. What about you, Frank? Any hopes and dreams for kids and a family?"

Now it was getting uncomfortably personal. He motioned for the waitress to bring their bill.

"Someday, maybe. I'm getting kind of old to be a dad. I'd be almost sixty by the time the kid graduated, and that's if it was born today."

The waitress placed the bill in front of the detective and

waited with the machine in her hand. "Cash or charge?" she asked.

"Um, credit card," he replied. He could probably write this off as part of the investigation. One of the perks of being a cop. He handed her his credit card, punched in his PIN, and took his card back.

She placed the receipt in front of him. "Have a nice day."

"You know, Detective, you would still be considered a catch." Ashley grinned at him and waggled her eyebrows.

"Yeah, right. Says you," he said as they stood to leave. "I'd better get you home."

They walked to his car in silence. Once they were on their way, Ashley looked over at him.

"Hey, Frank. Have you ever dated a suspect before?"

Colombo almost missed the light turning red. He slammed on the brakes.

"Ah, no. That's against the rules, Ashley. We can't date suspects or victims in any investigation."

"So . . . " she let her thought trail off, then picked it up again. "That either means this wasn't a date, or I'm not a suspect. I refuse to think of myself as a victim."

"How about none of the above," he said as they pulled into her driveway. He put the car in park and turned to Ashley. "Look. I think you're a pretty interesting lady. That much is true. But I've still got an open missing persons' case, and until that's solved, my mind will be strictly on finding your neighbor, or neighbors as the case may be."

Ashley nodded and opened her door.

"Good night, Detective Frank. Thanks for the non-date. We should do it again sometime." She shut the car door, and he watched as she opened her front door and went inside.

Once he'd pulled out of her driveway and driven a few blocks, he pulled over and smacked his open hand on the steering wheel. He really thought he could keep his emotions out of this, but she was fascinating. She was innocent yet experienced. She worked as a clerk in a plant store and, at the same time, got paid huge bucks for her artwork. She was a riddle wrapped inside an enigma. Or something like that.

He put the car in drive and headed toward home. Halfway there, he turned right toward the station. He needed to solve this missing persons case once and for all. There had to be some clue that he'd overlooked.

Once at the precinct, he took the steps two at a time and headed to his desk. He turned on his computer, and an alert popped up. About an hour ago Maria Wilson's credit card was used at a gas station two hundred miles away. Another alert popped up. Rocky Houston recently withdrew another two thousand dollars from his bank account.

He sat back in his chair, put his feet up, and put his hands behind his head. A smile escaped his lips and spread to his whole face. All evidence pointed to Maria and Rocky running away together. He'd go tell the wife in the morning. With any luck, they'd find the runaway lovers soon.

Chapter 25

Ashley awoke to the sun streaming on her face and her cat purring in her ear. Another day in paradise. She stretched and smiled as she recalled her meal with the detective. They were mismatched, but maybe, just maybe, he'd make good babies.

She grabbed Dudley, took him to his litter box, and prepared his breakfast. She slipped a pain pill into his food, then made herself a strong cup of coffee. Her head still hurt a little, and she needed it not to. She had to formulate a new plan. Either seduce the detective or hunt further afield for a sperm donor. Neither was at the top of her list. She missed the days of being able to just bring them home, get their seed, and wait. Sure, she had to dispose of a few here and there, but for the most part, bringing prey home had been an easier way to find out if the men were good and decent. It never occurred to her that men who came home with strange women after a few drinks were probably not the kind of guys she wanted as a baby daddy.

Coffee in hand, she opened the back door and walked over to the gate on the deck. She looked across the street and saw Beth pulling weeds from a small flower garden at the base of a huge fir tree. Beth looked up and waved. She put down her trowel and made her way over to Ashley's house.

"Hey neighbor, nice to see you up and around. It's been

quite the crazy few days in the neighborhood, hasn't it?" Beth approached the gate, and Ashley opened it to let her in.

"You can say that again," Ashley said. "Can I offer you a cup of coffee?"

"I'd say yes, but I've already had three. I've been up since sunrise, hoping Rocky would come home so I could divorce his sorry ass. I suppose you heard about that Maria woman. She's missing, too. Skank! I hope she realizes that if he cheated on me with her, he'll do the same to her."

Ashley nodded, not sure what to say. She'd never had a girlfriend before. Matt was the closest thing she had to a friend, and he was more like family.

"I hope they find them soon," Beth said, looking over at her yard. "The grass needs cutting, and Rocky always wanted to use a push mower, and I'll be damned if I'm pushing that old thing around and raking up the cuttings." She wandered over to Ashley's flower garden. "My goodness. These are simply beautiful."

Ashley joined her. "Yes, my new fertilizer worked great this year. The plants thrive on natural fertilizers. I only wish I had more room to grow more flowers."

Beth went farther into the yard, toward the vegetable garden. "Wow, these are huge already. And look at the beans and peas! Wow, Ashley, you do have a green thumb."

Ashley smiled and took another sip of her coffee. "Thanks. I like to think of myself as a nurturer. Someday, I hope to have a little gardener at my side to pass on my passion for creating and growing things."

"I'm sure you will," Beth assured her. "A pretty thing like you won't be single for long. What about that detective that's been around? He seems sweet on you. Thank goodness Rocky left with that tramp. If he hadn't, that nice detective wouldn't have caught that realtor who assaulted you."

Ashley gritted her teeth and took another sip of coffee.

"Oh," Beth looked at her. "I'm sorry. I hope I didn't upset you. I was just, oh, I don't know what the hell I was thinking. Things are pretty tense all around, aren't they? Men disappearing, your fiancé getting killed, my husband missing with that tart."

Ashley stared at the woman. How on earth did she think she could be friends with such a clueless bag of flesh? Thoughts of Randy and the future they could have had mixed with images of her recent assault. She closed her eyes in an attempt to stop whatever tears were lurking, ready to spill out. She couldn't cry, though. Crying was weak, and she was strong. She heard a car engine, turned away from Beth, and walked to the gate. The detective was getting out of his car in front of Beth's house.

"Detective Frank!" Ashley shouted. "She's over here. Do you have news?"

The detective stopped mid-stride, pivoted, and walked toward Ashley's house. She liked the way he walked. Confident but not cocky. Self-assured without a swagger. Perhaps he would make a good baby daddy.

"Good morning, Ashley," the detective said. "I hope you're feeling beter today."

"Good morning, Detective." Beth smiled as she made her way from the garden to the deck. "I was just admiring Ashley's garden. Do you have any news? Did you find them?"

"We can talk over at your place if you like," he said, nodding to Ashley.

"No, whatever you have to say, you can say in front of her. It's not like everyone in the neighborhood doesn't know what's been going on anyway. It's been the talk of the town for a while now."

"Can I get you a cup of coffee, Detective?" Ashley started toward the house.

"Yes, that'd be great. One sugar, one cream, please." The detective smiled and went over to Beth. Ashley went into the house and poured a fresh cup for the detective and filled her cup. By the time she came out, the news was sinking in, and Beth was not happy.

"So, he's alive then, and he's with her. Great, that's just great." She tried to swipe away a tear and missed. "I guess I'd better get to the bank and freeze our joint account. No way I want them to have access to my money."

"Beth, we'd appreciate it if you didn't do that. The only way we can track him is through his withdrawals. Don't you want to know where they are?" The detective took the offered cup and had a sip. He nodded and smiled at Ashley.

"No! I don't give a rat's rump where they are or what they're doing. I assume he's not a missing person anymore?" Beth pursed her lips and crossed her arms.

"Well, technically, he's still missing. Someone has to verify he's alive by seeing him in person. But because we have both her credit card and his bank withdrawal in the same city, it's a good sign. But no one has seen them. It's up to you if you want to keep the case open or not."

Beth paced back and forth across the deck. Ashley and the detective watched her for a moment.

Ashley finally spoke. "Detective, who can verify they're alive? Does it have to be a cop?"

Beth stopped pacing and stared at the pair. "Yes, can anyone besides a cop declare they've seen them?"

"No, there are a few options. In this case, a doctor or health care provider could do it. Or even a lawyer or legal advocate."

"What about a friend or a family member?" Beth waited for the response.

"No, it has to be someone approved by the law. People can't just say they were mistaken and say they are alive."

Ashley nodded, went over to Beth, and put an arm around her shoulder.

"Maybe she took him against his will? We don't know what happened. But I'm sure the detective here will figure it out."

Beth let out a half snort, half laugh. "Against his will? I don't think so. The man is as stubborn and willful as they come." Beth sighed as another tear trickled down her face.

"I understand you have to keep the case open and my bank account. I just wish it was a higher priority. If you get any more leads as to where they are, let me know. Maybe I can hire a private detective to track them down." Beth smiled at Ashley and stepped out from her embrace.

"I have to go. Thank you for the information, Detective."

Beth opened the gate and went home.

Ashley couldn't help but notice she'd stopped crying by the time she was at the end of the driveway. She shrugged and faced the detective.

"Poor thing. We were talking about how many crappy things are happening in our once-quiet neighborhood. I'm glad I'm selling. It's time to get away from people." She finished her cup of coffee and turned toward the house. "Coming in?" she asked as she stepped inside.

The detective followed and placed his half-finished cup of coffee on the counter. "Thanks, you make great coffee," he said.

Ashley watched him hesitate. "Anything else, Detective?" She put on her best smile.

"Yes, one small thing. The missing man you had at your home. The case has been transferred to another police force. Since you stated he left your home and Maria confirmed she saw someone fitting his description heading toward the highway, my boss decided to close our case and transfer it to his area, where his folks live. Less paperwork for us."

"So, I'm no longer a suspect or a person of interest in his disappearance, then?" Her smile grew wider as she leaned back against the counter and crossed her arms.

"Yes, that is correct. But there's still the case of your missing neighbor."

"What are you saying? I'm a suspect in Rocky's disappearance?"

"No, not a suspect, but as a neighbor who knew him and one of the last people to see him, you're still a person of interest.

There's something about these run-away lovers that doesn't add up. No one's seen the car, and we have it in the system."

"Maybe they rented one. Or maybe they parked it behind their lover's hideaway, and that's why no one's seen it," Ashley offered.

"You could be right," he said. "In the meantime, if you hear anyone talking about them that could help us, let me know. I'll let my boss know we'll still be monitoring their money trail and see where it leads."

Ashley's phone dinged, and she went into the living room to retrieve it. When she returned, she was frowning.

"Bad news?" the detective asked.

"Yes and no," Ashley said. "Matt was supposed to come back today with paint for the door and the fence. He just texted to say he can't make it today. Something came up. That's not like him. He's usually so reliable." Ashley's brows knit together as she thought about Matt's no-show.

"I'm sure he'll be here tomorrow," Colombo said. "What does he do? Maybe he had some work or something."

"Yeah, probably," Ashley said. "He mostly does side jobs for people. Hauling garbage, disposing of yard waste, delivering furniture, that kind of thing. Sometimes he gets the odd backyard mechanic job. He probably got a last-minute paying gig. I suppose I should have offered to pay him, but you know, family and all."

"Yeah," the detective agreed. "Family."

The two stood in the kitchen, not speaking. Ashley stared at her blank screen while the detective looked at his shoes.

"Um, well, I should be going."

Ashley looked up. "Yeah, of course, detective work to do and such. I think I'll check on Dudley and then head to the pet store and get him a treat. He hasn't had many of them lately."

"Okay then. Well, you have a nice day, and I'll be in touch if I need anything else from you." He turned on his heels and headed for the door. Before he got to it, Ashley touched his arm.

"Don't go."

He turned and looked down into her upturned face.

"Is there something you need?" he asked. The look on her face told him exactly what she wanted.

"It's just that," she hesitated. "I just feel so, well, I don't know. I know the douche is dead, and no one is coming to get me, but I can't help but feel like . . ." she let her words trail off, and she dropped her hand from his arm.

The detective placed his hands on her shoulders. "No one is going to hurt you. Tell you what, I've got some work to do at the office. I'll call to check up on you later this afternoon. Get Dudley his treats and rest a bit. You've had a pretty rough time of it."

Ashley turned her face up to his, her lips slightly parted. A precursor to a kiss she hoped would happen. The detective let her go and stared at her.

"Look, Ashley, I can't get involved with you. You've been through a lot lately, and I represent something safe in all the chaos. I don't think now is the time to start anything. You are a person of interest in two cases. I'm a good cop. I take pride in not crossing lines."

Ashley dropped her head and sighed. "Fine. I suppose you're right. But I will feel better if you at least call."

"I will," he said and headed out the door.

Ashley stood alone in her kitchen. Men were so complicated yet simplistic. Maybe she couldn't get him this time, but if she wasn't pregnant by this time next month, she knew where to find him.

She looked around the room and decided to text Matt back.

Did you pick up the paint yesterday?

A few seconds later, she received a one-word reply.

No.

She texted back.

I'm going out, so I'll go get it. I hope you're okay. Let me know when you're coming over.

Ashley went to her bedroom, grabbed her purse and keys, and headed for the door as her phone dinged.

Not today. I kinda hurt myself doing a job for a client yesterday. I'll be fine, but I can't make it over for a few days. Thanks for understanding.

Ashley stared at the text. How the heck did he hurt himself between leaving her place and this morning? She wanted to ask him but knew he'd let her know in his own time. If he said he was okay, then he was.

Ashley locked the door and headed for her car. She was glad she had a few more days off work. It was time to pick out some paint and get the house ready for sale. Maybe there'd be some prospects at the hardware store.

Chapter 26

The next few days passed quickly. Ashley finished painting her door and the casing with a lovely slate blue. She'd opted for a black stain for the fence, and much to her surprise, the dark color made the home look more inviting. Best of all, she'd met someone at the hardware store.

His name was Andrew, but he preferred Andy. He was from a neighboring small town. Andy was tall, dark, and almost handsome, with curly brown hair and deep-set brown eyes. Ashley assumed he worked there as he was helping someone out when she was in the paint aisle. When he was done, he helped her pick out the right paint and stain. Once he explained he didn't work there, they had a good laugh, and he'd asked her out. She agreed to meet him a few days later for a dinner picnic at a small park midway between their homes. After all, who was she to turn down a perfectly healthy and helpful man?

It was about a half-hour's drive to the park he'd suggested. She was to bring iced tea and a dessert. He would bring the main course. Ashley fed Dudley, then put a camping cooler filled with iced tea and rice crispy cakes in the back. She had one stop to make first.

Ten minutes later, she walked into her competitor's nursery. She wore an oversized hat and sunglasses as well as a

Cleansing Water

gaudy orange Mumu to hide her body shape. No use getting noticed when she didn't have to be. She'd called earlier and learned they had some monkshood in the herb section of their lot. She walked to the back corner, found it, and paid cash.

Once the plant was carefully placed behind the passenger seat, she headed for the highway. It was time to meet her possible baby daddy.

* * *

It was a decent date, as far as first dates go. Andy was a perfect gentleman. He'd brought cold chicken, a garden salad, and some fresh berries. They sat and made small talk about their respective towns, sports teams, and places to holiday in the summer. The conversation lagged but didn't feel awkward as they watched people come and go in the park.

"So, why were you helping so many people at the hardware store the other day?" Ashley asked.

"I dunno. I guess I just look like a guy who knows things." He laughed and reached for her hand. "I like you, Ashley. I can tell you're a special kinda gal."

"Why, thank you, Andy. You appear to be a special kinda guy, too." She laughed at how corny it sounded. But corny was good, right? It wasn't malicious or demeaning, or cruel. She needed more of that in her life. She cocked her head and watched him as she would a bug under a glass.

"So, tell me, Andy, what's your story? Are you single, divorced, have kids, want kids? What's your life plan?"

Andy took his hand away and sat up straighter. "Life

plan? Wow. I never thought we'd be discussing that on a first date. But yeah, someday I'd like a wife and kids. I just broke up with someone I dated for a couple of years. We just weren't compatible in the end. She loved to write and paint and grow stuff in her garden. I like to hike in the woods and ride my ATV. I just couldn't go to one more art gallery or book signing or plant sale. Don't get me wrong, those things are great, but not my thing."

Ashley grinned. "Pity, because I'm an artist and I love my garden. You're in luck, though. I don't write, but I do love a good book."

"Ah, crap." Andy shrugged and packed up his picnic supplies. Ashley followed his lead and put her containers back in her cooler.

"So, that's it then?" Ashley asked. "No more dates?"

"Honestly, that's why I hang out at hardware stores. I like meeting women who are into building things and painting things like fences and doors, not art. I like women who love the great outdoors, not just the space behind their houses. The girlfriend, before the last one, was a carpenter, made amazing cabinets, and dabbled in wooden puzzles. She loved to hike and fish, too, but she was also religious, and I'm not. I guess I'll just keep looking. No offense, but I don't see this going anywhere. I can't do another artsy garden fairy."

The couple stood up and walked toward their cars at the far end of the lot. The sun was still out, but there were no other people in the park. They'd gone home or headed out for parts unknown.

Ashley opened the back door of her car and placed her cooler on the floor. She turned to Andy. "So I guess sex is out of the question?" It didn't hurt to ask as she was ovulating, and there were no other prospects around.

Andy stopped, put his basket in the car, and stared at her. "Really. You want sex. Even though you know, there's no future with us. You really are a wild child, aren't you?"

Ashley smiled. "Give me your address. I'll meet you there if you're up for a quickie."

Andy grinned back. "Hell yeah, I'm not dead. And it won't be that quick. Don't you worry. I like my ladies to finish happy."

He wrote his address on a piece of paper and handed it to her.

"It's a bit out of the way, though. Take the first left after the last stop sign up this road." He pointed in the direction he wanted her to go. "Once you turn left, it's about a mile more. Nothing up there but acreages and farmland. I'm the last acreage on the right. You'll see a bright yellow sign that says *No Trespassing* by a wooden gate. I'll leave the gate open. I can stop and get a bottle of wine if you want."

"No wine for me," Ashley said. "So don't get any unless you want some."

"Nah, I'm good. I've got some scotch at home." He reached over and swatted her bum. "See you in about ten minutes."

Ashley kept the smile on her face as he drove away.

"Asswipe." she muttered as she brushed imaginary Andy cooties off her behind. She was pleased she bought the monkshood. All she had to do was figure out how to get him to take it.

* * *

Ashley thought about what Andy said as she drove toward his acreage. She wanted an acreage and to go hiking in nature and learn how to build and fix stuff. She wanted to be able to teach her son, or daughter, those things. Once he learned she was—what did he call her? An artsy garden fairy? Yeah, that was it. After that, he got cold and wrote her off as date or wife material. No matter. She only needed him for five or ten minutes, and then that would be that.

As she drove past the other gates and driveways, she didn't see any cars. That was good. There was no one around to write down her license plate. She knew people who lived in the country paid special attention to strangers.

She spotted the no-trespassing sign at the end of the road and the open gate. She drove through, then closed it, not wanting to be interrupted later. Ashley looked around. It was beautiful here. This was the kind of place she wanted someday. She should have told him that. Ashley liked to hike and build and fix stuff, too. She waited for a moment, then drove to the end of the driveway.

She stared up at the two-story ranch house and sighed. Yes, this was what she wanted. She could almost imagine her child running around in the yard chasing squirrels or something.

Ashley pulled the purple blooming plant out of car and knocked on the door. Andy greeted her with a smile that turned to a quizzical look.

"What's this?" he asked.

"Oh, I bought this before. You know, kind of a here's-a-houseplant-thanks-for-the-help gesture. But I think you're not a plant guy. If I could just water it, I'll take it back with me. It was in the car too long, I think."

Andy stepped aside and pointed her to the kitchen. "Sure, water is in there."

He already had a glass of scotch in his hand. She hoped he didn't drink too much. She didn't want the deed to last any longer than necessary. After watering the plant and placing it on the counter, she returned to the living room.

"Nice place you have here," she said. "You live alone?"

"Yeah, no roommates. It's quiet out here, and I like it that way." He paused and stared at her. "I didn't have you pegged for a casual sex person. But if you're up for it, so am I."

He gave her a grin that made her skin crawl just a little. He wasn't horrible, but he certainly wasn't husband material. She thought about the nature vs. nurture debate. She'd nurture the hell out of her kid. No way he'd grow up to be a jerk.

"Yeah, well, sometimes you just need to let go and do what you want. So—" she stopped speaking and looked around the living room. "Which way to the bedroom?"

Andy grinned, knocked back his scotch, and led the way. "Step into my parlor, said the spider to the fly."

Ashley gave a little laugh. If only he knew he was the fly and not the spider.

* * *

Ten minutes later, it was all over. He'd even made sure she enjoyed herself, which was a plus, considering how long it had been since she'd had an orgasm.

"How was that?" he asked, a big grin on his face.

"It was, ah, good," she replied. "Can I make a cup of tea? I don't want to overstay my welcome, but maybe we could go again in a few?"

Andy laughed and shook his head. "Sure thing, lady. Kettle and tea are in the kitchen. I'll rest up so we can go again."

Ashley flashed him her best smile and padded naked into the kitchen. She put the kettle on and put the monkshood in the sink. She found a pair of cleaning gloves, pulled the plant out of its pot, and thoroughly rinsed off the root. Before the kettle came to a boil, she had chopped the root into tiny pieces and placed them in a bowl.

"You almost done in there?" came a voice from the bedroom. "I'm almost ready!"

"Just a few more minutes. The kettle just boiled," she hollered back.

Ashley turned her attention back to the bowl. She had at least a gram of root, which she ground into a paste with a large spoon. It should be enough. She didn't want to put boiling water on it just yet, as that would partially neutralize the poison. Monkshood, sometimes called wolfbane, was highly poisonous in its raw state and could, at times, be fatal. It mimicked a heart attack and was hard to trace during an autopsy unless you knew what you were looking for. Now all she had to do was figure out a way to get him to take it.

She rummaged through the fridge and found some cheese. That might work. "You hungry?" she called. "I'll make us a snack."

"Sure, whatever," came the reply.

Ashley cut the cheese into bite-sized chunks and poked a hole in one end with a chopstick she found in the drawer. She carefully stuffed a few pieces with the root paste and put them on a plate, then added some crackers. The rest of the poison she placed into a cup and added the no longer boiling water.

"That should do it," she said to herself. "I just have to convince him to take enough of it." She stirred in three teaspoons of sugar, hoping to hide the bitter taste.

She came back to the bedroom with the plate and cup and sat it on the bedside table. "I have an idea," she said, carefully picking up a piece of the poisonous cheese. "The cheese looked a bit old. I hope it's okay. Taste it?" She opened her mouth and held the cheese in front of his mouth. He automatically opened up, and she popped the cheese bite in.

He bit down and made a face. "Yeah, it tastes a bit odd, kinda bitter."

"Well, it is old cheddar, probably a bit older than when you bought it." She carefully put another piece on a cracker and held it up to his mouth. He smiled and opened wide, chewing twice, then swallowing.

"Oh gawd, that tasted even worse? What the hell did you give me?"

"Well, I did say it was old. I cut off a bit of mold. Sorry about that. Here, have some tea." She passed him the cup and held her breath.

Her grabbed the cup and took three big swallows before his eyes opened wide. "What the hell? This tastes like shit, too. Are you trying to poison me? My mouth is all tingly and numb!"

"Yeah, about that. It wasn't supposed to do that. It was supposed to be like a male enhancement thing. I got it in Chinatown at an herbalist. He said it would help with, you know, keeping it up."

Andy glared at her. "Well, you could've told me before you made me eat that shit. You sure it's safe?"

Ashley nodded. "Perfectly. It's been used for years."

He relaxed a bit and stuck his tongue out. "Well, my tongue is numb, so no oral sex for you. But . . ." His voice trailed off as he looked down at the small tent under the sheet. "It looks like something else is working."

Ashley grinned and carefully picked up another piece of cheese. "Perfect. Have a couple more. You probably won't taste it now."

Andy opened wide, and Ashley fed him the last three pieces of cheese and helped him wash it down with the warm, sweet tea.

"Hop on, darlin'," he said with a grin. Let's take this herb for a test drive."

Ashley hesitated, then pulled back the sheet. The poison wouldn't be in his bloodstream quite yet, and definitely not in his sperm.

She hopped on, as he so eloquently put it, and rode him until he came. She raised herself off him and went to the bathroom to clean up. She stepped aside as Andy burst into the room.

"I'm going to be sick," he said before he unceremoniously threw up into the toilet. She looked at his vomit. It was mostly liquid, with very little cheese.

"Here, let me get you something to drink. Maybe that cheese was bad." Still naked, she went into the bedroom and grabbed the poisonous teacup, then rushed into the kitchen. Ashley put the last of the ground root into a glass, added some water then poured the rest of the sweet tea into it. She almost ran back to the bathroom. "Drink this."

Andy grabbed the glass and drank the last of the liquid. "Gawd, I feel like shit. Why is my mouth so numb? I can't feel a damn thing. It's worse than the dentist!"

"Let me get you back to bed." Ashley helped him up and put his arm around her shoulder. She got him back into bed and tucked him in. "You rest. I'll be back in a bit."

She gathered up the plate, grabbed the glass from the bathroom, and deposited them in the kitchen sink. Five minutes later, everything she'd used to create her concoctions was washed, dried, and put back into cupboards and drawers. She swept up any dirt on the counter and put it back into the pot.

She rummaged around under the sink and found two plastic bags. She placed the remains of the ground-up root, the plant, and the pot into one bag and put them by the front door. She'd use the other bag later.

Andy was looking worse for wear when she checked on him.

"I think I need to go to the hospital," he said. "I can't breathe very well, and I'm cold."

"Oh, don't you worry. I'll stay right here with you." She looked at the bed and saw a few of her hairs on the sheet. There were probably some skin cells, too. "I just need to tidy up a bit."

She carefully pulled the sheet off Andy and rolled him over onto his side. She managed to remove both the bottom and top sheets, then grabbed the pillowcases and left the room.

Ashley put the sheets in the wash and came back to the bedroom with a fresh set she found in the closet. She put on a fresh set of gloves and managed to remake the bed with Andy on it. It was tricky but not impossible. Thank goodness he was still conscious and could help.

"Why are you changing the sheets," he asked as he tried to catch his breath. "And why are you wearing yellow cleaning gloves?"

"I just want you to be comfy," she said, ignoring the second question. She smiled and put on her clothes. "I'll get you a blanket, too. You look cold."

Ashley found a blanket and brought it back to the bedroom. She removed a rubber glove and checked Andy's pulse. It was slow but still had some strength to it. There was still time. It had only been twenty minutes.

"I'll be right back."

Ashley put the glove back on and headed out to the yard. She looked around but couldn't find a burning barrel. The garbage would be too easy to go through. She decided to put the remnants of the plant in her car and dispose of it later.

She came back into the house and grabbed a bucket, a cloth, and some bleach. She added just enough hot water and cleaned down the kitchen counters and cupboards. Then she decided to wipe down the cup and glass again, too. She pulled them out, gave them a good wipe inside and out, then rinsed them and placed them on a tea towel. What else? She looked around the room and wiped down the door handle to the fridge. She reached into the garbage and pulled out the cheese wrapper, wiped it down, and put it back.

Next stop, the bathroom. Ashley wiped down the toilet and sink, then cleaned the floor with her rag. Ten minutes later, she was back in the bedroom where she wiped down the bedside table. A girl had to be careful.

"What's happening to me?" Andy asked. "Do I know you?"

Ashley nodded. The confusion stage had set in. "Yes, I'm the housekeeper, remember? You're sick, and you asked me to come clean up while you recuperated."

"I don't feel good. I think you should call an—" Andy's sentence was cut off by a convulsion, and spittle gathered at the corners of his mouth. He gasped and reached for Ashley, but she stood back, watching safely from a distance. His convulsion stopped, but he had a hard time catching his breath.

"It won't be long now," she said matter-of-factly. "Just go with it."

Andy stared at her, his eyes wide with fear and confusion. "Why?" was all he managed to say.

"Because you dismissed me without getting to really know

me. Did you know I wanted an acreage just like this? Did you ask me if I liked hiking or nature or making stuff? No, you did not. You assumed I was a one-dimensional character. An artsy garden fairy. Well, guess what, Andy. Even artsy garden fairies can build things and be outdoorsy and like fishing. You wrote me off because I didn't fit your version of the perfect woman. You were quick to judge. Well, time's up. There won't be a perfect woman for you. In fact, there are no women in your future."

Andy stared at her as he gasped for breath. "But . . ."

"No buts, Andy, you have no future. You'll be dead soon, and they'll find you in a few days, maybe a few weeks. By then, no one will remember me talking to you at the hardware store. I wore a big ole hat and sunglasses and that awful Mumu. No one will be able to describe me either. No one will even think to look into your death. Do you know why? Because by the time they find you, you'll have started to rot. And when they do an autopsy, they'll see your heart is a mess. It'll look like you had a heart attack."

Ashley took off one of the rubber gloves and checked Andy's pulse. "Hmmm, about thirty beats per minute. I bet your blood pressure is really low, too." Ashley took her hand away and put her glove back on. "Back in a bit." She hummed a random tune and headed back to the kitchen.

She put the sheets into the dryer and rewiped all the surfaces she may have touched. When she was done, she poured the bleach water down the drain in the kitchen, hung the rag over the faucet, and looked out the window. Poisoning someone took so long. She much preferred a quick knife to the jugular, but she no longer had that luxury.

It was dusk, and she could see her reflection in the kitchen window. Outside, the birds serenaded the setting sun. She studied her face in the window. What had she become? A caricature of a female murderer choosing poison to dispose of her victims.

She wondered if the experts knew the reason women chose poison to kill. Maybe it was because it was so damn hard to get rid of bodies bigger than them.

She missed the days of feeding Dudley his favorite treats, but she hated the not being pregnant part. Perhaps this was it. Maybe using poison used by witches of old was the way to do it. Maybe her ancestors were burned at the stake or drowned. Maybe she was simply getting revenge for all of them.

Ashley shook her head to bring herself back to the present. Her car lights would be noticed soon. She had to leave before anyone saw her.

She went back to check on Andy and watched as he had another convulsion. His eyes were bloodshot and open. Spittle ran from the corners of his mouth, and his body was pulled into the fetal position. He wouldn't be making any more snap judgments or slapping any asses any time soon.

She took off her glove and checked for his pulse. Nothing on his wrist. She checked his neck. Nothing. She waited another twenty seconds. Nothing. That was that. It was time to go. She found her alcohol wipes, took one out and methodically cleaned his member. Satisfied there was no DNA left; she stuffed the damp wipe in her pocket. She put the glove back on, opened the bedroom window a few inches, and left the room.

Ashley checked the dryer on her way out. The sheets were done, so she folded them and placed them in the closet. She turned off all the lights, turned off the air conditioning, and made sure she had everything with her. After a final look around, she pressed the lock for the door and closed it.

Once in the car, she took off her rubber gloves and put them and the wipe in the empty plastic bag. She'd find a dumpster on the way home.

Chapter 27

Ashley got out of her car and retrieved the takeaway bag from the passenger seat. She'd dumped her other clothes and the plastic bags in separate dumpsters miles away. Now she was hungry.

As she approached the door, she saw Matt sitting on her stoop. His left hand was loosely wrapped in white gauze.

"What are you doing here, Matt?" Ashley asked as she unlocked the front door.

"What? Can't I pop over and visit my sister?"

Ashley opened the front door and went into the kitchen. She opened the bag, took out the containers, and retrieved two plates from the cupboard. She rummaged around in a drawer and retrieved three serving spoons and two forks.

"Don't just stand there," she said to Matt. "Sit down. Eat. I bought plenty."

Matt did as he was told.

"So, tell me, what happened to your hand?" Ashley scooped out a big helping of mixed veggies and put them on her plate, then did the same for Matt.

"It was stupid." He scooped some mystery meat in sauce out of a container and put it on his plate. He did the same for Ashley. They both reached for the rice. Ashley pulled back and let him serve her, then himself.

"Well, accidents usually aren't planned, are they, and sometimes they are stupid. What's up?"

"I burned it on a Holley three-barrel carburetor. I was helping a friend build a custom muscle car, and well, I got careless." He held up his wrapped hand. "It's mostly the fingertips, a bit on the palm. It should heal nicely in a week or so."

"Well, I should hope so," Ashley said. "I might need a bit more help sprucing this place up. You know, a few minor repairs here and there, and you are the handiest guy I know." She smiled and dropped the subject.

Matt shoveled food into his mouth, and when he finally stopped, it was because his plate was empty. "Thanks, sis. I didn't realize how hungry I was." He got up, put his plate in the sink, and brought them both back a glass of water. "So, how're things on the baby-making front? Any news?"

Ashley shrugged. "Still too early to tell. I'll let you know next week. In the meantime, I want to fix this place up just a little more and get it ready for sale. I've decided that a couple of acres would be perfect for us. I've got the realtor looking into it now."

"Oh?" Matt raised an eyebrow. "I thought that was just talk, but cool. What area are you looking in? Somewhere close by?"

"Not sure. As long as it's no more than a fifteen-minute drive to a hospital, doctor, and grocery store, I'll be happy."

"Alrighty then, I'll keep my ears open, too. Hey, have you heard any more about your neighbors' disappearance?"

"Yeah, I think they ran off together. The detective stopped by to tell Beth her husband used his bank card for another withdrawal, and that woman used her credit card for gas. Beth is upset."

"Why? The cheater is gone, and she can get on with her life."

"Because if she can't find him, she can't get the divorce papers signed, and she can't get on with her life. It would've been better if he were dead. Then she'd get everything."

A small smile crept onto Matt's face. He raised his water glass and clinked it with Ashley's. "Well, here's to the cheater being dead then."

Ashley stared at her brother. "Matt, did you have anything to do with them disappearing? I mean, if you did, I don't care. I just want to know what I may have to deny."

Matt shook his head. "Aw, c'mon now. You know I don't disappear people, unless they're dead. And no one has asked me to take away their bodies. So, to answer your question, I had nothing to do with it."

Ashley shook her head. "It's just so darn strange. I can't wait to get out of this town and into a home surrounded by nature. Somewhere less . . ." she paused to get the right word. "less peoplely."

Matt laughed. "I'm with you, sis. The only people I want to be around are you and your kid."

Ashley put a hand on her belly. A vision of her latest sperm donor writhing in pain flashed briefly in her mind. "Well, here's hoping."

* * *

Ashley had an uneventful ten days back at the nursery. Work was busy as it usually was near the end of August. They had several last-minute sales on leftover flowers and vegetables. Plus, there was the ever-popular planting of fall bulbs. She got to chat with people who loved plants, and that always made her day.

There were no more visits from the detective, and Beth had thankfully left her alone. Even Matt stayed away while his hand healed. He'd be over on Saturday to help her.

After work, Ashley headed to a chain hardware store where she rented a floor sander and bought a couple of gallons of varnish and some rollers. She could do the work herself for less than two grand, and she'd use the saved money for baby clothes. Tomorrow would be a good day. Fresh floors and maybe a baby.

* * *

Ashley slept fitfully and got up shortly after sunrise. Today should be the first day of her period. She mentally examined her body. There was no cramping, and she didn't feel bloated. She knew testing was too early, but the package said it was early detection.

She gave Dudley a tummy rub and padded into the bathroom. Peeing on a piece of plastic had become almost too commonplace for her. She hoped today would be the day. It was a full month before the fall equinox, and she was hoping for a spring baby. Carrying a baby in the summer would be too uncomfortable. She peed on the test strip and set it down.

Dudley hobbled to the door of the bathroom and meowed loudly.

"Yes, boss. I'll feed you. And stop looking so pathetic. You've got at least two more weeks in that cast."

Ashley went into the kitchen and put on the kettle. She stared at her Google Home and plugged it in.

"Hey Google, play "Beautiful Boy" by John Lennon." The music started up, and Ashley sang along as she prepared herself a decaf coffee and made Dudley his breakfast. She imagined playing with her son in an open meadow and then collecting eggs with him from a chicken coop. She was looking forward to being the best mom ever.

She put the dish down as Dudley hobbled into the kitchen. He sniffed the food and looked at her with pure disdain.

She should have taken a souvenir from the hardware guy. It had been months since she'd been able to give Dudley his favorite treat, and he was not amused.

"Sorry, kiddo. No special treats today. Maybe another day."

Ashley took a sip of her coffee then walked into the bathroom. She stared at the test strip. One solid pink line, and there, right beside it, a faint pink line.

"Oh, my gawd!" Ashley stared at herself in the mirror. "I'm pregnant!"

She ran for her phtook a photo of the test, and texted Matt.

Couldn't wait to see you and tell you. Look!
I'm pregnant!

She attached the photo and ran into the kitchen. She picked up a startled Dudley and danced around the room.

"You're going to be a brother!" she squealed. She put the cat down and stood in the center of the kitchen, grinning like a maniac.

"Hey, Google! Play "Happy" by Pharrell Williams."

The upbeat tune played as Ashley danced and giggled. It was barely six in the morning, but she wanted to shout it from her yard, shout it to her neighbors. She was going to be a mom!

Ashley danced wildly until the song was over, then unplugged her Google Home. It was time for a shower.

There was so much to do and such little time to do it in. She did a quick mental calculation. She'd be just a little pregnant for the rest of the summer. Then she'd spend the fall and winter incubating her little miracle, and by spring, they'd be in a new home, and she'd have a family, a real family.

Chapter 28

Ashley sat in the gynecologist's office, impatiently flipping through a magazine. She'd taken the day off work. Three days since she'd taken the test, and still no period. This was it. But she wanted to be sure. Matt was at the house sanding the wood floors in the spare room. She had to be out of the house anyway, just in case. Once he'd finished sanding, he'd apply the varnish. Another reason she had to stay away all day. She couldn't risk hurting the wee one growing inside of her.

Ashley whispered to her belly. "Hang in there, little bean, my little nugget. Just nine more months, and you'll come out to meet the world."

A woman beside her, who looked to be full-term, smiled. "I used to call my belly pet names. I like Bean and Nugget. Cute."

Ashley smiled at the woman. "It's pretty new yet, so that's as far as I've got. What else do you call him or her? Sorry, it's none of my business."

"No worries," the woman said. "It's a her. She's due in two weeks. When I first got pregnant, we called her Bun, then Bunny, and Bug. As I got larger, my husband started calling her Cletus the fetus. Then we found out it was a her, so that stopped, and he came up with Chicken Little. Now I call her my

Little Spawn and Thumper. Mostly Thumper."

Ashley watched as the woman winced and the outline of a foot pushed against her maternity top.

"Oh wow!" Ashley stared at the wave of movement across the woman's belly.

"Yeah, you say that now." The woman smiled and tried to find a more comfortable position. "Do you want to feel her? It's okay. I don't mind."

Ashley nodded and tentatively put her hand on the woman's lower abdomen. She waited a few seconds and was rewarded with a swift kick that sent her hand flying off the woman's belly.

"Oh my!" Ashley grinned from ear to ear. "I can hardly wait for that to be me. Thank you."

A nurse entered the waiting room. "Ashley Taylor. Come with me, please."

Ashley stood. "That's me. Nice meeting you." She followed the nurse into the doctor's office.

She handed Ashley a clear plastic cup with a pink lid.

"Here you go. The bathroom is right there. Pee in this cup and place it on the counter over there. Then come back to that room." She pointed to the patient room beside the bathroom. "Put on the exam gown and hop up on the table. The doctor will be with you as soon as we test your urine."

Ashley took the cup and headed into the bathroom. The deed done, she came out, placed the half-full sample on the counter, and entered the exam room. She sat on the table kicking her feet back and forth. She didn't know why she was nervous. She wanted this with all her heart and soul. The moments crawled by as she waited for the doctor to come speak to her.

Ten minutes later, there was a light knock on the door, and the doctor entered.

"Good morning, Ashley. Good to see you." He sat down in a chair across from her as a nurse wheeled an ultrasound machine into the room. Ashley sat there, waiting to hear the words she already knew were true. She was going to be a mother.

"Ashley, we tested your urine. It does show a low level of hCG, the pregnancy hormone. But it's not as high as we'd like to see at the beginning of a healthy pregnancy."

Ashley's heart skipped a beat, and she held her breath. "But I'm pregnant, right?"

The doctor smiled at her, then looked back down at her chart. "That's what we are going to find out. Lie back and lift the gown just above your belly button."

Ashley did as she was told.

"This is going to be a bit cold."

Ashley tensed as the cold gel hit her belly. A few seconds later, the ultrasound probe was searching for its target. The doctor watched the monitor closely, avoiding Ashley's gaze. After a full minute, he handed her a tissue and turned off the machine. Ashley wiped off her belly and sat up.

"So, is he okay?"

"Ashley," the doctor said. "I'm afraid you aren't pregnant."

"But I took a test, and you just said my urine test was positive." She could feel something akin to panic rise inside her.

"You probably were pregnant and quite recently. Sometimes the embryo doesn't implant. We call that a chemical pregnancy. It's quite common, and if you'd waited another day or two, you'd have gotten your period. That's why we suggest you don't take these tests until you are at least a week late with your period."

"But the pregnancy test said early detection." Ashley started to cry quietly. The doctor handed her another tissue.

"Yes, and they are quite good. Most have a ninety-eight to ninety-nine percent accuracy rate. But, in this case, it was a false positive. I'm sorry. Better luck next time. But please, don't take the early detection tests. The regular ones work just fine if you wait until your period is at least a week late."

Ashley nodded. "Okay."

"Have you been under any stress lately?"

"Well, maybe a little. I'm getting my house ready to sell, and there have been some strange things going on in my neighborhood, and . . ." she let her voice trail off.

"And what, Ashley?" The doctor stopped writing and looked at her.

"Well, a few weeks ago, actually almost a month now, I guess, maybe more, I don't know." She stopped and tried to picture a calendar in her head. "It doesn't matter. About a month ago, I was attacked in my home. They got the guy. He didn't rape me, and, well, he's dead now."

The doctor stared at Ashley, then made some notes. "I see. Well, that is certainly an awful lot of stress. Go home and take it easy. Have a nice hot bath or a glass of wine. Heck, have both."

"It's morning," Ashley said. "Too early for wine." She hopped off the table. "I guess I'll just go help my brother refinish the floors then."

"I'm so sorry, Ashley. You're still young and healthy. It will happen. Just not this time." The doctor closed the file and left the room.

Ashley got dressed and kept her head down as she walked through the waiting room. Damn, that realtor for stressing her out. If he wasn't dead already, she would likely have killed him with her bare hands.

She picked up her phone and sent Matt a quick text.

> False positive. Not pregnant. Don't want to
> talk about it.

Chapter 29

Ashley spent the next few weeks working, washing walls, and patching nail holes. Her period came three days late, and she cursed every time she had to change her tampon. Life wasn't fair. Matt's hand healed and he was over every couple of days to help her. So far, they'd painted the spare room, the living room, and the kitchen. All they had left to do was the laundry room, bathroom, and her bedroom.

She went into the laundry room and surveyed the walls. The only thing on the walls here was a calendar stuck to the wall with a push pin and a poster that said, "Laundry Room. Home of the disappearing socks." Ashley thought it funny when she first got it. Now it just mocked her. The only socks she'd be washing in the near future were hers.

She pulled push pins out of the poster and the calendar and put them in a container. She crumpled up the poster and put it in the recycle bin.

Calendar in hand, she sat down at the kitchen table and stared at the dates she'd circled for her period and ovulation dates. Now it was all out of whack thanks to a three-day delay in her last period. She could hardly believe it was already early September. Another month gone without a baby in her belly. She grabbed her pencil crayons and adjusted the dates with new colors. According to her calculations, she should be ovulating right about now. But there was too much to do with the house, so hunting had to wait. She had to place her attention on fixing her place up and then finding a new home.

The doorbell rang, and Ashley reluctantly got up to see who it was. It was Kate, her realtor.

"Hey Ashley, I just came by to see how the upgrades were going. Can I come in?"

"Sure." Ashley motioned to the kitchen. "Care for a coffee while I give you the tour?"

"Absolutely," Kate said, looking around the room. "The living room looks great. I love the new colors. Where'd you put your paintings?" she asked as she followed Ashley to the kitchen.

"Oh, they're in storage. Waiting to be unboxed at our new home. Any updates on an acreage?"

"Well," Kate said as she seated herself at the table. "There might be one coming up in a few weeks. The owner died unexpectedly, and his next of kin doesn't want it, so they are selling. It's about an hour from here. Nice place, a two-story rancher located at the end of a road that leads to other three and four-acre lots. It's rustic, fully fenced, and—"

Ashley interrupted as she set down the coffee. "Wait, you said the owner died?"

"Yes, a few weeks ago. Heart attack or something of the sort. Young guy, too. One of those DIY mountain men that spent their days hiking in the woods and fields. Anyway, it would be perfect for you. Lots of trees, too."

Ashley took a sip of her coffee. "But I bet there's no big

garage or bunkhouse or chicken coop."

The realtor nodded. "You're right, there isn't, but there could be."

Ashley put down her cup. "I have a feeling it's not the right one," she said as a vision of Andy's cozy ranch house came to mind. "I like the rancher style, and if you could find something, say, two or three hours away, I'd be interested. Preferably a bit farther north, but not up in the hills or mountains. Somewhere with very little snow."

The realtor nodded. "Of course. I'll keep looking. Oh, and before I forget, I have a couple who may be interested in this place. They want to start a family, and this is the perfect size for them. Especially with a garden, and so close to the highway. They can easily commute to work, and the yard is a great place for the kids."

Ashley tried not to let her face show what she was feeling. She'd thought this place would be perfect, too. But no matter how hard she tried or how much she hoped, her dreams had yet to come true.

"I want a family someday soon, too," Ashley said. "That's why I want the acreage. Somewhere my kid can run free, slightly supervised, of course. Gotta watch out for coyotes and bears." Ashley smiled and stood. "Come, I'll show you the refinished floor in the spare room."

Kate followed her out of the kitchen. The pair stood at the door and admired Matt and Ashley's handiwork.

"Wow, this is just beautiful," Kate said. "And the way the sun is streaming in here right now is perfect. I'll make sure to make a note to show the house around this time of day, well, at least for the next month or so. When do you think you'll be ready to sell?"

Ashley moved over to her bedroom door. "Soon, I hope." She opened the door and walked in. "I was thinking of redoing this room as well. There's probably a wood floor under the carpet, and I'd paint it a nice light blue or gray blue. What do you think?"

Kate looked around the room. "That would work. The lighter the color, the better." She paced the room and looked around. "Is this the same size as the other room?"

"I think so," Ashley said. "I'd have to check the papers from when I bought it. Why?"

"If you decluttered some of your knickknacks and moved your bed and side table into the other room and put the dresser in the closet, we could stage this as a kid's room. I think it's a bit bigger, and we could put in a desk and a set of bunk beds."

"But, I—"

Kate cut her off. "Oh, don't worry, I have a storage locker full of extra furniture. I've even got the perfect rug for the side of your bed in the other room. You get things done, floors, walls, etc., and give me a call. I'll bring the furniture over, and we'll stage it for a quick sale."

"Oh, okay." Ashley stared at the realtor. This was a woman who knew how to get things done. She was glad they met.

"Good." Kate left the room and entered the kitchen. She pulled a contract out of her briefcase and set it on the table. "Let's go through the paperwork, and we'll decide on a date for your open house. After that, it shouldn't be too hard to sell."

Ashley stared at her. Was it going to happen that quickly? She wasn't even pregnant yet. "But I wanted to wait until I found a place to move to."

"That won't be a problem, Ashley. We'll make it a long possession date. If the prospective buyer doesn't like that, we can ask for an extra ten grand for living expenses for you until you find a place." Kate handed her a pen and slid the papers across to Ashley. "I've already filled most of it out."

Ashley stared at the contract. Her eyes opened wide when she saw the asking price. "Seven hundred thousand dollars? Are you sure? You said six hundred thousand before, and even with renos, that would bring it to what, six fifty at the most?"

Kate nodded. "Yes, but that was before we learned a new Costco and a new stadium is going in up the road. This is going to be one hot property in a month or so. Trust me."

It sounded too good to be true, but Ashley signed the papers anyway. "As for my dream home, I've decided it can be anywhere, just not too far south. I still want all four seasons and a bit of rain in the spring. But, like I said, not too much snow. Am I asking too much?"

"No, you're not." Kate signed her sheets and handed copies to Ashley. "I'll be in touch next week. Let me know when you're done with the renos and moving furniture."

Ashley walked her to the door. When she opened it to let Kate out, the detective was standing there, arm raised as if he were about the knock.

Kate took a step back, laughed, and made her way past

the detective. Ashley stepped aside to let him in.

"To what do I owe the pleasure, Detective, er, Frank? Sorry, it's really hard not to call you Detective."

"That's okay, Ashley. I was just talking to Beth and thought I'd stop by."

"Any news on her cheating husband?" Ashley asked as she closed the door.

"Not really, and I can't talk about it. We may find him yet." The detective looked around and smiled. "Wow, you've done a great job. Love the paint color."

"Come," Ashley said. "Let me show you what used to be my art room."

Colombo followed her and stood in the doorway admiring the work. "Nicely done, Ashley. I love these floors! You did a great job."

He turned and walked back to the living room. "Well, I just wanted to stop by and see how you were doing."

"I'm good, but—" she stopped, cocked her head, and looked at the detective. "You're a strong guy, right? Are you off duty?"

"I could be. Why?"

"Want to help me move some furniture?"

* * *

An hour later, Ashley had her bedroom emptied and a new setup in the new room. The dresser was tucked into the closet, and the only things in the room were a made bed, a side table, a lamp, and a clock.

"Nicely done, Frank," she said as she fell back on the bed. "I hope I can sleep okay in here. I've never spent more than a few hours at a time in this room for the past ten years or so."

Frank stared at her on the bed. He was happy to see her smiling. She'd had a rough few months. His protective side wanted to gather her up in his arms and look after her. The cop in him wanted to interrogate her.

Ashley interrupted his thoughts. "Why are you looking at me like that?" she asked.

He shook his head. "The light in here, it's, well, it's beautiful."

Ashley blushed a little and then patted the bed beside her. "Sit," she commanded.

"I shouldn't. Look. You are a beautiful woman, and I'm an old cranky cop. I don't think this is a good idea. I'll show myself out." He didn't want to feel the way he did. She could still be a suspect in the missing persons' case. He was a cop, and cops didn't get involved with the women who were persons of interest. But damn, she looked so good.

"You're not old." She got up off the bed. "You're what, forty? That's eight years older than me. Not old at all."

He stopped in the doorway and turned to look at her. She smiled, and his willpower waned.

Don't do it. You're a professional, damn it!

Ashley slipped her hand in his and led him to the bed.

"C'mon, Frank. You helped me move it, and it's all made up with fresh, clean sheets. You aren't afraid of cooties, are you?"

"No, it's not that. It's just, well, there are things that

are still up in the air when it comes to you and what's been happening around here." He sat down on the bed beside her.

"Okay, well, as you said before, my attacker is dead, my old date's case has been transferred, and my missing neighbor is obviously off living his best life without his wife. So, what else is there?"

He thought hard for a moment. It was against regulations to be involved with anyone involved in any ongoing case, no matter how tenuous the connection was. He'd been a good cop his entire work life. Never once strayed from the rules. She probably had nothing to do with her neighbors' disappearance, but she was still a person of interest, and that meant no romantic or sexual contact. He could lose his job.

He felt a small hole form in his resolve as he stared into her eyes.

On the surface, she didn't look like she had any connection to the runaway lovers. Besides, there was something about her that niggled at the back of his brain. If she'd stop smiling at him, he just might be able to put his finger on it.

"Nothing, I guess. It's just that, Ashley, I barely know you. I'm investigating a case that you're involved in. And even if we solve this, even if you're no longer part of the investigation, you don't know me. I'm a cop, and dating a cop is hard work for the one dating them. I keep shitty hours, I'm obsessed with finding answers, and I have a hard time trusting people. You don't want to do this. I think it's some transference thing or something or other. I stopped you from being raped, and you feel indebted. We shouldn't do this."

Ashley sighed. "Look, Frank. I promise you I had absolutely, positively, nothing to do with Rocky's disappearance, or Maria for that matter. You may have noticed I'm a loner. I don't like or let too many people into my space. I've had shitty relationships with men all my life. The fact you will rarely be around, keep odd hours, and don't trust until you get answers, is a plus for me. I'm the same way. The trust part, anyway. Plus, some days, when I get into my painting or get obsessed with my garden, I keep odd hours, too. And besides, I'll be moving soon, but I don't know where. This may go nowhere, or things might work out. But, as some wise person somewhere once said, 'You never know until you try.'"

Colombo stared at her. It would be nice to have someone to come home to or somewhere to go after work. Someone to just relax with. But not until after this case was over.

Dudley hobbled into the room and tried to jump on the bed.

"And I'm allergic to cats." He watched as Ashley picked up her cat and left the room. She came back with a cat bed and placed it on the floor at the foot of the bed. Dudley climbed in and went to sleep.

"Okay, how's this then," Ashley pushed him back onto the pillows and straddled him. "Let's just be lovers then. Two people who are tired of being alone, giving each other a bit of pleasure until it doesn't work anymore. Can we do that?" She playfully leaned over and kissed his neck, just under his ear.

Colombo groaned. It had been a long time since a woman touched him. Even longer since he'd been intimate with one. He tried to sit up.

"Ashley, this isn't a good idea. I could get fired. Besides, I'm too old for you, and I don't know if I can do casual or temporary or whatever."

She finished unbuttoning his shirt and ran her finger down from his lips to his chest. She giggled as she played with his chest hairs.

"Seriously, Ashley. I could lose my job, and I'm not good for you. I, well—" He stopped as she eased herself off his groin and sat on his upper thighs. Her hands skillfully opened his pants and pulled down the zipper. He watched as a big grin spread across her face as she reached in to find her prize. He groaned.

"Ah, what the hell," he said and, in one quick move, flipped her over onto her back. Ashley giggled and licked her lips. Within seconds he had her shirt off and was gazing at her naked breasts. "You are so beautiful," he said as he went in for a taste.

Chapter 30

Ashley stared at the calendar on her kitchen counter. It was hard to believe the autumn equinox was just a week away. Fall was right around the corner. She double-checked the new dates. They were correct, and she'd been quite active with the detective since their first liaison. He wasn't a great lover, but he was good at some things, and above all else, he came every time, and that was what mattered.

He believed her when she told him she was on birth control, and he'd admitted he was afraid of getting a vasectomy. She learned he'd been married once, eighteen years prior, and it only lasted a year. She couldn't handle being married to a cop, even if he was just a beat cop at the time.

The doctor's words ran through her head. No testing for at least a week after her missed period. Today was the day she should get it, but so far, nothing. She'd spent the entire day at work without even a twinge, let alone a cramp. But she'd be patient. She had to be. She couldn't go through another false positive again.

Matt was over a few times and helped her pull the carpet from what used to be her bedroom. The floor underneath was in much better shape than the one in the spare room. All they needed was a good cleaning and polishing. In the evenings,

Frank helped her fill cracks and holes and paint the room a light blue-gray. He'd even come shopping with her to get some curtains.

Her phone dinged. She picked it up and saw a text from Kate.

> I should be there about 9 a.m. tomorrow.
> You're not working, right? I'll have my truck
> with the bunkbeds, dresser, some cute
> things for the wall, and your bedroom rug.
> Are we still on?

She texted back.

> We repainted all the rooms. The floors look
> great too. See you at 9.

Things were moving along nicely. Her open house was in a week. Frank was over almost every night for baby-making, and Matt hadn't been around unless he was asked to come to help out. Life was good.

She smiled, knowing this might be it. How ironic would it be if her baby daddy turned out to be the cop who investigated crimes that may or may not be related to her. Ashley didn't think of herself as a criminal. She felt more like an exterminator, ridding the world of those who shouldn't be around anyway. In her mind, she was the good guy, if not the hero.

She hopped into the shower to ready herself for her

evening date with Frank. That's what they called them. Dates, not sleepovers or screw-fests. They were dates. It's just that most of the date happened in the bedroom. He said it was because they couldn't be seen out together, but she knew it was because he wanted her to himself.

She thought it ironic she was trying to make a baby in the room where so many men had paid for their shitty attitudes after failing to impregnate her.

The water washed over her, soothing her psyche. She did her usual ritual, imagining the water taking away all her pain, all her frustration, and all her sadness. By the time she was done, she felt like a kid fresh from the confessional. Sin- and guilt-free, she was ready to tackle whatever life had to offer.

She wrapped herself in a towel and headed for the bedroom as the doorbell rang.

"It's me, Ashley," came a familiar voice.

Ashley thought it was odd that he didn't knock. He always knocked. She opened the door. Something was wrong.

"Hey sexy, what's up? Why no knock?"

The detective came in and paced the room. "Look, I shouldn't be telling you this, but." He stopped. "Do you have any whiskey?"

"Yeah, sure, bottom middle cupboard." Ashley pointed to the kitchen and headed for the bedroom. She slipped on a T-shirt and some capris and joined Frank in the kitchen. She watched as he downed a shot of scotch and poured himself another.

"You want one?" he asked as he downed the second shot.

"Ah, no, thank you," she said and sat down. "What's wrong, Frank?" She put her hand on his.

"They found Maria Wilson's car," he said and gulped the second shot.

Ashley poured him another, then put the lid back on the scotch and put it out of reach.

"Who is Maria Wilson?" she asked.

"Your almost neighbor. The one who lives up the next block and may have run away with your neighbor Rocky. They found her car. It was burned pretty badly, but we got the VIN off it. It was transferred into someone else's name just after they disappeared. Same last name, Wilson, but the first name was Nathanial."

Ashley waited for more, but he stopped talking.

"And? Why has this got you so shaken up?"

"One of my guys is into woo woo stuff. He told me Nathanial is the angel of purification and fire. The car was burned almost beyond recognition. They found it a couple of hundred miles away, near where Maria first used her credit card to get gas."

Ashley stared at him, not understanding why he was so upset. "And?"

"And Maria Wilson didn't have any relatives named Nathanial, or Nate or Nat or any variation thereof. It's too much of a coincidence. Investigators think it might have been there a few weeks, which puts it around the time Maria and Rocky disappeared. We're putting more people on the case."

"And?" Ashley still didn't understand why he was so upset.

So some guy had the car registered in his name, and then it ended up on fire. Shit happens.

"And." The detective tossed back the third shot of the scotch. "You are still a person of interest as you were one of the last people to see Rocky. I can't see you anymore until this case is wrapped up. I could lose my job."

"Shit." Ashley got up and poured herself a glass of water. "But that doesn't change anything between us, right?"

"I'm afraid it does. I've been battling with seeing you since, well, you know, that first night. Now things are looking more like foul play. I can't see you anymore. I just came by to tell you." He hung his head, then banged his fist on the table. "Damn it!"

"But—" Ashley stopped. His temper frightened her, reminding her of her drunken father and what he'd done to her. She stayed over by the sink, not wanting to get in his way.

"Okay then. But you just had three shots on an empty stomach. You're a big guy, but I don't think you should drive. How about I feed you, and then you can go on your way? Have you told Beth?"

"Yeah." He took a deep breath. "I just came from there. We should have the warrant to search Maria's house by morning. I can't, shouldn't, be around you. At least not until this is all wrapped up. I'm sorry."

"Okay," was all Ashley managed to say. She turned and opened the fridge and pulled out ingredients for a sandwich. Once it was made she placed it in front of him. She stepped away and leaned against the wall.

"Eat."

"Thanks," Colombo muttered as he wolfed down the sandwich. A minute later, he pushed the plate away and stood. "I'm sorry. I have to go to the office. I'll, well, I'll be in touch."

"Okay." Ashley watched him get up and leave. She didn't like this side of Detective Frank Colombo. Maybe she'd misjudged him as a baby daddy. Maybe he was like all the rest.

Chapter 31

At precisely nine a.m. Ashley's doorbell rang. She opened it to a smiling Kate. "Hey there. Care to give me a hand?" she asked.

Ashley grinned. "You bet."

There was a slight chill to the early September air, but it certainly wasn't long pants and jacket weather. She met Kate by the truck bed and whistled when she saw the contents.

"Wow, you sure do have great taste in kid's stuff." Ashley stood by the tailgate as Kate wrestled with part of the bunk bed. She grabbed the end of what she presumed was one of the bed frames and held it steady while Kate jumped off the truck.

It only took twenty minutes, and all the furniture, rugs, and framed posters were out of the truck and in various places in Ashley's bedroom and living room.

"Damn, I forgot the screws. Can you go get them, Ashley? They're in the glove box. I'll put the rug by your bed and get the base of the bunkbeds set up."

"Sure thing," Ashley said as she bounded out the door. The sun was shining, her place was taking shape, and she still hadn't got her period. As she closed the door to the truck, an envelope of screws in hand, she noticed Colombo pull up to Beth's house. She waved, but he didn't wave back. She watched from her front door as he spoke to Beth and got back into his car.

Ashley shrugged and headed back to what was to be the new kid's room. She tossed Kate the screws, and the two of them made swift work of assembling the furniture. The framed posters looked great, the knickknacks were minimal, and best of all, they looked neither boyish nor girlish. Perfect for setting the scene for a prospective owner.

"Great job, Kate," Ashley said as she walked Kate to the truck. She glanced down the street toward where Maria lived. She thought she saw an ambulance but couldn't be sure. "So, open house on Saturday then?"

"You bet," Kate said. "It's online, and I've let my fellow realtors know via our bulletin board that this is a great space. Plus, it's back-to-school time, so parents can book to see the place while their kids are at school or bring them along for the open house. You okay with kids wandering about?"

"Yeah, sure, I love kids. If you don't mind, I'll be here, but out in the garden. I've got to start my end-of-season cleanup. I can answer any questions you don't have answers to. I know you don't normally let homeowners hang around, but I promise I'll stay out of the way. Besides, Dudley will just have gotten his cast off, so I want to keep him close by outside with me. Let him catch the last of the summer rays."

"No problem. I have no idea what is happening in the garden, so feel free to answer any questions, but make sure you don't divulge where the bodies are buried." Kate laughed.

"There are no bodies." Ashley felt her heart pound, and fear seeped into her bones.

"I was joking!" Kate laughed again. "I highly doubt that

you're some kind of murderer who buries people in her yard. It wouldn't be good for the plants." Kate smiled and stared at Ashley.

"Yeah, right, decomposing bodies would be bad for the garden. No bodies here." Ashley smiled as Kate got into the cab of the truck.

"See you Saturday, if not before," Kate called as she pulled away.

Ashley walked to the end of her driveway and noticed a For Sale sign. She hoped it wouldn't be there long, and she'd be pregnant and off enjoying her new life soon.

Curiosity got the best of her, and she started walking toward Maria Wilson's house. The closer she got, the more it looked like something was going on. Three or four cars were on the lawn, and an ambulance. When she was half a block away she saw Frank. She waved, but he ignored her.

"This can't be good," she said to herself.

She watched as Colombo walked toward the house. Not good at all. She stopped walking and stared at the scene. If something had happened to Rocky and/or Maria, this was going to put a major dent into her sexy time with the detective. She turned and headed for home.

* * *

Detective Colombo informed Beth they had a search warrant for Maria's house. He instructed Beth to stay home and wait for him to return to give her whatever news he might have. Under no circumstances should she to come to Maria's house.

He knew something was off the moment they managed to get the door open. A putrid stench wafted its way around him as he entered the home. It grew stronger as he approached the door to the basement, something between rotten eggs, rotting meat, and garlic. He'd have to stay away from pasta for a bit.

He pulled a surgical face mask from his pocket and opened the door. He found the light, put on the mask, and peered into the basement. From where he stood, it looked fine, but the smell was much stronger here. He motioned for two uniforms to come with him and told two others to stand at the front and back doors. A minute later, his fear was confirmed. There, lying in a corner, were the semi-bloated bodies of a man and a woman. Colombo assumed they were Rocky and Maria, but he couldn't be sure. He made his way back upstairs and quickly went outside. He wanted to puke.

"Hey, hey you!" he motioned for one of the ambulance attendants. "They are most certainly dead, but I need you to confirm, okay? I'll call the coroner."

He leaned against a tree and took in big gulps of fresh air. This wasn't good. Not good at all. If he'd been more on the ball, he would have asked for a search warrant earlier, or at least as soon as they found the car. But it wasn't in her name, and there was a paper trail of purchases.

"Damn it!" he hollered into the sky. He looked down at his shoes. All he wanted to do was go see Ashley. Now he had to go tell some poor woman her cheating bastard husband was dead. Today was not a good day to be a cop.

The paramedics returned to the yard, shaking their heads.

"We didn't touch anything, sir, but you are correct. They are quite dead. We'll wait for the coroner." The paramedic grabbed a metal clipboard from the cab of the ambulance and started writing. They had a pretty shitty job some days, too.

Colombo dialed the coroner's office and let them know the situation. Ten minutes later, a black panel van with no markings arrived. He was glad it didn't have coroner written on it in big letters. Nothing like freaking out the neighbors any more than he had to.

"Good morning," he said, approaching the vehicle. The coroner stepped out of the van, case in hand. "It's pretty bad in there. Looks like they've been there a few weeks. All I need from you right now is ID if you can get it without disturbing the scene."

"You the lead on this?" the coroner asked as the photographer joined them.

"Yeah, that'd be me." He followed them back into the house. "My partner should be here shortly."

The detective and the coroner stood back and watched as the photographer took shots from every angle, leaving markers on the ground for perspective. When he was done, he motioned for the coroner to come over.

The coroner shook his head. "These fine folks have been dead at least a couple of weeks by the looks of it. But it's pretty cool down here. That would have slowed down the decomp." He set his case down, pulled on his gloves, and examined the bodies.

"Detective, here's your ID." The coroner held out a wallet. It looked damp. "Extra gloves are in there." The coroner motioned toward the case.

Colombo put on a pair and took the wallet. The smell

made him gag, but he opened it and looked inside. The driver's license told him all he needed to know. It was Rocky, all right. Now he had to go tell the wife. Some days his job sucked. The photographer was now standing beside the body, an open plastic Ziploc bag in hand. The detective kept the driver's license and dropped the wallet into the bag.

He looked around the room. No purse or ID, but he was fairly certain the woman was Maria Wilson.

"Any idea what they died from?" Colombo asked.

"At first glance, there are no signs of entry from a bullet or a knife. Clothing is intact, no blood. That goo on the floor is probably intestinal in origin. They are too far gone to do much of an exam here." He pulled a stray hair off the floor beside the body. The photographer walked over with another baggie and sealed it once the hair was inside.

The coroner nodded to the photographer, and he left the basement. He returned shortly with one of the ambulance attendants and a black gurney, complete with an empty body bag. Colombo couldn't watch and went back outside.

"Hey, Frank!" Tate Sparks called as he got out of an unmarked police car. "Sorry, I'm late. No excuse really, but—" He stopped speaking when he saw the look on Colombo's face.

"Hey, Tate," Colombo replied. "It's not pretty in there. We no longer have a missing persons case. It's now a murder investigation."

"Murder/suicide?" Sparks asked.

"Too early to know," Colombo replied. "But no visible wounds, no nothing. Just two dead, bloated, stinking bodies in a corner of the basement. The coroner believes at least two weeks, could be more. Basement is pretty cool. Could have been poison. We'll know when we get the autopsy results."

"Damn." Sparks shook his head. "So the wife and that Ashley woman were two of the last people to see Rocky alive, then?"

Colombo let out an audible sigh. "Yeah. I'll tell the wife, but I need you to question the neighbors and Ashley. You okay with that?"

"Yeah, sure. I think you got too close to her anyway." Sparks looked up and down the street. "This looks like such a nice neighborhood. Don't know if I'd want to live here after all the shit that's gone down the last few months."

Colombo let out another audible sigh. "Okay, I have to go inform the wife. You okay securing the scene?"

"Yep." Sparks gave his friend a pat on the back. "See you back at the office."

Colombo headed for his car—thankful he'd parked up the street. No way he wanted to wait for cop cars and ambulances to move out of his way. He made the short trip to Beth's house in a minute flat. Now came the hard part.

Chapter 32

Ashley watched from her window as Colombo got out of his car and walked up to Beth's door. A part of her wanted to run to him and get answers. The other part knew better, so she stayed where she was. She watched as her lover went inside and closed the door.

She knew she'd be called in and asked questions, but she didn't have anything to tell. She had more questions than answers. Her phone dinged, and she looked down to see a text from Matt.

> Hey sis. Are you free for dinner tonight? My treat!

She stared at the phone. He was such a good brother, but she had no idea if she'd be home or being questioned at dinner time.

> Not sure, Matt. I think they found bodies in the house up the street. Cops are everywhere. Could be Rocky. I don't know anything yet, but they might be questioning me. Not sure.

She hit send and watched for the three bouncing dots. They briefly appeared, then stopped. She shook her head.

Those three bouncing dots were the lamest torture treatment of the twenty-first century. They created angst and impatience. She hated them.

The dots reappeared and then stopped. She waited. Ten seconds later, she tossed the phone on the couch and went to find Dudley.

"Hey Dudley, where you at, little man?" She found him curled up in his bed on the floor by her bed. She bent down and stroked his fur. "Mama might have to go away for a bit today. I'll fix your dinner now, but don't eat it yet. Wait for supper time."

The cat opened one eye, looked at her, yawned, and went back to sleep.

"Nice chat as always, Dudley." She left the room and went to prepare him some food, just in case.

Her phone dinged again just as she set down the food. She retrieved her phone and stared at the screen.

> Wow, that sucks. ● Keep me posted. I can pick something up and bring it over if you like. Text me when you know.

Ashley sighed and tapped on the tiny keyboard.

> Will do. If I'm free, let's get something from that Thai place at the mall.

She put the phone in her back pocket and looked out the window. Colombo was leaving Beth's house. He didn't even look her way.

* * *

Three hours later, there was a knock at her door. Ashley jumped up, hoping it was Colombo. Detective Sparks stood at the door, his face a mask of normalcy.

"Good afternoon. I'm Detective Tate Sparks. Can I come in?" He flashed her a badge.

Ashley steeled herself. "Sure thing, Detective. I saw all the emergency vehicles in front of Maria's place. I've been waiting for you. I thought you'd drag me downtown, as they say."

"No need to drag anyone anywhere, at least not yet," he said as he walked in. "Nice house. Can we sit at the table?"

"Sure thing, follow me. Can I get you anything? Coffee, tea, water?" She headed for the cupboard and pulled out a glass.

"Water would be fine," he said.

She took down another glass, filled them both, and returned to the table. "I assume you found something, or you wouldn't be here. I went for a walk earlier and saw all the commotion down the street. Are they okay?"

"Until we have more information, I'm not at liberty to say, ma'am." Sparks took a sip of water and pulled out his notebook. "I understand you were one of the last people to see Mr. Houston before he disappeared."

"Mr. who? Oh, you mean Rocky. Yeah, I saw him. I can't tell you what day, though. I was over at their place looking at their garden a few weeks ago. And I saw him walking down the street toward Maria's a couple of times, but that's about it."

"What did you two talk about when you were at the house?" Sparks asked, his pen poised above the paper.

"I didn't talk to him much. Mostly her. He was in the garage tinkering with his boy toys. Beth and I talked about plants. I'd given Rocky my fertilizer recipe, and the plants still weren't doing well, so I went over."

"Did you talk about anything else?" Sparks stared at her.

Ashley squirmed a little. There was no way she was going to tell him about his wandering eyes, his thinly veiled advances, and Beth's suspicions. She didn't want to be involved in this at all.

"Nope, just plants. Some were over-watered, and some under-watered. I told her how to check the soil, and that was about it."

"Were the Houston's having any marital problems?"

"Not that I know of. I mean, what couple doesn't have problems?"

"Okay. Did Rocky ever mention anything about your neighbor up the street, Maria?"

"No, we didn't have that kind of relationship. We talked about plants and fertilizer, and that's about it. I'm a pretty private person, Detective. I don't gossip, and I hope my neighbors don't gossip about me."

She watched as the detective, not the one she wanted to be here, flipped through his notes.

"Well, I have here that about five or six months ago, a

date of yours disappeared from here. It appears your neighbor, Rocky, thought he saw him that night. And your neighbor up the street a bit, Maria, may have seen him walking past her house that night. But we can't ask them anything about that now, can we?"

Ashley gave the detective an, *are you kidding me*, look.

"Wait, are you still looking for that guy? I thought the case was closed or transferred or something. Why are you bringing this up?" Ashley paused and narrowed her eyes. "Wait, Maria's dead?"

Ashley pushed her chair back and went to the sink to refill her almost full water glass. This couldn't be happening. Both eyewitnesses that cleared her were dead. What the hell was happening?

"I didn't say she was dead. I said we can't ask her anything right now." He closed his notebook and got up from the table.

"I'll be in touch. Don't leave town. We may have more questions for you." Sparks headed toward the door, then stopped. "If you think of anything that might help, here's my card."

Ashley followed him and reluctantly took the card.

"I'm not going anywhere, Detective Sparks. I'll be here if you need me." She plastered on her best smile and watched as he walked out the door. She closed it and leaned against it. Ashley was used to things being tied up in nice little bows and dealt with. This was not good at all.

She went back into the kitchen, drank her water, and put her and the detective's glass in the dishwasher. It wasn't full, but she threw in a dishwashing tablet and turned it on anyway.

Water would wash away all evidence of him ever being here. She felt a sense of relief as she heard the machine fill with water, then hum.

"Ashley? Are you in here?" a voice called from the living room.

Ashley went to the door to find Beth standing there. Her eyes were a bit puffy, but she looked okay otherwise.

"Beth, oh my goodness, are you okay?" Ashley closed the door behind her and motioned for her to sit on the couch.

"I don't know," was all she could say. Then the corners of her lips turned up ever so slightly. "He's dead. That cheating bastard is dead. No divorce. No mountains of paperwork. No lawyer bills. He's dead."

"Oh, Beth, I'm so sorry. I didn't know. The detective just left. He didn't tell me much, just asked a bunch of questions about the last time I saw him and you."

"You didn't tell him what I said, did you?" Beth leaned forward on the couch.

"You mean about you wanting a divorce and knowing he was cheating? Absolutely not. It wasn't my place to do so."

"Thank goodness. It would be so messy if you did." Beth gave an audible sigh of relief. "I should be sadder than I am, or at least I think I should be. But a part of me is relieved he's gone."

"Did Detective Colombo tell you what happened?" Ashley would give anything to know something.

"Not really. They said they're still investigating. They aren't ruling out foul play, but it could have been a murder/

suicide. Not sure who killed who or if they did it together, or if it was a robbery gone bad. They need an autopsy to find out. I gave permission for Rocky's. No idea who Maria's next of kin is, and quite frankly, I don't care."

"Well, don't you worry, Beth. I won't say a thing to that detective."

"What about your detective?" Beth sat back on the couch, hands in her lap.

"My detective?" Ashley tried to feign innocence but knew it was no use. "Oh, Frank. I never said anything to him, or at least I don't remember saying anything."

"Good, let's keep that between ourselves. I don't want anything else to make this mess even messier." Beth stood and headed for the door. "You're a good friend, Ash." She waved as she left, closing the door behind her.

Chapter 33

Matt rang the doorbell and patiently waited. The smell of pad Thai and yellow curry with prawns wafted up to his nose. He pressed the doorbell again as his stomach growled.

"Coming!" came a voice from inside.

"Hurry up, I'm starving." Matt tried the door handle. Locked.

Ashley opened the door with a towel around her head. "Sorry about that. I decided I needed another shower. Just to get the stink of today off me. Let's eat in the kitchen."

Matt followed her and took containers out of the bag while she grabbed serving spoons, plates, and utensils.

"Water?" she asked.

"Sure," he said, taking the rice container out of the bag and opening it.

Ashley put the plates and utensils on the table and sat opposite Matt.

"So, tell me. What was all the fuss down the street today? Did they find your neighbor?"

Ashley spooned some rice onto her plate and then put a healthy serving of yellow curry on top. "It's been a strange day all around. Detective Frank wouldn't even talk to me, and this other detective came over and told me not to leave town. I think they're dead, Rocky and what's-her-name." Ashley dished up a healthy serving of pad Thai and started to eat. "Oh, my gawd. This is so good. I love that place!"

Matt smiled at her. He loved seeing his sister happy. He would do anything to keep her that way.

"They suspect you?" Matt asked as he helped himself to the food.

"No, I don't think so. Hey, where's the chicken satay?"

Matt reached into the bag and took out the last container. "Oops, I forgot to take it out. Here you go."

Ashley smiled and grabbed the container. "Anyway, then Beth came over and wanted to make sure I was all hush-hush about her wanting to divorce Rocky. Things are getting way too complicated in this neighborhood. I'm so glad I'm moving."

"Well, no one has called me yet, so I guess I'm not a suspect." Matt dipped his chicken skewer into the peanut sauce.

"Why would you be a suspect?" Ashley stopped chewing and stared at her brother. "Matt, did you . . . " She left the question unasked.

"Did I what? Did I have anything to do with their deaths? C'mon Ash, I'm a disposal guy, not the one who needs a disposal guy."

"Does that mean you think I did it?" Ashley frowned at her brother.

"Good gawd. Ash, no. I just meant that . . ." He shrugged and took another bite.

"Meant what?" She stared at him.

"I just meant that I don't have the expertise some people

have, and let's leave it at that."

He grabbed his water and took a sip. "You're very sensitive today. A little PMS, perhaps, or did you get your period? If you did, I'm sorry."

Ashley's frown turned upward. "Nope. And today is around period day, but the doctor said to wait a week. So, I'll wait."

The pair finished their dinner in silence. Each lost in their thoughts. Finally, Matt spoke. "Have any names picked out?"

Ashley stared at him. "Yes, and no. I'm going to wait until I know what it is, get over the five-month hump, and then start thinking about it."

"What about Rowan or Riley?" he suggested.

Ashley glared at him. "Yeah, like I want another male starting with an R in my life. No thanks!"

Matt hung his head. She was either PMSing or mad at him. There was so much he wanted to tell her. So much he wanted to say, but he held his tongue. She'd know soon enough. Then she'd understand just how much he loved her.

Chapter 34

Frank Colombo paced the halls of the coroner's office. They should have the test results by now. There was no stomach left, no contents to test. Now they had to wait on the tissue samples, and there were dozens of them. Some took longer than others, and as the bodies were in bad shape, they could prove inconclusive.

Frank looked up as the coroner approached him. "Hey Frank, sorry we took so long. Well, I have good news and bad news."

"Give me the bad news first. I'd like to end the day on a good note." Colombo tried to force a smile. He missed Ashley, and he wanted this case over with.

"The bad news is the bodies were too far gone to be positive on the cause of death." The coroner held up a plastic bag with some evergreen needles in it.

"What's that?" Colombo asked.

"Taxus Baccata, or yew leaves. They look a little like pine leaves," the coroner replied. "Your men bagged everything they could find in the kitchen, bedrooms, etc. They found a few of these in the U trap under the kitchen sink and brought them here, just in case."

"Okay, and why is this good news?"

"Well, Taxus Baccata is commonly known as the suicide tree. The leaves and berries can be ground up, put in tea or food, or eaten on their own."

"So you think it's suicide?" Colombo was hopeful.

"Well, this plant has been used for literally centuries as a way to kill enemies or oneself. It's fast acting. If intervention isn't available within the first thirty to ninety minutes, depending on the amount taken, then it's usually fatal. Basically, it causes a huge amount of damage to the cardiovascular system, and people usually die within two to twelve hours of ingesting it, usually from heart failure."

"But no way to know if it was a murder/suicide or double suicide or a murder?" He hated leaving loose ends in cases like this. He simply wanted to get back to Ashley, have a stiff drink, and call it a day.

"Well, I sent a team back to look at the yard, and there are no yew trees in Maria's yard, but there is one next door, close to the fence. It could have easily been reached from her side."

"What are you saying then? They killed themselves?"

"We found some berries still on the tree. The berries aren't poisonous, but the seeds are, and so are the leaves. You'd have to be an avid gardener to know they were poisonous. Was either of the deceased gardeners?"

"Yeah, I believe Rocky was a bit of a gardener. His neighbor was over there admiring his garden just before he disappeared."

"How old was the female?"

"How old? I don't know, maybe mid-forties? Why?"

"Despite yews being highly poisonous, in smaller doses,

it could be used to cause spontaneous abortion. But the female was in her mid-forties, so that's probably not the case. Plus, we have two dead bodies, not one."

The detective scratched his head. It was all a bit much. "So you're telling me it was either a murder/suicide or a double suicide or a homemade abortion gone wrong, or maybe a murder. Geez, Doc, throw me a bone here. There's got to be something. How are you going to classify the deaths?"

"Well, I honestly doubt it was a murder. Someone would have to have been in the house, made the tea, and convinced them to drink it. There were two teacups in the sink, not three. There were no ligature marks on the wrists or ankles. Those two drank the tea without being forced, as far as the evidence shows."

"For gawd sake, Doc, how are you ruling on this? Can I close the case or not?" Colombo just wanted to go home, better yet, to Ashley's. Her open house was tomorrow, and he wanted to help her with it.

The coroner looked at his file again. "I'm going to have to rule double suicide based on the evidence at hand."

"Yes!" Colombo started to give a high-five, then slowly lowered his hand. "I mean, I'll head back to the office now and inform the others working on the case. They'll be glad to know this one is closed."

"Have a nice night, Detective. I'm sorry this took so long." The coroner shook his hand, turned, and walked back to his office.

Colombo smiled all the way to the precinct and continued to do so as he filed his report. He'd have to be serious when he informed the widow. His partner would get a hold of Maria's next of kin. He picked up his phone and texted Ashley.

Case closed. Can I come over?

He watched and waited for the three little dots. A moment later, they appeared, quickly followed by,

YES!

Colombo turned off his computer, placed the closed file on his boss's desk, and left to go tell Beth Houston the news. In less than an hour, he'd have his arms wrapped around a naked Ashley.

Chapter 35

Ashley watched as Colombo parked on the street in front of her house. He got out, glanced in her direction, and walked across the street to Beth's. She found her lighter, lit some candles, then ran into the bedroom. She lit two more candles, dimmed the lights, and pulled back the covers on the bed. Dudley, fresh out of his cast, jumped up.

"No, Dudley, bad cat!" She picked him off the bed and took him to the laundry room. He didn't like it in there, but his litter box was there, and that's where she'd also been keeping his food and water lately. She put some kitty treats in his bowl, tossed a few cloth mice into the room, along with Dudley, and closed the door. She couldn't have her lover sneezing in her mouth while they were being intimate.

Ashley went into the bathroom, brushed her hair and teeth, then checked her makeup. She looked fabulous, and she knew it. She almost believed she was glowing, but she wanted to wait until tomorrow to take the test. However, she was over a week late, and she felt different. A knock on the door interrupted her thoughts.

She rushed to the door and flung it open. Matt stood there, a big grin on his face.

"Matt? What are you doing here?" She looked around

him to see Colombo's car still outside, but he was nowhere to be seen.

"I brought you this!" he said excitedly as he held out a bottle of vanilla extract.

"Ummm, why?" she asked as he stepped into the living room.

"For tomorrow, just put a few drops on a cookie sheet, put the oven on low, and the entire house will smell like cookies. Puts people in the mood to buy." He looked around the room.

"Oh, candles. Damn, did I come at a bad time? There were no cars in the driveway, so I thought—" He stopped mid-sentence. The only sound was that of Dudley batting a cloth mouse around the laundry room. "Ah shit, so sorry, sis. I'll leave." He handed her the vanilla extract and headed for the door. "Let me know how it goes tomorrow!" he called as he left.

Ashley closed the door, went and checked her hair and face again, then stood by the window to watch for her lover. Moments later, he left Beth's house, crossed the street, and bounded up the driveway and stairs to her door. She opened it before he could knock.

"Hey there," he said as he looked into her smiling face. "I was in the neighborhood and—"

Ashley cut him off and grabbed him by the shirt collar. "Shhh. Not a word."

She let go of his collar and led him into the bedroom. Once there, she playfully shoved him back on the bed and proceeded to undress him.

Somewhere in the back of her mind, she knew it wasn't

necessary. She was probably pregnant, and she could be done with this cop. But she wanted to celebrate. She was cleared of any wrongdoings, not that she'd done anything wrong, at least to Rocky and Maria.

Once she'd removed all of Colombo's clothing, she did a slow strip tease, loving how it affected him. She could get used to having a man around. It was nice. It wasn't often she had sex for pleasure, but she was enjoying it.

"Damn, woman, you are so hot!"

"Shhh," Ashley whispered. "Just shut up."

Twenty minutes later, it was all over. Ashley was happy, and Colombo had a huge grin on his face. Tomorrow she would find out if she was pregnant and hopefully sell her house.

Chapter 36

Ashley hummed as she showered. Frank asked if he could get anything ready to help her with the open house, but she shooed him out the door. She didn't want him there when she took the test or when the realtor showed up.

She watched as the water flowed off her body and down the drain. So cleansing, so freeing. Water was like the confessional at a Catholic church. It washed all her sins away.

She'd peed on the plastic pregnancy test just before hopping in the shower. There was no way she wanted to go through the tension and stress of watching for a plus sign. When she stepped out of the shower, it beckoned to her, teasing her to come and take a look. She ignored it, dried herself off, brushed her hair, and went into the bedroom to get dressed. Dudley was lounging on the bed, somehow stretching his little cat body completely across it.

"Sorry buddy, you have to go outside today. Don't worry, it's not too hot, and I put catnip in your carrier." She scooped up the cat, carried him to the carrier, and put him inside. He immediately rolled around in the cat nip.

Ashley opened the back door to let in some fresh air. Then she remembered the vanilla. Kate would be there in twenty minutes, so she still had time. She quickly placed Dudley in a shaded area in the yard, turned the oven to 250°F, and pulled out a cookie sheet. She laid down some parchment paper and let a dozen vanilla extract drops drip onto it before she placed it in the oven. There was just enough time to put on makeup, make the bed, and get out to the garden before the lookie-loos arrived.

She raced back to the bathroom and pulled out her mascara. The pregnancy test caught her eye.

"Nope," she said aloud. "I've got to get everything ready first." She finished her makeup, made the bed, and went back to the kitchen. It smelled heavenly. She turned off the oven and opened the door slightly but left the cookie sheet inside. One quick look around the house confirmed it was ready. Kate would be there in five minutes. Just long enough to get the results and scream for joy or cry in anguish and then compose herself.

It was time. She took a deep breath, walked to the bathroom, and picked up the test. Tears welled up in her eyes. She'd never been so happy to see a plus sign in her entire life.

"Woooo hoooo!" she shouted and did a little dance around the living room, test in hand. "Oh, My. Gawd! I did it! I'm going to have a baby!"

She touched her hand to her belly and whispered. "Sorry about that, little one. I'm just so excited. I know you're the size of a bean right now, but little bean, you and I are going to have a fabulous life together."

Ashley almost floated into the kitchen, where she deposited the positive pregnancy test in the garbage. Then she changed her mind, pulled it out, and put it in her back pocket. She'd figure out how to tell the detective later and if she wanted or needed to tell him.

He'd done his job, and it was a temporary arrangement. He knew she was moving.

The doorbell rang, and she dashed to answer it, a big grin on her face.

"Hey there!" Kate bustled past her, setting up plastic stands with information and putting her cards in various locations around the house. "All set? Ready to head outside?"

"You bet," Ashley said, her face a permanent grin. "It's going to sell today. I can feel it," she said as she opened the back door. "I'll be in the garden if you need me, or if you want me to leave, I can take Dudley for a ride."

"I think I'll need you for any questions I can't answer about the garden. Stick around for a bit, and let's see how it goes."

Ashley gave her a wave and headed into the garden with visions of blue onesies dancing in her head. Now she could start thinking of a name. Maybe a gender-neutral one, that way, if for some reason they couldn't see the sex of the baby, she'd be ready.

* * *

The day passed quickly as Ashley puttered in her garden. She weeded, pruned, uprooted and tilled where necessary. She'd spoken to two or three couples who had questions about the garden, but nothing that made her feel like they wanted the place. She recognized a few of her neighbors come to the door, then try and hide when they stepped outside and saw Ashley. She merely shook her head. She'd be gone soon enough.

Dudley came out of his carrier and Ashley put him in his halter so he could snoop around the freshly uprooted pea and bean plants. He explored the pile of dead foliage Ashley collected, ready to take to the far corner compost bin. It was a beautiful fall day, almost summer, but with a hint of winter to come. When the last prospective client left, Ashley poked her head in the door.

"Can I come in now? I have to pee!" She giggled, knowing she'd be doing a lot more peeing in the future. Being pregnant was going to be great.

"Yes, of course," Kate called. "I'm just finishing up some paperwork. Go pee and come sit at the table with me."

Ashley grabbed Dudley and his carrier and brought them both inside. She shut the back door and rushed to the bathroom. As she relieved herself, she thought about how she'd decorate the baby's room. She didn't have a place to live yet, but that would come soon. She could feel it in her entire being.

She finished up, washed the garden dirt off her hands, and grabbed a glass of water before sitting down at the table. Before Kate could say anything, there was a knock at the door.

"Be right back," Ashley said and bounded out of her chair. Maybe it was Frank. Maybe she was ready to tell him. She opened the door to a pair of strangers. "Oh, hello. The open house is over, but you can make an appointment to see it later if you like."

The woman spoke first. "We wanted to speak to the realtor if she's still here."

Kate came and stood beside Ashley. "I'm the realtor. How

can I help you?"

The man spoke this time. "We need to talk to you privately about this house." He made a motion toward Ashley, suggesting she not be there.

"Oh, well, it's up to Ashley. We were just finishing up and—"

"It's really important," the woman said, her eyes pleading for Ashley to agree.

"Sure, why not," Ashley said. "I need to run to the store to get something for dinner anyway. Just don't let the cat out. I'll be back in fifteen minutes." She went to the bedroom, retrieved her purse, and shut the door after ensuring Dudley was safe on her bed, snoozing away.

* * *

Ashley returned home, satisfied she had enough mineral and vitamin-enriched foods to ensure a healthy baby. She even bought a chocolate bar, dark chocolate, for the baby. Kate was still there, sitting at the table, a stack of papers in front of her. Once Ashley put all the groceries away, she sat at the table.

"So, how did it go? What did they want?"

Kate couldn't control her enthusiasm. "We got two offers on the house today. Two of them!"

"Wow, that's great," Ashley said. "So, were they close to the asking price?"

"No, no, they weren't," Kate replied. She paused and waited for Ashley to speak, but the smile on her face told Ashley the news was good.

"Over asking?" Ashley held her breath. "How much?"

Kate pushed a piece of paper toward Ashley. "This one put in an offer of $710,000, and they want a possession date of February fifteenth. That's about five months from now."

"Wow, nice price. Okay, I should be able to find a place by then, but moving in February, yuck." Ashley's mind spun. The extra cash would pay for moving expenses and a brand-new crib for the baby. But February was a crappy month to move. She'd hoped for April.

"What was the second offer?"

Kate pulled out the second offer and put it in front of Ashley. "This one is for $750,000." She waited for Ashley's response.

Ashley's mouth fell open. She took a breath and closed it. "Are you kidding me?"

She wouldn't have to work for a year after the baby was born with that kind of money, depending on the cost of her new acreage.

"Not kidding you. There is a caveat, though. They want to move in, in less than a month. Possession date would be October fifteenth at nine a.m."

"Wow," was all Ashley managed to say. She sat there, stunned. It had been quite the day.

"So, which do you prefer? Long possession for less money, or quick possession with $40K more?"

"Well, I'd have to give notice at work, but that's only two weeks," Ashley thought about all she'd have to do in one month. "Plus, I don't even know where I want to live, let alone see the place, put in an offer, and move."

Kate interrupted her musings. "I have a friend who's a realtor about 250 miles northeast of here. She sent me this listing yesterday." Kate pulled out her tablet and opened the listing. "It's five acres, three of them useable, with four bedrooms in the main house, plus a lower family room that could easily be turned into a painting studio. It's at the back of the house and gets the morning light. There are three bathrooms, a dining room with an open kitchen, and a nice large living room with a wood-burning fireplace."

"But does it have a workshop, or a barn, or a garden?"

"It does." Kate flipped through the photos. "It has a three-car garage and a workshop. The workshop has a one-bedroom suite above it. The only catch is the owners have a live-in farm helper who resides in the suite. He only works about ten hours a week, and in exchange, they give him eggs and free room and board. He looks after the garden, as it's almost an acre in size. He also tends to the chickens and animals every morning. He also heads south, way south, for the winter months, so he'll be leaving in November, not back until mid-April. The couple that lives there rescued a donkey and a pot-belly pig, which they hope you'll keep." Kate showed Ashley the photos.

"Okay, but where would my brother live? I guess he could live in the house until the farm guy left. I'm assuming the pig, donkey, and chickens are in a barn?"

"That they are, yes, and it's heated."

Ashley flipped through the photos. It was in the right area, just a little bit north, so she'd get all four seasons, but not high

Cleansing Water

up, so little snow. She didn't like the idea of having a stranger on her property, but then again, if Matt used the garage for his car business, she could keep someone else on. After all, she did want more than one child, and having Matt pay his way and having a helper might be nice.

"What do we know about this guy, this part-time farm hand?"

Kate took the tablet back and pulled up his Facebook profile. She handed it to Ashley. He was a nice-looking fellow, probably early thirties. He painted as well, and from a quick look at his profile, he was pretty good at it. No wife and no photos with him and other women. She put the tablet down and looked at Kate, trying to decide.

"Can I meet him when we view the property? If I like him, then he can stay. I might need help. If I don't, then he packs up and goes shortly after we move in. Would that be fair?"

Kate grinned. "Yes, and if you like, we can extend the time limit on accepting these offers to forty-eight hours, and we can go see the place tomorrow. I'll drive."

Ashley grinned. Could this really be happening? She thought she should talk to Matt or Frank or someone about it, but the reality was she was doing this for her and the baby. It was her money, her life. Not theirs.

"Okay, I'm in. I'll strongly consider offer number two, and if I like the place and we can have a quick possession date." She took a deep breath and grinned. "I'm in!"

Kate grabbed her phone and typed a quick message. A few seconds later, it dinged.

"We are all set. Pick you up at 7:30 tomorrow morning. It's about a four-and-a-half-hour drive from here, an hour to view the place, and four and a half hours back. We'll stop somewhere to eat there and back. Are you up for it? I'd have you home by 7:30 p.m.

Ashley clutched her belly. The butterflies she felt were threatening to escape, and she was light-headed. "Wow, seriously. This is happening?" She got up and hugged Kate. "Let's do this!"

Kate stood and returned the hug. "I have to do a lot of paperwork yet today, but I'll have an offer drawn up, just in case."

"Wait? How much is this place anyway? You know I have a budget. Is it close?"

Kate grinned at her. "The owners are looking for a quick, cash sale, and have it listed at one million even. You could probably get it for $900,000."

"Oh, my gawd! Really? I could kiss you!" Ashley beamed and opened the door for Kate. "I'll see you in the morning!"

Chapter 37

Frank Colombo flipped through the notes on the Houston/ Wilson file. Something wasn't quite right. He barely slept because he knew there was something he was missing, but he couldn't put his finger on it. The coroner ruled it an intentional double suicide. Maybe the couple didn't want to live without each other. Maybe Houston's wife, Beth, knew about the affair and threatened them. Something didn't add up.

"Whatcha looking at that for?" Detective Sparks walked up behind Colombo and put a fresh cup of coffee on his desk.

"Something's off, Tate. You might say my Spidey senses are tingling on this one." He looked at the crime scene photos, the bodies, the cups in the sink, and the lack of any kind of mess in the kitchen. There was nothing but the cups in the sink, no spoons, and the teapot was rinsed and drying on the side. "It's not quite right. I think someone else was there. It's too clean. Depressed people ready to kill themselves don't care about cleaning up afterward."

"Do you think your girlfriend had anything to do with it?"

Colombo glared at Sparks. "No, I don't think that. We were together too much around that time. I would have sensed something. But maybe Maria had another lover, or maybe the wife found out. That Matt fellow, Ashley's brother, gives me the creeps. There's something off about him. I think I'm going to do a bit more digging."

"Fill your boots," Tate said, then walked away laughing.

Colombo grabbed his keys off the desk and the fresh cup of coffee. He'd pay another visit to the widow and see if he could track down Matt and question him.

* * *

Colombo parked across the street from Ashley's house. Her For Sale sign swung in the slight breeze. He briefly wondered if the house sold and how long she'd be around. He'd grown fond of her, but he could tell that to her, he was a distraction. He didn't mind. He got the companionship he was lacking and a few rolls in the hay to boot. He stepped out of the car as Beth emerged from her house.

"She's not home," she called. "I saw her leave with the realtor around 7:30 this morning."

"That's okay," he said. "I'm here to see you anyway. Do you have a moment?" He reached back inside the car and retrieved his takeaway coffee cup and what was left of her dead husband's belongings. "I brought you these," he said and held up a Ziploc baggie.

"Oh." Beth's smile disappeared. "Sure, come on in." She turned and walked into her house. "Can I get you a coffee or anything?"

He held up his cup. "No thanks, I brought my own, but I might need a top-up."

They sat quietly at the kitchen table as Beth went through Rocky's belongings. There wasn't much there. A watch, a cell phone, and his wedding ring. She lined them up on the table.

"Hard to believe this is all that's left of him." She fingered the ring. "Well, they do say until death do us part. I guess this is us: parted."

Colombo watched her closely, looking for a tear, a sigh, anything that showed her grief. Everyone grieved differently, but Beth acted numb, emotionless even. He stood and walked to the window that looked out over the backyard. He froze. There in the yard were the remnants of a yew tree. Only a few sticks and needles were left, with a few red berries dotting the lawn.

"I didn't know you had a yew tree," he said and went back to the table. "Why'd you chop it down?"

"It killed Rocky," Beth said, her voice flat.

"That particular tree killed Rocky?" Colombo was intrigued by her choice of words.

"No, of course not." Beth took a deep breath and sat up straighter. "Just the same kind of tree. The coroner told me. I didn't want it around, no matter how pretty it is. I'll clean up the rest of it after you leave. The tree guys took most of it yesterday afternoon."

"Are you doing okay?" Colombo asked.

"About as well as one could expect." Beth picked up the watch and put it back into the bag. She did the same with the cell phone and zipped it shut. "I canceled his account yesterday. No use paying for the phone if he's not using it."

Colombo nodded and watched as she headed to the

garbage and deposited the baggie into its depths.

"Why are you throwing them away?" he asked.

"Because they smell bad, Detective and I'm not about to try and clean the stench of death off them." Beth glared and him as a tear formed in her eye.

Maybe he was wrong about her. Maybe his Spidey senses were off. Maybe it was Matt he should be talking to. He changed the subject.

"Do you ever talk to Ashley's brother, Matt?"

"Yeah, now and then." She went to the cupboard and pulled out a tin of coffee. "Top up, Detective?"

"Don't make a new pot on my account." He finished the last of the coffee in his cup.

"It's no bother. I want some, too." She scooped out the coffee, added it to a fresh filter, filled the back of the machine with water, and turned it on. Soon the smell of freshly brewed coffee filled the room. She sat as she waited for the pot to finish brewing.

"I get Matt to do dump runs for me sometimes. He has a pickup, and he's affordable. Lord knows I couldn't get Rocky to do it. He was always too busy. Now I know what he was busy with." She shook her head and took the takeaway cup from the detective. "Cream and sugar?"

"Yes, please, one of each." He watched as she put the cream and sugar in his takeaway cup and a bit of both in her cup. The machine made a gurgling sound, signaling it was finished. She filled his cup, stirred, and poured herself a cup.

As she set the cup in front of Colombo, she hesitated, then

sat. "Detective, could you not smell what was on the phone and the watch? Didn't it upset your stomach? It sure upset mine."

"Sure, I smelled it, but I don't have the best sense of smell, or taste for that matter." He sipped his coffee. "Now this tastes good, a little bitter, just like I like it. Dark roast?"

She smiled. "I think so. Now tell me, Detective, why are you really here? Anyone could have brought these to me, or I could have retrieved them from the coroner's office." She watched as he took another sip of the coffee.

"Well, something's been bugging me about the case. Specifically, who was using the credit cards, withdrawing the cash, and who drove the car? We tried to find this Nathanial Wilson person, but we think it was an alias. Now the boss thinks this person, whoever it was, somehow got Maria to sign over the car. But it's odd. If they were killing themselves, why would they give him her credit card and his bank card, and the PINs to go with them? It just doesn't make sense. I think this Nathanial person had something to do with their deaths. But I can't prove it."

Beth stared at the detective as he took another sip of coffee.

"Well, Detective, maybe, since they knew they'd be dead soon, maybe they gave it to him. Kind of a screw you to the credit card company and me."

"Could be." Colombo took another big swig of coffee. "My theory is whoever got the car stole the credit card and the bank card and somehow got the PINs from them before they died. I just haven't figured out how."

"Wait, are you saying it wasn't a double suicide? It was a robbery gone wrong? What kind of robber would make them drink poisoned tea? That's a pretty far-fetched idea."

Colombo looked at his watch. He'd been there about ten minutes, and he had no new leads except the chopped-down yew tree.

"You said she left around 7:30 this morning? Any idea when she'll be back?"

"Who? Oh, we're talking about Ashley now. Okay. It's hard to keep up with you, Detective. One minute you're all credit cards and robbery, and the next, wondering when your sweetheart will be home. How's that going anyway?"

"It's okay, but it's not too serious," he replied. "But we shouldn't talk about Ashley when she's not here. It feels like gossip."

"Oh, the whole neighborhood gossips about you two. We even have bets to see how long you'll last. Now that she's moving, the speculations are flying. Will you go with her? Will she move before the year is out? Will she wait until spring? I have the chart if you want to place a friendly bet."

Beth stood, went to the dining room, and brought back a chart. Sure enough, there were dates for both the move and for how long the relationship would last. There were only six empty spots farther down the calendar.

"Wow. It looks like my odds aren't that great." He chuckled. He hated neighborhood gossip, but it was also a great way to get tips and info.

He wasn't sure how he felt about the odds against him,

but he sure as hell wasn't going to bet on any of this.

"So, what else do the neighbors say? Any ideas or tips on what else might have happened to Rocky and Maria?"

Beth stiffened. "Please, don't mention that woman's name. It's hard enough talking about Rocky, let alone her."

The detective nodded and drank the rest of his coffee. "Okay, I'll make you a deal. You tell me what you've heard, and I won't mention her name."

Beth eyed him suspiciously. "Well, according to the Wheelers down the street, they think she and Rocky were together for at least four months, maybe more. The Larsons think Ashley's brother, Matt, had something to do with it. Someone said they saw someone who looked a little like him drive the car away in the wee hours of the morning. Then there's the Rolands. She swears she saw Ashley at the house, but that couldn't be because I know when Ashley leaves her house. She only went to work or was at home when they disappeared. It's all quite overwhelming when you think of it. Everyone suspects everyone else."

She picked up her coffee cup and brought it to the sink. She dumped out the liquid, added some dish soap, washed and rinsed it, and set it on the side to dry.

"Can I take that from you, Detective?" Beth grabbed his takeaway cup and washed and rinsed it, too.

"Why did you do that?" he asked.

"Did what?"

"You washed my takeaway cup. Why'd you do that?" The room wasn't as in focus as it once was, and he had a headache.

Darcy Nybo   299

"Oh, it's for the recycling. I don't put anything into it unless it's cleaned." She smiled at the detective. "Are you feeling okay? You look a bit pale. Maybe too much coffee?"

"Maybe," he replied. "My stomach is a bit upset, too."

"Let me get you some water." Beth got up, poured him a glass of water, and set it in front of him. "Drink up, it should flush that coffee through your system, and you won't feel so bad."

The detective picked up the water glass and noticed a slight tremor in his hand and arm. He took a few sips and tried to focus.

He watched numbly as Beth stood, emptied the coffee pot into the sink, and tossed the filter into the trash. She opened the cupboard, pulled out the coffee tin, and also emptied it into the garbage. As with the cups, she rinsed out the pot and the tin and set them on the side to dry.

The room spun as she smiled at Colombo, pulled the bag out of the trash can, and tied the top in a knot.

"Why'd you do that?" He tried to stand and was instantly dizzy. "I think I'd better go." He held onto the table and made his way out of the kitchen. He was having difficulty breathing, and the pain in his stomach was almost more than he could bear.

"Here, let me help you." Beth guided him to the door with the trash bag in one hand. "Are you sure you're all right? I could call an ambulance."

"No, no. I'll be fine. You're right. Too much coffee. Now where did I put my car keys?"

He noticed Beth watching him as he searched for his keys. Was that a smile on her face? Had she poisoned him?

"Beth, the berries from that tree, did you destroy them all?" His dizziness was worse, and his breath came in gasps.

"No, not all of them," she said with a smile. "I dried out the berries, took out the seeds and carefully ground them up, and put them in the coffee. They're the most potent part. I wore gloves, of course. That stuff's highly poisonous. Silly man, you didn't even notice that I didn't drink my coffee."

She opened the front door, walked out, and deposited the bag into the trash can at the curb. The truck should be there in about twenty minutes to haul it all away. She came back to find the detective leaning against the doorway.

"Here," she said. "Let me help you to your car."

He stumbled a few times, but she managed to get him seated. She took his keys out of his hand and started the car for him.

"I think you've got about ten minutes to make it to the hospital. But I don't think you'll make it. I have a sneaking suspicion you'll crash before then, and by the time the paramedics arrive and get you into the ambulance and over to the hospital, it will be too late. Your heart will stop, and even if they get it going again, you'll sink into a coma. It shouldn't hurt too much, though."

Colombo stared up at the sweet-looking widow. How the hell had he missed the clues? Maybe because there weren't any.

"Wait," he gasped, trying to stay focused. "Did you poison your husband and Maria?"

"Of course. I caught them in flagrante, as they say on the TV cop shows. I told them to get dressed, and I'd be back to speak to them, and we could come to a reasonable solution to this mess. I came home, grabbed my stash of dried yew seeds, and went back to the house. Through the alley, of course. I couldn't have anyone see me there. They looked rather guilty when I got back. I told them to sit while I made them a nice pot of herbal tea. I probably gave them too much, but they were pretty scared of me. Oh, did I mention I held a gun on them when I got back?" She patted the detective on the shoulder. "You should get going if you want to live," she said.

"So, what? You took the credit card and bank card and got their PINs, then made them go downstairs?"

"Yes, of course. They were feeling a lot like you are right now. Confused, dazed, weak. So, I helped each of them down the stairs and left them there. Then I went back upstairs and cleaned the mess and washed the teapot and rinsed out the cups. While I was doing the dishes, I saw the neighbor also had a yew tree. I put on some rubber gloves, pulled off a few needles, and gently put them down the sink to make sure they'd be found. You got the cause of death right, just not which part of the yew and who fed it to them. Now run along, Detective. You have about nine minutes left, and the hospital is about that far away, if not more."

"But," Colombo looked at her through slightly unfocused eyes. His stomach had him contorting in pain. His curiosity got the best of him, and instead of leaving, he asked, "The car, the cards?"

Beth laughed. "Detective, I told you Matt hauls things away for me sometimes. I gave him the car and the cards and sent him on his way. It wasn't even that expensive. He used to haul things for his sister, too. As I said, I know what goes on in Ashley's house. I have the perfect view. Now, off you go." She put his hands on the steering wheel, put the car in drive, and closed the door. "Go on then."

To anyone watching, it looked like she was having a friendly chat with that nice police officer who worked on her dead husband's case. She waved as his car slowly made it down the street.

Colombo concentrated on the road. The highway was three or four blocks away. If he could get there, then he could get to the hospital in time. His vision blurred, but he made it to the on-ramp. He tried to focus on the speedometer and the road as he merged into the fast-moving traffic. The last thing he remembered was being struck from behind.

Chapter 38

The next day, Ashley crawled out of bed at seven a.m., still tired but happy. The viewing had gone splendidly. The acreage was just what she needed. It was an easy twelve-minute drive to a neighboring small town that had, as she wanted, a doctor, a school, and a grocery store. A larger city lay forty miles to the south. A good place to look for baby-daddy number two if necessary. She'd have to revise her hunting and disposal technique, but she was up for the challenge.

It felt surreal. She'd accepted the early possession offer, and the owners of the acreage would let her move in on the fourteenth of October. She'd met the man who helped out at the acreage, and she was pleased to note he was quite pleasant, very polite, and showed no signs of drug use, alcohol abuse, or misogyny. Things were finally going her way.

Now all she had to do was decide whether or not to tell the detective she was pregnant. He wasn't the kind of guy she wanted to stick around anyway. His job was here, not where she was moving. She pulled on her jeans and reached into the back pocket. She pulled out the pregnancy test and tossed it in the garbage once she reached the kitchen. Dudley followed her and yowled in front of his dish.

"No treats, not this early." Ashley poured dry kibble into

his dish and refreshed his water. "We are going somewhere soon, and you, my fine furry friend, are going to have a brand-new home. I may even ask that handy guy to build you a catio. Maybe we can build it just off the family room so you can watch me paint. We might even be able to enclose it a little for the winter. I think you'd like an outdoor enclosure. Maybe the odd mouse will wander in."

There was a knock on the door, and she steeled herself. She would tell him she was leaving in a month, and they were done.

Instead of Colombo, the dour face of Tate Sparks greeted her.

"Detective Sparks? What are you doing here?" She opened the door and let the detective in. "Can I get you something? A coffee, tea, water? I was just about to make breakfast, but it can wait."

"No, this isn't a social call," he said and stepped into the living room. "I'm just going to come right out and say it. People die around you. I don't know how you were involved, but my gut says you were." He glared at Ashley. It looked like he'd been crying. He certainly smelled like he hadn't changed clothes in the past twenty-four hours.

"What are you talking about?" She didn't like being spoken to like that. Especially since she'd done nothing wrong. Her happy mood faded. She crossed her arms and glared at the unwelcome detective. "Does Frank know you're here?"

"Oh, that's a good one, lady, a real good one. How'd you do it?"

"Do what!" Ashley was losing her temper. Even Dudley sensed the mood change and slunk into the bedroom to hide.

"He's dead, and I know you had something to do with it." Sparks looked at her hard and long.

"What? Who's dead? Frank? No way. He's coming over for breakfast this morning. I was going to tell him about the house and everything. He's not dead. What is wrong with you?" Ashley stood her ground, not letting the detective farther into the house.

His shoulders slumped. "Look, I don't know how you did it, but you did. Where were you yesterday?"

"I was 250 miles away looking at a new home, Detective. Would you like me to call my realtor?"

"Yes, as a matter of fact, I would."

Ashley grabbed one of the extra business cards and handed it to the cop. He had some nerve coming in here and accusing her of whatever he was accusing her of. Frank couldn't be dead. He was fine the last time she saw him.

Sparks pulled out his phone and dialed the number on the card. He put the phone on speaker. "Kate Johnson here. How can I help you?" came the cheery voice.

"Ms. Johnson, this is Detective Sparks. Were you with Ashley Taylor yesterday?"

"Yes, I was. We left around 7:30 in the morning, drove out to an acreage she was interested in, and were back here by around seven last night. Why do you ask?"

"It doesn't matter, ma'am. Thanks for your help." Sparks hung up and put the phone and her card into his pocket. "This isn't over." He pointed at Ashley, turned on his heels, and started out the door.

"Wait! Where's Frank? What's going on?"

Sparks turned and shook his head. "I told you, he's dead. His car was hit as he merged onto the freeway not far from your house. He died en route to the hospital. He wasn't wearing a seat belt, which he would never do. He always wore one. Witnesses say he was swerving and merged onto the highway barely going twenty-five miles an hour. His spine was broken, and he had major head trauma. I don't know if you fought, or you dumped him, or maybe you even poisoned him, but he's dead, and I know it's your fault." With that, Sparks turned and left the house.

Ashley stood, stunned into silence. Dead? How could he be dead? She stared at the open door, dumbfounded.

A few moments later, Beth appeared. "Are you okay, honey? What's wrong?" She stepped into the living room and helped Ashley to a chair.

"He's dead," Ashley said, not fully comprehending what just happened. "That Sparks cop, he said Frank was killed in a car accident, and it was my fault. How could it be my fault, Beth? I wasn't even here."

"Oh honey, it wasn't your fault. Let me make you a cup of tea or something." She started for the kitchen.

"No, don't." Ashley looked at her with pleading eyes. "Why do people I care about leave me?"

Beth went to her side. "Oh, sweetie, it's not your fault. Randy's death was an accident. And the detective's death was, too. You just have really bad luck. I'm so sorry. I didn't know you were in love with him."

"I wasn't," she said in a whisper. "But I loved Randy, and I loved my mom. She wasn't a good mom, but I loved her. And I could have maybe loved Frank." Ashley stared at Beth. "I'm so glad I'm moving. This neighborhood is tainted. I can't wait to move. There are too many people dying, and it's not my fault!" Ashley put her head in her hands and quietly sobbed.

"I know, sweetie. I think it's time for me to move, too. You're right. There's bad energy in this neighborhood. I think I'll move into a smaller house with lots of garden space. Do you have your realtor's card handy?"

Ashley looked up and sighed. "Yeah, there's a couple over there."

Beth smiled at her and picked up a card on the way to the door. "It's a shame we can't still be neighbors anymore," she said as she walked out the door. "I liked you and your brother."

Ashley watched her go, still stunned by the latest turn of events.

Chapter 39

Ashley looked around her living room. She loved the way her furniture looked in her new home. There were a few holes to patch and paint to apply, but for the most part, the two-level rancher was in great shape. She set up a studio in the back family room, and Pete, her boarder/helper, built Dudley a catio with sliding doors before he left.

She'd decided to keep Pete on as Matt had big plans for restoring classic cars, and that would take up most of his time. There was a bathroom and a large, heated storage room in the garage. It was big enough for a studio apartment, and Matt made it his own.

Pete was gone for the winter, and Ashley had the house to herself. Matt would be over shortly for dinner to celebrate their move. She hummed to herself as she prepared the meal. The smell of chicken and fresh vegetables cooking filled the air. Dudley wound his way around her ankles, hoping something would drop to the floor.

Ashley looked out the kitchen window. Light snow was falling, not too little, not too much. This truly was the perfect place for her and her baby. She turned as Matt came into the room.

"Hey bro, how goes it? All settled into your new place?"

"Yep, all done. I put weather stripping around the door so the fumes from the garage won't get in. It's perfect. I can't thank you enough." Matt looked around and gave a happy sigh. "I finally feel like I'm home. It's been a long haul, but we made it." He plopped himself down in a chair and started to pick at the salad on the table.

Ashley walked over and slapped his hand. "Did you wash up?" she said with a smile.

"Yes, ma'am," Matt said and made sure to keep his hands away from the food.

Ashley served up a delicious chicken stir-fry to go with the salad. Life was good.

Ashley sat and started to eat. She hadn't been hungry the last few weeks, but now her appetite had returned. She still missed Frank, but there were a few options in town she had her eye on.

"This is nice," Matt said. "It sure feels good to be out of the disposal business." He shoved a forkful of salad into his mouth. "We wouldn't have this," he made a sweeping gesture, fork in hand, "if Frank or Randy were still around. I guess it's a good thing they're gone." He smiled at Ashley.

"What do you mean by that?" Ashley set down her fork and stared at him.

Matt took a deep breath. "Look, I have to tell you some things, and you might be mad at me, but I want us to have a fresh start. You, me, the baby. I want us to be a strong family unit and to do that, I have to be honest with you."

"Go on," Ashley prompted.

"Well, to start, you weren't the only person I helped dispose of things."

"I know, you had other clients. Why is this new news?" Ashley stabbed at her salad and pulled it off her fork with her teeth. She chewed slowly, watching Matt carefully. Something felt off. She kept her face neutral, just in case.

"Well, I helped Beth with some things." He shoveled a forkful of stir-fry into his mouth and chewed with gusto. "This is so good, Ash."

"What things? Like garden stuff?" Ashley poked a piece of chicken and put it in her mouth, chewing slowly. She didn't like where this was going.

"Well." Matt put down his fork. "I took Maria's car, her credit card, and Rocky's bank card and drove as far away as possible. Then I filled the car up with gas, with her credit card, then took money out of his bank account. After that, I found a vacant lot, hidden by trees and such, where I set the car on fire. I hitchhiked around for a bit, using the credit card and taking out cash in a few places. That's why I couldn't be there to help with the fence. I was disposing of things."

Ashley took another bite of salad. "Is that how you burned your hand?"

"Yeah, that was a dumb move." He picked up his fork and stuffed another mouthful in. "Yep, really good."

Ashley put her fork down and smiled at Matt. "It's nice to know you helped Beth with her problem. Did you help her with Frank, too?"

Matt laughed. "Nope, that was all her. Who knew yew

trees were so toxic."

"Wait, Frank didn't die because of the car crash?" She waited for an answer.

"Nope, well, maybe. She poisoned him like she poisoned Rocky and Maria. I mean, what are the odds there would be two women in the same neighborhood who are not afraid to take matters into their own hands? I admire you two."

Ashley looked at her plate. It wasn't like Matt to keep things from her. She wondered what else he'd done. "Well, I'm happy you're happy," she said and put a morsel of food in her mouth. She'd lost her appetite. How could she not have known about Beth? She looked up at Matt.

"I feel like there's something you're not telling me, Matty. What is it? You know you can tell me anything, right?"

She watched as he struggled to decide what to tell her.

"Okay, but you have to promise not to be mad at me. I did it for your own good, for our good. Your baby, whoever the biological father is, deserves a good daddy like me. Someone who knows how not to be a shithead."

Ashley's stomach tightened. What the hell else had he done?

He put his fork down and placed both hands on the table.

"Okay, I'll tell. I did some work for a guy where Randy took his car. He owed me cash for some disposal work. When you said Randy was going to the local mechanic, I called in a favor. Ash, I didn't like Randy. I could just tell he was going to try and take you away from me. I couldn't let that happen. I love you, you're my sister, but I love you in other ways, too. I just couldn't let him take you away."

Ashley closed her eyes and steadied herself. Now was not the time to get angry. That would come later. Now she had another problem on her hands. Would there ever be a day she wasn't disappointed by men?

"So, you were responsible for what happened to his brakes. You put a hit on my fiancé?" She held her breath.

Matt hung his head. "Yes. I did." He stood and paced the full length of the kitchen. "Ash, you've got to understand. It's been you and me forever. I couldn't let that change. Now look at us. You have this great house, a great career as a recluse artist, and you've got a kid on the way. I've got my own place with a huge garage to restore classic cars, and you've got some guy you don't even have to pay to help around the barn and garden. It's perfect, Ash. We, us, we wouldn't have this if Randy was here. I'd be pushed out, and I couldn't let that happen." He stopped pacing and pleaded for understanding with his eyes.

"I see." Ashley stood and gathered up the plates. "Help me clear the table, would you? I want to bring the scraps out to the chickens and Petunia and George."

Matt hesitated, then picked up his plate. "So, are we good?" He took the plate to the sink and scraped the scraps into a child's bucket beside the sink.

"Yeah, we're good." Ashley scraped the leftover salad and stir-fry into the bucket. "Take this out to the barn, would you? I need to pee, then I'll join you, and we can distribute this amongst the chickens, pig, and donkey."

Matt went over to Ashley and pulled her into a bear hug.

She hugged him back.

"You are the best sister ever. If you ever see me as something more than a brother, I'll be here. I love you, Ash." He pulled back and kissed her on the cheek. He smiled and grabbed the bucket. "See you in a bit."

"Don't feed them without me," she hollered from the bathroom door. "Just be a sec. And don't forget your coat!"

Ashley waited until he was outside before she went to the sink and splashed cold water on her face. A pang of anguish stabbed her gut, and the grief she thought she'd buried rose to the surface. She pulled her coat off the hook, grabbed her favorite butcher knife, and tucked it into the sleeve of her coat as she headed out the door.

Chapter 40

Ashley waddled around the kitchen, making her special treat for Dudley. The chickens, and Petunia, the pot-bellied pig, ate well over the winter. She learned that George, her donkey, wasn't fond of meat. It didn't matter. He had plenty of hay and other treats.

She looked out the window and marveled at the birds scratching in the yard. She smiled at the new growth coming up around the flower garden. She loved spring.

Ashley went to the stove and checked the contents of the pot. It was ready.

Dudley wove his way around Ashley's ankles, excited to get his favorite treat. She rinsed the treats in cold water and watched as little fat and small bits of skin made their way down the drain.

Water. It never let her down. In a few moments, Dudley would eat the last of his treats. When he was done, she'd put the pot and his dish into the dishwasher. All evidence would vanish within a couple of hours.

"Maroooowrrrrrr!"

"Oh, be patient, Dudley, please!" She admonished the cat but knew it wouldn't do any good. She realized this special treat might be his last. Pete would be back at the end of April to help with the garden and the animals. Just in time, too, as she was due near the end of May. She needed him around, so he was safe, for now.

She plugged in her Google Home. "Hey, Google, play "Flowers" by Mylie Cyrus." She danced around the kitchen and sang as she pulled one baby toe and one ring finger from the pot and put them in the cat's dish. Then she rinsed out the pot and put it in the dishwasher. Dudley gave a little growl as he munched on his favorite treat. She watched as he stripped the bones clean on both appendages and went back to chew on the bones.

"Nope, no bones for you." Ashley picked up his dish, headed out back to a fifty-gallon drum and tossed the bones in. They'd be absorbed into the rest of her homemade fertilizer soon. Once it was done, she'd dilute it with water and use it in her wonderfully large garden.

The baby gave a kick as she walked back into the kitchen. She winced and patted her oversized belly.

"Careful little girl. Don't hurt your mommy. How about a nice hot shower to wash away our stresses?"

Ashley's initial disappointment at having a daughter gave way to acceptance. What if, despite her efforts, a son was influenced by his friends and turned into someone she didn't like? She couldn't have that. Now that she was having a girl, she would teach her everything about gardening, plants, and men.

Ashley walked into the bathroom and turned on the shower. She stepped in and tilted her head back as the water washed away all her sins.

Afterword

This book was originally a short story that wouldn't leave my head. It happened after a particularly pleasing dinner party where I enjoyed a meal with my circle of friends during COVID. The next day I opened up the dishwasher and put away the dishes and when I was done, a sad wave of realization hit me. Every bit of evidence about that pleasant evening with wonderful people was gone. All I had left was a great memory.

After I wrote the short story, I filed it away and forgot about it.

I teach creative writing online, and on several occasions I had students and coaching clients ask me if it would be hard to create a protagonist who was an anti-hero. Was crafting a relatable anti-heroes feasible for authors? I said I thought it was highly possible.

A year later a friend of mine in the movie industry approached me and asked if I had any horror stories. I told him about, *Cleansing Water,* and he asked if I could expand it. I outlined the rest of the story almost as it is presented here. It morphed into a contemporary crime drama; graphic but not horror. Stories sometimes assume a life separate from their creators. I love it when that happens.

Anti-heroes like Dexter from the TV show, *Dexter,* and

Joe from the Netflix series, *You*, helped inspire me to write this book.

Dexter in particular is the perfect likable, relatable, anti-hero. He was broken but he could love and be quite sweet and protective at times. He also had a code he killed by, as does Ashley.

I usually write fun children's books or short stories. I even wrote a metaphysical novel. So why this? Well, like many authors I write all kinds of stories. Writing is my passion. Once characters emerge, I must write, irrespective of genre.

I hope you enjoyed this book and the characters, as some may reappear in future books. If you liked the book, please leave a review on Amazon or Goodreads or wherever you like to leave reviews.

If you didn't like it, let me know why. Feedback is always welcome. You can find me on Facebook at facebook.com/DarcyNyboAuthor or on Instagram @write.warrior.

About the Author

Darcy Nybo developed a love for writing in Grade 2. She believes her writing skills have improved somewhat since then, as evident by her successes.

She is a self-proclaimed word nerd who loves to put words together to evoke emotion, inspire, entertain, and educate.

Darcy received several awards for her short stories and as a local freelance writer. She's also a book editor, writing coach, and university writing instructor. If words are involved, you'll find her there. She runs two word-related companies: alwayswrite.ca and artisticwarrior.com.

She will probably never retire. As a friend once said, "retirement is doing what you want, when you want, with who you want."

When she's not writing you'll find her teaching, coaching, editing, putzing around in the garden, cooking up delicious meals, visiting with her daughter and granddaughter, looking after dogs and hanging out with family and friends.

You can find all her books online.

Acknowledgments

A big thank you to all my beta readers: Audrey, Nelson, Susan, Darlene, Cat, Annie, Stephanie, and Marilyn.

Big gratitude to my friend Jonas for his encouragement and his proofreading skills. I knew in the depths of my being we'd both end up doing what we're passionate about. To think it all started in a writers' group in a tea shop. You rock!